The Dwarf

MODERN KOREAN FICTION

Bruce Fulton, General Editor

TREES ON A SLOPE
Hwang Sun-wŏn

THE DWARF
Cho Se-hŭi

Cho Se-hŭi

THE
DWARF

Translated by Bruce and Ju-Chan Fulton

University of Hawai'i Press

Honolulu

This book has been published with the assistance of the
Sunshik Min Endowment for the Advancement of Korean
Literature, Korea Institute, Harvard University, and
the Daesan Foundation, Seoul, Korea.

Printed in the United States of America
11   6   5   4   3   2

An earlier version of "Knifeblade" was published in
Modern Korean Fiction: An Anthology (2005).

Library of Congress Cataloging-in-Publication Data
Cho, Se-hŭi.
[Nanjangi ka ssoa ollin chagŭn kong. English]
The dwarf / Cho Se-hŭi; translated by Bruce and Ju-Chan Fulton.
p. cm.—(Modern Korean fiction)
ISBN-13: 978-0-8248-2940-7 (hardcover : alk. paper)
ISBN-10: 0-8248-2940-9 (hardcover : alk. paper)
ISBN-13: 978-0-8248-3101-1 (pbk. : alk. paper)
ISBN-10: 0-8248-3101-2 (pbk. : alk. paper)
I. Fulton, Bruce.   II. Fulton, Ju-Chan.   III. Title.   IV. Series.
PL992.17.S4N3613 2007
895.7'34—dc22
                                        2006015040

University of Hawai'i Press books are printed on acid-free
paper and meet the guidelines for permanence and durability
of the Council on Library Resources.

Designed by University of Hawai'i Press production staff

Printed by The Maple-Vail Book Manufacturing Group

Contents

The Möbius Strip

THE MATHEMATICS TEACHER entered the classroom. The students noticed that he hadn't brought the textbook. They trusted this teacher. In this school he was the only teacher to have won the students' trust.

"Gentlemen," he began. "This has been a challenging year. You've really put your heart into your studies, all of you. And so for this last class I'd like to talk about something that's not related to the college entrance exam. I've been looking through some books and I found something I'd like to share with you. Let me start by putting it to you in the form of a question: Two boys have just finished cleaning a chimney. One of them comes down with his face black as night. The other comes down without a trace of soot. Now, gentlemen, which of the boys do you suppose will wash his face?"

The students looked up at their teacher standing on the podium at the head of the classroom. None was quick to answer.

After a momentary silence one of the students rose.

"The one with the dirty face."

"I'm afraid not," said the teacher.

"Why not?" asked another student.

The teacher explained. "Two boys come down the chimney, one

with a clean face, one with a dirty face. The boy with the dirty face sees the boy with the clean face and decides his face is clean, too. And the boy with the clean face sees the boy with the dirty face and decides his face is dirty, too."

The students gasped in surprise. Every pair of eyes remained fixed on the teacher standing on the podium.

"Let's try it a second time: Two boys have just finished cleaning a chimney. One of them comes down with his face black as night. The other comes down without a trace of soot. Now, gentlemen, which of the boys do you suppose will wash his face?"

The very same question. This time a student immediately rose.

"Now we know. The boy with the clean face."

The students waited expectantly for the teacher to respond.

"No, that's wrong."

"Why?"

"You won't have to answer that question again, so please listen carefully. Two boys, together, cleaned the very same chimney. And so it's not possible that one of them had a clean face and the other a dirty face."

The teacher now took up some chalk and wrote "Möbius strip" on the chalkboard.

"Gentlemen, this is something you know from your textbook. But it's not related to the college entrance exam either, so just relax and listen to what I'm about to say. Now a surface can be inner or outer. For example—paper has a front and a back; the earth has an interior and an exterior. If you take a plain sheet of paper and cut away a long rectangular strip, then paste the two ends of that strip together, you get the same thing—an inner and an outer surface. But if you give that strip of paper a twist and *then* paste the ends together, you can no longer distinguish inner from outer. What you have now is a single curved surface. And this, gentlemen, is the Möbius strip you know so well from your textbook. Now I'd like you to think about this curved surface that has no separate interior and exterior."

Squatlegs entered the bean field. In the lingering daylight he was able to pick several fully ripe stalks. There were weeds everywhere. Holding the stalks in his armpit, Squatlegs scooted along between the furrows on hands and crippled legs. It was so quiet he could almost hear the seeds falling from the weeds. Bean field? More like a weed field. Squatlegs came out on the ocher-colored dirt road and took the beanstalks in his hand. He smelled the burning wood, a good smell. The sky had begun to darken. The wood he had set ablaze before venturing into the bean field now burned bright red. He placed a piece of sheet metal over the fire, then shelled the beans and roasted them. The wood was bone dry and burned with scarcely a wisp of smoke. Just a few hours before, this wood had been part of Humpback's veranda.

They had torn down Humpback's house, the men with the sledgehammers. They had pulverized one of the walls, then stepped back, and the north-facing roof had simply collapsed. That was all they had to do to his house. Humpback had been sitting where the prince's-feather grew beside the poplar tree. He had risen and gazed at the sky. His wife and their four children were picking the ears of corn left for seed on the cornstalks bordering their yard. Before the men with the sledgehammers moved to the next house they had watched the woman and children in silence. The woman and children hadn't opposed the men, they hadn't cried. The men had found this disturbing.

Night was falling. Squatlegs heard from the fields the whisper of wings—a spiraling flock of goatsuckers hunting insects. He continued to shell beans onto the piece of sheet metal. He enjoyed the smell of the wood burning, the beans roasting. People passed along the other side of the lake—a group of laborers working on the new apartments. Squatlegs watched as their silhouettes cut across the field beside the lake and on toward the bus stop.

Listening for Humpback's footsteps he removed the piece of sheet metal from the fire. Still no sign of him. Humpback's wife, their oldest boy, the other children—they'd exercised self-restraint, all of them. Squatlegs chewed on a cooked bean. Humpback's veranda was burning briskly. The others in the neighborhood hadn't restrained themselves. They had clutched at the men with the sledgehammers and wailed. They believed they wouldn't be held responsible if they acted as a group. They had seized one of the men with the sledgehammers and had kicked and butted him. Minutes later the man rose, bleeding. He shook his fist at them and spit the blood collecting in his mouth. His front teeth were broken and bloody.

When the men with the sledgehammers had approached, Squatlegs had made way for them, pointing out his house. He had withdrawn to the side of the road where the cosmos were in full bloom and there he had sat. His wife and children hadn't been as composed as Humpback's family. His wife had squatted behind their pump and shielded her face with the hem of her soiled skirt. Beside her the children had kept rubbing their teary eyes. In no time the roof and walls were leveled, leaving only dust.

Squatlegs heard Humpback's footsteps. Humpback appeared with a plastic container and set it down away from the fire. The container was filled with gasoline. He had toted this heavy container for two or three miles along the darkening road. Where the road ended at a vacant lot, people were peddling worm medicine wrapped in aluminum foil.

The tonic peddlers drove around in an old junker purchased from an auto graveyard. Inside were lauan timbers, hard rocks, beer bottles, spikes, knives with long blades honed to a fine edge. These were the tools of trade of the man they called The Master. This man could break a rock or a beer bottle with the chop of a hand, he could snap a lauan timber in two, with his teeth he could draw out a spike driven so deep into wood that the head was bent. When he strapped the blade of one of the knives to his palm with nylon cord, pressed the tip to his stomach, and then released it, people had the sensation that their body tissues, skin and all, were being shredded by the blade. But The Master was unscathed.

The Master's strength was awesome. Humpback had obtained the gasoline from The Master. He had closely observed the interior of the car. Squatlegs noticed Humpback looking back toward their village, now veiled in darkness. Humpback hunched down and Squatlegs pushed the piece of sheet metal toward him. Humpback put a bean to his mouth but instead of eating it he spoke in an undertone.

"What's that?"

"Hmm?"

"I thought I heard something."

For a second the two of them held their breath.

"Birds," said Squatlegs. "Goatsuckers flying around for food."

"At night?"

"They sleep during the day. Stick to the trees and sleep."

Humpback put back the bean he was about to eat. Squatlegs watched as he lit a cigarette with trembling hands.

"What's the matter?" asked Squatlegs.

"Nothing."

"Scared?"

"Nothing to be scared of."

"If you don't feel up to it, go on back."

Humpback shook his head. His children were asleep in the tent. Before going to sleep they had made a fire in front of the tent. Squatlegs' children had contributed their kitchen door to the flames. The door was in pieces, couldn't be sold.

It was pitch black inside the tent. The village people standing in front of the fire had gone their separate ways and the troubled land where once their houses had stood was draped in darkness. Some of the grown-ups had made their way toward a hazy column of light.

A car was parked in the vacant lot in front of the checkpoint manned by the night guards. Inside the car a man looked over some documents along with notarized impressions of personal seals. The man passed money out through the window. The people who had given him the documents squatted in front of the car and counted the money.

Squatlegs returned the piece of scrap metal to the fire and shelled more beans onto it. He would have been happier if Humpback had at least eaten some of them. These last few days he hadn't seen Humpback eat a thing.

"About time he left, isn't it?" Humpback asked. The cigarette, mostly ash, hung from his fingertips.

"Yeah," said Squatlegs. "Don't let him kill me. This guy is fat as a pig. If he gets on top of me, he'll smother me."

"Then why did you tell me to go home?"

"If you go home, I'll have to come up with another plan."

"Another plan?"

"Forget it."

Squatlegs looked around. His field of vision was screened by the apartments. The dark skeletons of the buildings filled the expanse from east to west. Humpback scooped sand onto the fire. Squatlegs removed the piece of sheet metal, then looked on, mute, until the other had put out the fire. With the last ember covered, gloom enveloped the surroundings.

Humpback said, "His lights are on."

Squatlegs looked toward the village. The car's headlights swirled in the evening sky, then slowly moved toward them.

Squatlegs pushed the piece of sheet metal toward Humpback.

"Eat."

Humpback kicked it into the bean field. Container of gasoline in hand, he started walking. Squatlegs followed quickly. Water had gathered in a large hollow in the road. There were two stepping stones, and Humpback hopped across, feeling his way. He waited. Squatlegs avoided the puddle, scooting over the roadside weeds until he came to where Humpback was standing. He sat himself squarely in the middle of the road. He produced a length of electric cord from each pocket and displayed them both to his friend. Humpback nodded, crossed to the right side of the road, and hid himself in the bean field. Silence lay in every direction and Squatlegs grew fearful. He felt like talking to his friend.

"Did you find out the going price today?"

"Yeah," came Humpback's disembodied voice.

"How much?"

"Three hundred eighty thousand *wŏn*."

Squatlegs no longer felt like talking.

"Look there," came Humpback's voice from the bean field.

Squatlegs saw two columns of light approaching, churning the evening sky. He closed his eyes. All that remained of the bright lights was thick gloom on his retina. He didn't budge—not when the car entered the puddle, not when the horn sounded. The bumper pushed up against his chin and finally the car stopped. Curses poured out from the man inside.

Humpback hugged the ground.

The man emerged from the car. Still blinded by the headlights, Squatlegs pivoted to the side and squinted up at the man.

"What do you think you're doing!"

Squatlegs mumbled something in a small voice.

The man bent down.

"What?"

"I want to die," said Squatlegs. "Run me over—pretend I'm not here."

The man had to hunch down beside Squatlegs to make out what he was saying.

"What the hell for? There has to be a reason."

"You remember me?"

"Sure. You sold me your right of possession."

"Yes. For a hundred and sixty thousand *wŏn*."

"You have a problem with that? I gave you ten thousand more than you would have gotten from the city."

"No. No problem at all," said Squatlegs. "We used it to pay back the deposit to the people who rented from us."

The man said, "Fine. Now get out of the road."

Squatlegs turned his face away.

"Now that we've given away that money, there's nothing left."

"You didn't have enough money for an apartment, so you sold your right of possession. What's the point?"

"Did you see what happened to our house?"

"Yeah, I saw." The man's voice now had an edge to it.

"Our house is gone." Still the same small voice. "You owe me another two hundred thousand, mister."

"What!"

"Just because I don't know much doesn't mean you can get away with what you did. You bought something worth three-eighty for one-sixty, then sold it for a two-twenty profit. You can't do that. Give me two hundred thousand, and you've still got twenty thousand for yourself. And don't forget—you bought up everyone's right of possession."

The man rose.

"Move! Or else I'll do it for you."

"Be my guest."

For the briefest instant Squatlegs lost his presence of mind. The man's shoes had struck him in the chest. Instinctively, Squatlegs clutched and hung to the shoes that kept coming at him. But he was too weak. The man pummeled his face with heavy fists, then hurled him easily into a patch of grass.

Knocked practically upside down, Squatlegs tried to crawl back onto the road. The man noticed and turned toward his car. He would have to get by this obstacle before it regrouped.

He bent over to climb inside. And then a dark shadow slammed into the pit of his stomach. The man's large body slumped to the ground. Humpback, emerging from his hiding place in the field, had kicked the man with murderous force.

"I'll give you the money!" the man wanted to say. But he couldn't speak. Humpback had already taped his mouth shut. Nor could he move. He was tied fast with the electric cord. The man watched Humpback help Squatlegs past the front of the car. Squatlegs' face, revealed in the headlights, was a bloody mess. Humpback wiped it for him. Squatlegs was weeping.

"Was it fun watching me get laid out like that?" said Squatlegs. "What took you so long? You wanted to see me get laid out, didn't you?"

"Knock it off," said Humpback as he turned and walked toward the car. "We have to get this guy into the car. And we need to find his briefcase."

"All right, load him in."

The man thrashed about, then lay quiet, exhausted.

Humpback climbed in and the two columns of light slanting across the evening sky vanished. He cut the engine. The black briefcase was beneath the seat on the driver's side.

Outside, Squatlegs had propped the man up in a sitting position. Humpback emerged from the car, took the man around the waist, and stood him up. The two friends walked the man to his car and sat him in the driver's seat.

Squatlegs said, "Let me sit next to him."

Humpback lifted Squatlegs and set him in the passenger seat. He himself climbed in back and opened the black briefcase. The man watched silently.

Humpback said, "Money and papers."

"Let me see."

The man realized that Squatlegs and Humpback had found everything.

Squatlegs rummaged through the briefcase. "He's already sold ours."

The man blinked.

"Look some more."

"He's got our names written down in a notebook. And some of the names are crossed out—must be the ones he sold."

Squatlegs looked hard at the man. The man nodded.

"For three hundred and eighty thousand—right?"

Again the man nodded.

Humpback said, "Count the money."

Squatlegs began counting. He produced two piles of exactly two hundred thousand *wŏn* each.

"Our money," he said.

The man nodded once more. He watched as Squatlegs passed one of the piles to his friend in the back seat.

Squatlegs' hands trembled. As did Humpback's. Their hearts pounded.

Squatlegs unbuttoned his shirt, put the money in an inside pocket, then buttoned the shirt and tidied it. Humpback put his share in the outer right-hand pocket of his shirt. His clothes had no inner pockets.

With the money accounted for, Humpback recalled what he had to do the following day. Likewise with Squatlegs. His children were asleep in the tent.

Squatlegs said, "Fetch me that container." In his hand was the remaining length of electric cord.

Humpback found the plastic container in the bean field. He watched the face of his friend. Watched it to the exclusion of everything else. Then he set off toward the village. The night was unusually quiet. Not a point of light could be seen. He couldn't even tell where the village lay. By and by he paused and listened hard, wondering if Squatlegs was scooting along behind.

Squatlegs ought to be curling himself up and dropping out of the car. He ought to be closing the door with a *thunk,* putting his hands quickly to work, and scooting out onto the ocher soil of the road now layered with darkness.

As he walked along, Humpback thought of his own normal pace and of how fast Squatlegs could go when his hands worked quickly.

Arriving at the village, Humpback proceeded to what remained of an out-of-the-way house and pressed down on the handle of a pump. He cupped the water in his palms and moistened his lips. He felt the outside pocket of his shirt. Squatlegs was scooting toward him, breathing hard. Humpback met him, looked into his face; it was hard to make out in the gloom.

Squatlegs reeked of gasoline. Humpback worked the pump and washed Squatlegs' face. Face smarting, Squatlegs closed his eyes. But the pain was nothing. He thought about the money inside his shirt and what he had to do the following day. From the far end of the dirt road flames shot up. His friend tried to rise and Squatlegs sat him back down.

Humpback's family certainly had restrained themselves when the men with the sledgehammers arrived. His own family hadn't been as composed. Squatlegs didn't like his friend jerking up like that. He himself was startled by the explosion. But presently it was over. The distant flames subsided, the boom of the explosion died out.

Darkness, silence enveloped the two men. Humpback set out. Squatlegs followed.

"Lots of things to buy," said Squatlegs. "A motorbike, a pull-cart, and a popper. All you have to do is drive. Then nobody has to see me scooting around anymore."

Squatlegs waited for his friend's reaction. But Humpback had nothing to say.

"What's up?" Squatlegs caught up with Humpback and grabbed his pantleg. "Hey, what's up with you?"

"Nothing."

"Scared?" Squatlegs asked.

"No way," said Humpback. "But it's weird. I've never felt like this before."

"Then everything's fine."

"No, it isn't."

Squatlegs had never heard his friend speak in such calm tones.

"I'm not going with you," said Humpback.

"What!"

"I said I'm not going with you."

"What's this all of a sudden? Look, tomorrow we'll go to Samyang-dong or Kŏyŏ-dong. Lots of vacant rooms there. We get the families settled and then we go around with the popper. Once we buy the motorbike we can go anywhere. Remember the time we went to Karhyŏn-dong? All the families who turned out with stuff to pop? We had the popper working nonstop till nine o'clock. It wasn't the popcorn they wanted. They just got to thinking about the old days and decided to bring the kids out. All we need to do is find a place like that. Every few days we'll bring home a pile of money that'll make the little woman's mouth drop. So what's on your mind?"

"I reckon I'll go with The Master."

"That tonic peddler?"

"Mmm-hmm."

"You're out of your mind. How much peddling you figure to do at your age?"

"Not too many people are perfect. He's one of them. He does that scary routine with the knife to draw a crowd, works himself to the bone peddling, and lives on the proceeds. That worm medicine he sells is the real thing. And he knows my physical condition is an added attraction." And after a pause: "The thing that scares me is your state of mind."

"I get the message. Go, then. I'm not going to stop you. But remember, I didn't kill anyone."

"Sooner or later, though," Humpback said, turning back, "we have to find a solution."

Squatlegs heard only footsteps as darkness enveloped his friend. Before long the footsteps were gone as well. He scooted off in search of the tent where his children were sleeping. He clenched his jaws so he wouldn't cry. But tears streamed unchecked from his eyes. Another long night—when would it end?

The teacher rested his hands on the lectern. He spoke to the students.

"Ask yourselves whether there exists a solid whose inner and outer parts can't be distinguished. Imagine a solid where you can't divide inner and outer—a Möbius-type solid. The universe—infinite, endless—we can't seem to tell its inside from its outside. This simple Möbius strip conceals many truths. I'm confident, gentlemen, that you'll give some thought to why I brought up the chimney story and the Möbius strip in this, your last class. It will gradually become clear to you that human knowledge is often put to extraordinarily evil uses. Soon you'll be in college and there you will learn much more. Make absolutely sure, gentlemen, that you never compromise your knowledge for the sake of self-interest. I've tried to teach you according to the standard curriculum, but I've also tried to teach you to see things correctly. I think it's time now for you to test yourselves on how my efforts have turned out. So how about a simple goodbye and let's leave it at that."

The class monitor sprang to his feet.

"Attention! . . . Salute!"

The teacher returned the students' bows, stepped down from the podium, and left the classroom.

The winter sun slanted down and the classroom grew dark.

Knifeblade

THERE ARE THREE KNIVES in Shin-ae's kitchen. Two are kitchen knives—one large and one small. Once a year Shin-ae calls a knife sharpener to put a new edge on the large one. A good sharpener knows knives. There are some who don't. Those who don't will start with the grindstone for the first sharpening. Shin-ae snatches the knife from such sharpeners and goes inside. When the ones who know knives take this one in hand their eyes open wide and they silently observe it. Knife sharpeners are struck by the sight of a good knife. They start by gently putting the blade to a fine whetstone. Sharpeners these days will say that a person could live and die a hundred times and never produce such a knife. To make this knife, they say, the blacksmith would have tempered the blade numerous times, hammered it countless times. His son would have worked the bellows. Who knows, the son might still be alive. If so, he would be a grandfather by now. And someday he will die. The smith will have long since passed on. Shin-ae's mother-in-law, who had this knife made for her own use when the smith was alive and hammering—she too has passed on. Shin-ae is forty-six. It's no good having the large knife sharpened by an amateur. With the small one it's all right. It's a run-of-the-mill knife she bought several years ago. There's not much to say about a knife like that. She bought it for a hundred and eighty *wŏn* from a knife peddler who was hawking his wares in the usual way by scraping the blades of two knives together. It's a run-of-the-mill knife you can buy for a similar price just about anywhere.

The third knife in Shin-ae's kitchen is a fillet knife. It's frightening to behold. Taut blade, three millimeters at the back; pointed tip; thirty-two centimeters long. It doesn't seem like a knife made for kitchen work. The thoughts that come to mind when she takes it by the handle are truly frightening. Hyŏn-u, Shin-ae's husband, bought it the previous spring. Why did he buy such a knife?

She couldn't figure it out. Shin-ae likes to compare herself and her husband to dwarfs. *We're tiny dwarfs—dwarfs.*

"Well, aren't we?" she asked her husband, who was home from work. "Am I wrong?"

"Well . . ." Her husband was reading the newspaper.

High officials call for social reforms; no party restructuring, declares opposition head; commentary on National Security Law; UN Secretary-General calls for ROK-DPRK talks; U.S.-USSR spacecraft stage dramatic docking high above Elbe River; violent crime up 800 percent over past decade; foundation head embezzles 100 million *wŏn* from school; South Vietnamese refugees in U.S. demonstrate against extravagant ways of former officials; employment outlook dim despite recovery; add-ons boost budget to 1.52 trillion *wŏn;* new Yŏŭido National Assembly Building rests on twenty-four pillars costing 10 million *wŏn* each; residents of condemned dwellings in redevelopment zone lack 300,000 *wŏn*, give up apartment rights, seek new housing; Kunsan tearooms cite defense tax, hike cost of phone calls; "dead" man revived at graveside; armed robbery; rape; forgery; timber thieves; red pepper cut with sawdust; fishmongers add dye, pump up fish; pop song "Too Much" found indecent, banned; winning number for housing lottery; actress bares all; "For Whose Sake Chastity?" reads ad; university professor calls unfair distribution of profits an invitation to crime and consumerism. Nothing different here from yesterday's paper. Nothing out of the ordinary in these stories. And yet people read the same newspaper day after day. Her husband was reading that newspaper.

"Am I?"

"Hmm?"

"Will you _please_ put down that paper?"

Such is life, Shin-ae told herself yet again. Last night her husband tossed and turned, unable to sleep, till the owl in the wall clock hooted two in the morning. He leaves early in the morning. Spends twelve or thirteen hours away from home. What he does at work, what happens to him there, the anxiety, doubt, fatigue that follow him around constantly—his hopes have evaporated. From the radio in her daughter's room across the way came the voice of a foreign singer whose face Shin-ae couldn't picture, singing in whatever language those people spoke. Someday that girl would be _thinking_ in a different language. Shin-ae worried about her daughter. If only their situation were a bit different. Why so much anxiety about managing their small family? Her husband was reading the newspaper as if he wished to add to the fatigue that had already accumulated. He was exasperated with himself and the life he led. He felt ill at ease in society and out of place in his times. He had studied history. He had read many books. The thoughts written down in those many books had once upon a time influenced young Hyŏn-u.

He had wanted to talk about all he had learned from books. And then suddenly he became taciturn. He grew up. Likewise Shin-ae had once been a girl of many dreams. A bright and pretty girl. One who grew up using her mind. Hyŏn-u had said, the first time she met him, that his greatest desire was to write a good book. The two of them fell deeply in love. And so they married. They knew each other's ideals and they held high hopes. But in the face of reality those ideals, those hopes, were of no help to them. The husband found it necessary to earn money—the thing he hated most. To earn this despised money he found it necessary to work like a dog. For his mother had fallen ill. It was her stomach. She died of stomach cancer. The mother having passed on, the father became ill. It was an illness the doctors couldn't identify. The father suffered terrible pain. Not even morphine injections offered relief. The doctors said he would soon die from the mysterious disease. But he lived another two years, fighting the terrible pain. He died at the mental hospital where he spent his last months. The father had lived his entire life at odds with society and the times. Shin-ae was well aware that her husband was cut from the same cloth. The man whose greatest desire had been to write a good book couldn't compose a single line. He decided he was aphasic. Although he worked with deadly determination to earn his detested money, all he had to show for it was debt. The hospital, while offering no cure for his parents, was forever demanding utterly prohibitive sums from the proceeds of that deadly determination. He was too drained to weep when his father finally passed on. As they consoled each other, husband and wife sold the Ch'ŏngjin-dong home in downtown Seoul, their home for so many years, and paid off the debts. With what remained they had bought a small house here in the outskirts of the city. The problem was the water. There wasn't any last night, or the night before. Three nights ago, only a little came out. Shin-ae had squatted in front of the faucet in the yard, waiting for the water. And at two-thirty in the morning it had finally come on. It had trickled out, the tiniest amount, from the faucet there by the front gate, the lowest area of their lot. She had filled a bucket using a small earthenware jar and taken it into the washroom. Before she could half fill the bathtub, though, the faucet gurgled and the water stopped. At four-thirty the heavens began to brighten. Sleepless and thinking dark thoughts, she forced herself to prepare breakfast.

　　Her husband didn't put down the newspaper. He had told her that at work, in pedestrian underpasses, when viewed by indifferent passersby, when surrounded by exhaust from vehicle tailpipes, he felt driven and confused. He had said that every day without fail when he commuted on the packed buses he saw city garbage trucks leaving on their rounds several at a time. Shin-ae understands what her husband is saying. She wonders how many souls a day are loaded into those garbage trucks and then disposed of. But no one in this world talks in that manner.

　　Fatigue had accumulated on her husband's eyelids like covers on a bed. He put the newspaper aside. He looked like he was about to faint dead away.

"You haven't listened to a word I've said."

It seems to her now that even the members of her own family each speak a different language. What they say never gets through.

"What in the world are you talking about?" her husband asked.

"I'm saying we're dwarfs!" Shin-ae said, practically shouting.

"How come we're dwarfs?" came her daughter's voice from the veranda.

Followed by the idiotic blaring of a television. The family in the house behind theirs had turned on their set. _What are they, deaf? It's so loud. Aren't there any normal people anymore?_ At the same hour each night the woman of that house called her young children, and the housekeeper too before she had finished the dishes, and sat them down, and they all proceeded to sniffle. First the housekeeper weeps, then the woman weeps, and finally the children sniffle. When they aren't crying they're laughing. And if it's not crying or laughing then it's singing. "Why, Why Do You Call Me?" or else "Nothing Better" or else "Darling, You Don't Know."

The children who live in that house read weekly magazines in bed. Among the articles they read is this one: "'Sexy Sounds' from a Car—Orgasmic Outcries and Heavy Breathing, Recorded Live."

The soap opera continued to blare from the TV. Two members of that family weren't home yet: the man of the house and the eldest daughter. The man is an inspector at the tax office. What's lacking in that family is one thing alone—a soul. There's always plenty of everything else. Well, perhaps the "always" part isn't quite accurate.

Misconduct, corruption, bureaucratic cleanup—there was a time when those words appeared almost daily in the newspaper. Only then did the family in back lower the volume on their TV. They stowed away their refrigerator, washer, piano, tape player, and other such possessions in the basement and brought out their old clothes to wear in public. The newspaper often quoted a high official as saying that any government official whose misconduct came to light would be dealt with in accordance with the law. But the misconduct of the man of the house in back must not have come to light, for he emerged unscathed. "If misconduct comes to light"—these words smacked of a very peculiar irony.

In any event, the family in back emerged unscathed, the television soap opera continued, and the man of the house and the eldest daughter still hadn't returned. Where could that man be at this hour, and what could he be doing? Where could the eldest daughter be, and what could *she* be doing?

The eldest daughter had taken a drug. Fortunately they had found her shortly thereafter and managed to save her. A doctor arrived, put a rubber tube down her throat, and flushed out the poison. The tax inspector and his wife heaved a sigh of relief. The doctor, though, shook his head.

"Too early. If you let her stay here, she'll take it again."

"Then what should we do, Doctor?" asked the woman of the house in back. She trembled pathetically.

"With all due respect, you should take her to a clinic."

"Excuse me?"

"A clinic."

"Couldn't you have her admitted to your clinic, Doctor?"

"I'm afraid I can't help you," said the doctor. "You need to find an obstetrics clinic."

At the time, the eldest daughter was wearing a long skirt.

That morning Shin-ae had seen her leave the house in long, loose-fitting pants that swept back and forth as she walked down the alley.

If you go by the government pay scale, the salary of the man of the house in back is quite a bit less than that of Shin-ae's husband. Shin-ae's small family lives humbly on a larger salary but their large family lives extravagantly on a smaller salary. How do you explain it? *We've heard about the good life till our ears ache, but the family in back seem to be the only ones enjoying it.* No poverty there. And so Shin-ae asks herself: *For goodness' sake, which side is that family on? And which side are we on? Which side is good, and which is bad? And for goodness' sake, can you even say there's a good side to this world?*

Feeling edgier by the minute, Shin-ae clapped her hands over her ears trying to block out the sound of the TV from the house in back.

"Hye-yŏng," she said, raising her voice to her daughter in the room across the way. "How about turning off the radio?"

"Is that better?"

The sound grew softer but the English-language song from her daughter's radio was still audible among the actors' voices from the TV.

"Kill it."

"Mom, you're acting weird tonight."

Her daughter approached. She was in her pajamas. She was holding her math notebook.

"If you're going to study, the radio has to be off."

"Mom, you're saying that because you don't know any better."

"I don't? Are you telling me I'm wrong?"

"You're wrong."

Shin-ae heard her heart drop. "All right, then, how am I wrong?"

Again she considered her age and her daughter's. They live in the same world yet fail to understand each other. It's because they think differently. She grew morose.

In the meantime her husband had fallen asleep. His face wore a scowl. _He'll be better come morning._ What sort of anxieties kept him up so late last night?

"It's too loud!" called out her son from the room between his parents' and sister's rooms.

Shin-ae, daughter in tow, went out.

"What's the fuss?"

"We've got to move! Listen to that racket. We get it from the front and we get it from the back. Why should we put up with it?"

The TV from the house across the alley sounded louder in the middle room. Shin-ae hadn't been paying attention to the sound of that TV that evening.

"At least _we_ can try to be quiet," said Shin-ae. "Father's sleeping."

"Are you kidding? How can he sleep through this?"

"You're not old enough to know what it means to be exhausted."

In her son's hand was a black notebook several times thicker than her daughter's math notebook. Her son's classes are more advanced than her daughter's. It's amazing the variety of knowledge that's accumulating in such orderly fashion inside his head. At this rate, a few more years of study and he'll have a chance for more status and income than anyone else his age.

But Shin-ae felt stifled when she mulled over her son's future. She sensed that for some time now her son believed that nothing was right except what he learned at school. The schoolteachers taught that everything is good. This was the accepted way of thinking in society at large. But to Shin-ae's son it was an absurd lie that concealed a lot.

The son had absorbed too much influence from his father. He would probably suffer on account of the ideas passed on to him by his father. Wouldn't those ideas, so forthright, so righteous, prove to be yet another source of aggravation for her son? It was clear that he'd meet with a frightful shock when he ventured out into the world.

"Your father couldn't get to sleep last night," said Shin-ae.

The TV from across the alley was as loud as ever.

She recalled the face of the man of that house. This man works in the advertising department of a baking company. Shin-ae was among those who had received a box of cookies from him. The wife had distributed a box to each of the neighbors, saying her husband had been promoted to assistant director.

"Just a little something—see how you like them," the woman said. "Daddy's assistant director now."

She was volunteering information.

"Things are looking up. People who know about our good fortune are making a big fuss because we haven't done anything for them. And it's understandable, since the budget for the ad department is several billion *wŏn*. The people who handle TV, radio, and newspaper ads have started coming around. And people from the ad agencies, too. It's not just cookies—his company produces ice cream and milk, too, and that's why they have such an unbelievable budget for advertising."

"Billions? I'll say it's unbelievable. But why do these people come to your house?"

The woman stared at Shin-ae. And then she spoke quickly. "They want him to buy ads. They want his business, and to get it they come loaded with money. People who know our situation realize that in six months Daddy's going to make a bundle."

"A bundle of what?"

"Money, that's what."

"How much of a bundle?"

That was the start of it. The family across the alley grew noisy. And more than just noisy, the house was unusually well lit and produced new smells. From the vent window of the kitchen, which faced Shin-ae's yard, the smell of broiling meat rode the breeze to Shin-ae's house. When her family sits down to dinner around their humble meal dominated by vegetable dishes, the aroma of grilled short ribs wafts across their yard.

The sound of voices comes in, too.

"Children, eat your dinner."

"I don't want it."

"I cooked some ribs for you."

"I said I don't want any!"

"Well, later then. Pok-sun, why don't you bring everybody a glass of orange juice."

Like the neighbors in back, those across the alley became a scourge to Shin-ae.

"Would you like to see our new TV?" the woman had said not long afterward.

This was the TV that was blaring now.

"If a problem is important then you need to sit yourself down till you solve it," Shin-ae told her son. "You can do anything you put your mind to. Don't let yourself be bothered by the sound of a TV in someone else's house. If you do, then it means your mind is drifting. Didn't you say you wanted a job where you could make a difference? The great people of the past, they didn't dedicate their lives to outmoded notions. I think I heard that from you. You say such things and yet you let little things get to you. If you can't study, then go outside and get some fresh air."

Her son said nothing. He wore a pained expression.

Shin-ae had spoken and now her heart ached. She closed the door to her son's room.

Her daughter had stepped down to the yard. Shin-ae saw her turn on the faucet at the front of the yard.

"Not a peep out of it," her daughter said.

"No reason why there should be."

Shin-ae approached and her daughter observed her.

"Please go to bed early tonight," her daughter said.

"Why?"

"I'll get the water."

"What's this all about?" Shin-ae demanded.

"I want to do it, that's all."

"It doesn't come on until two in the morning."

"Still, I can sleep afterward. Every night I go to bed early and it bothers me to think about you sitting there in front of the faucet. You're out here in the middle of the night when other moms are sound asleep. Other moms let their housekeeper get the water; *they* go to bed early. The people in front and back of us, they have their own water supply—they don't need much from the city. It upsets me to think that every night when I'm going to sleep my mom is out here like someone on a desert island. Please go to bed early tonight—I'll take care of the water for you."

"You'll be dozing off in class."

Shin-ae spoke like this, but her heart thrilled. *All of a sudden our Hye-yŏng is so mature! And before I know it she'll be old enough to say, "Mom, I'm tired of everything."*

"But I'm still wondering about what you said earlier. Why am I wrong?"

"Did I say that?"

"Yes—when I said you have to turn off the radio when you study, you told me I was wrong."

"Really, Mom." Her daughter blushed.

On the TVs, front and back, a commercial jingle came to a climax.

"I'd already forgotten," said her daughter. "But Mom, please try to be a little more understanding."

"About what?"

"I feel like I can study better when I'm listening to a pop song."

"That's a new one."

"Honest, Mom, that's how I feel."

"All of a sudden the world you two live in seems so narrow."

"You mean it was different when you were young?"

"Yes, it was. When your dad and I were your age we took part in campaigns in the farm villages—we were all quite devoted. And they tell me your grandfather spent time in China, Manchuria, Siberia, even Hawaii. Now there's a man who had a hard time of it."

"But why?"

"Why?" Shin-ae looked into her daughter's face. "For the country—that's why."

"But I don't understand why Grandfather was unhappy till the end of his life."

"The way things worked out didn't please him. Bring me that bucket," said Shin-ae. "For you kids, there isn't a country to save anymore."

"Mom, why don't you go inside now," her daughter said again. "I'll go to bed after I get the water."

"Well, we could both get it."

"Is it on already?"

Shin-ae squatted, almost kneeling, at the front of the yard and lifted the iron lid of the water meter hole. Then she bent over. "Goodness—now how did I forget that?"

To her daughter she sounded uncommonly composed. From the hole she retrieved the fillet knife.

"I was using it this afternoon and I guess I left it there."

"Mom, that's blood, isn't it?"

"It's all right," Shin-ae said. "I had a little accident this afternoon." Her voice was still composed.

The daughter looked into her mom's face.

Shin-ae thought of the dwarf. Earlier that day the dwarf had been standing in front of the two neighbor women, toolbag draped over his shoulder.

"Trust me, ma'am," said the dwarf. "Please trust me and let me take care of it."

The woman of the house in back shook her head. "I don't trust you."

The dwarf said nothing.

The woman inspected the dwarf. "How old are you?"

"Fifty-two, ma'am."

"Good lord, is that right!" She inspected him once again.

The dwarf spoke up: "I can't find work anymore. And my kids lost their jobs at the factory and *they're* out of work. Please let me do this— I'll give you an honest job."

But the two women, looming over him like giants, shook their heads. The dwarf did not even come up to their shoulders.

Shin-ae had been looking out the vent window of her kitchen. The dwarf stood silently, toolbag over his shoulder.

"Mister?" Shin-ae spoke impulsively. "Could you do something for us?" She had said this without knowing what the dwarf did or what work she could give him to do in the house.

"He's lying," said the woman from across the alley before the dwarf could answer. "He says he can put in a new faucet so we can have water sooner. Have you ever heard of such a thing?"

"Why is it a lie?" said Shin-ae. Her voice sounded louder than she had intended.

"Go ahead, then. You have him do it and see what happens," said the woman from the house in back.

"Thank you, we will," Shin-ae said as she closed the vent window.

She emerged from the kitchen and stepped down to the yard. In the sunshine stood the faucet, bone dry. There wasn't a drop of moisture in the house. Out she went. But it was the strangest thing. No one was there. The dwarf was nowhere to be seen. As Shin-ae walked up the alley she looked toward the side street that connected with the main street. The dwarf had left the alley and was turning right onto the main street, where the bus ran.

Shin-ae scurried toward the main street. The dwarf was out of sight. She was met with the ear-splitting sound of a stereo from an appliance shop. She followed the main street until she arrived at a weathered sign. On it were painted a faucet and a pump.

"What can we do for you, ma'am?" said a man inside the shop. "Are you planning to dig a well?" he asked politely.

"No."

Shin-ae peered inside.

"Come on in."

"We're not getting any water from the city line."

Shin-ae entered the shop like someone being pushed from behind.

"Then you ought to have a well dug." The man was standing in front of a heap of metal pipe. "Once you have the well, you put in your own water service. We've put in practically every private service in the neighborhood. Where do you live, ma'am?"

"Down below the grape patch."

"We've done a lot of work there. Hooked up the gentleman who works at the tax office."

"The missus here lives just this side of them," said another man. Half a dozen men were playing flower cards at the foot of the pile of pipe.

"Well, then, you probably know all about us, ma'am. We hooked up the baking company gentleman, too. Turn on the tap and the water gushes out, anytime you want. No different from using the city water line."

As the man spoke, a chipped front tooth came into view. His right arm sported a tattoo of a nude woman. Again he spoke, revealing the chipped tooth.

"Don't let the cost of it be your priority, or you'll end up worrying about water the rest of your life. Just try it and see how you like it. We had a gentleman ask us to come and look at his water line—well, you can look till the cows come home but what good will it do? While we're on the subject, I might add that we did a job up there where the president of the wig factory lives. They have a big swimming pool and they fill it with their own water. It sounds simple, but when I tell people that an automatic pump does the filling, they're always surprised."

"What if we put in a new faucet? Won't we get our water sooner that way?"

"Hell, no—doesn't make sense."

Shin-ae regretted having entered the shop. "Well, that's all I wanted to know." Best be gone quickly, she told herself.

"Hey!"

The man's shout made Shin-ae's heart drop.

"You—I'm talking to you!"

With a frightening scowl the man hefted a cast-iron pump by the bottom. To Shin-ae the change in the man's behavior was inconceivable. The dwarf had appeared outside and the man was about to run out after him. Steadying the heavy toolbag on his shoulder, the dwarf stepped backward hesitantly, then walked quickly out of sight. Shin-ae nudged the man aside and left. The man said something, revealing his chipped tooth, and followed Shin-ae. She couldn't understand what he was saying. The dwarf was taking the main street. Shin-ae ran along, not looking back. From the shopfront the man shouted something. Shin-ae pursued the dwarf while trying to calm her racing heart. Presently the man's voice could no longer be heard. The dwarf stepped clear of a cultivator emerging from an alley on the left. This was the last place you would expect to see a cultivator, a machine manufactured at a farm equipment factory, transporting a load of coal briquettes.

Shin-ae walked right up to the dwarf. "So here you are."

The dwarf scanned the surroundings, then stepped into the alley. Shin-ae, remaining where the dwarf had stood, saw the man in front of the pump shop glaring in her direction.

"Is he still there?" the dwarf asked, not stirring from the alley.

"He went back inside," Shin-ae said.

The dwarf set down his toolbag and mopped the sweat from his face.

"Why are you scared of him?" Shin-ae asked.

The dwarf blinked like a scared rabbit.

What could possibly have inspired such terror? Shin-ae wondered. Several people stood in front of a drugstore waiting to use a pay phone.

As she turned to look at them the dwarf moved his hand. He tore off a piece of pastry from his pocket and put it in his mouth.

"Could you help us out, mister?" said Shin-ae.

Tight-lipped, the dwarf observed her.

Shin-ae turned and walked off. Behind her she heard the steps of the still silent dwarf.

"I'm sorry," he said by and by. "I was afraid you and the neighbor women would get into a fight on my account, so I left."

The dwarf's toolbag, which he had slung over his shoulder, contained a variety of well-worn tools. That toolbag was much too heavy for him.

"Why don't you set it down," said Shin-ae.

The dwarf set to work. He removed the iron lid and examined the water meter. Then he produced a measuring stick and measured its depth. He also measured the height of the faucet above the ground in front of the soy crock terrace.

"Ma'am, look," said the dwarf. "This spigot's six feet or so above your water line. And it's about five feet above where the line joins your meter. The other problem is, the city doesn't have enough water for everybody. And the pressure's low. So I'm going to put in a new spigot for you that's lower. That way you'll get your water before those other families, because their spigots are high, too. I'm not a liar, ma'am."

"I know," said Shin-ae, her heart pounding.

"We'll keep the new spigot behind the meter," said the dwarf. "Can't put it in front. That would be cheating—same as stealing. You'll have to get down on your stomach to fetch water, but that's better than staying up all night. I imagine you'll get your water three or four hours before the other families. That will get you by for the time being. One of these days we'll live in a world where everyone has enough water."

The dwarf produced his well-worn tools and set to work. Shin-ae's heart was still racing. The dwarf bent over so far he looked as if he were planted upside down, and cut through the city water line. His tools had been used so long they were pretty much useless now. That seemed to make his work more difficult. He had one advantage, though: His small build enabled him to work bent over inside the cramped water meter hole.

Shin-ae squatted beside the meter and made conversation.

"Where do you live, mister?" she asked politely.

"Over there, below the brick factory," said the dwarf. "You can see the smokestack from here. There's a bunch of houses clustered below, all with a big number painted on them. Out front there's a sewer ditch. Come on down sometime. It's kind of a mess there, but we manage to have fun. The neighbor children don't grow right, so they look real small, but they're cute kids. The wife drives pigs down the bank of the sewer ditch to wash 'em."

"You raise pigs too?"

"People next door do. If our kids hadn't been fired from the factory, I could have bought a few for us to raise ourselves."

"How many children do you have?"

"Three." The dwarf came to a stop. "*They* aren't dwarfs."

"Now why do you say that?"

"Well, look at me."

"Mister?" said Shin-ae. "I like a person like you. I was just thinking how nice it would be to have you for a next-door neighbor."

Shin-ae felt a lump in her throat. The dwarf bent over and returned to work.

"Once the kids catch on at another factory, the first thing we're thinking to do is buy a few pigs. Why don't you come over then?"

While the dwarf worked, Shin-ae passed her hands over the tools and the sections of cast iron from his bag. These consisted of a pipe cutter, monkey wrench, socket wrench, screwdriver, hammer, faucets, pump valves, a selection of screws, T-joints, U-joints, and hacksaw. Metal and nothing else. All of it resembled the dwarf. These instruments that resemble the dwarf probably rest quietly in the shadow of the brick factory's smokestack while he sleeps. His family, too, they'll all be sleeping quietly. On windy nights the rippling of water in the sewer ditch will carry over the wall to the yard of the dwarf's family, all of them quietly sleeping. On windy days they'll tremble uneasily, all of them, because the brick factory smokestack looms too high for them to sleep peacefully. For the dwarf, there lies yet another danger just one step outside his neighborhood. That danger takes several forms. This world is not a safe place for the dwarf. Could that be the reason for what happened next?

The dwarf finished his work, and when he had gathered all of his tools into his toolbag, one by one, the man appeared. The man with the chipped tooth, the man with the arm sporting the tattoo of the naked woman—the man from the pump shop. It was hard to believe, but he kicked open the gate and entered. Slap went his hand against the face of the dwarf, who had turned toward the man in surprise. The dwarf's face snapped backward. And then forward, from a slap to the opposite side of his face. The dwarf crumpled up, blood streaming from his nose. It was frightening. Shin-ae took the dwarf in her arms. She felt a choking sensation. "What are you doing!" she shouted. "Who do you think you are!" The man yanked Shin-ae by the arm. Helplessly she was dragged clear and thrown to the ground. With one hand the man picked up the dwarf. His fists drove into the dwarf's chest—_thunk! thunk!_—and then he lifted the dwarf with both hands and tossed him to the ground. The dwarf fell like a dead stump. He resembled a dead thing. But he wasn't dead; he was squirming. The man dealt with the dwarf as if he were an insect. He placed a foot on the dwarf's stomach. "What are you sniffing around here for? You got some kind of magic for making the water run? What do you think you're doing messing with houses that need wells? I think we need to fix you. How about it? Huh? How about it?" he said, stomping on the dwarf's stomach. The dwarf's face was a bloody mess. It had all taken place in the space of a few breaths. He was killing the dwarf, thought Shin-ae. And now he was kicking him in the ribs. The dwarf rolled over twice, then curled up like an inchworm. She had to save him, thought Shin-ae, and she ran. She sprang onto the veranda, then down to the kitchen. She picked up the big knife and the fillet knife. The big knife, tempered numerous times, hammered countless times by the smith while his little boy pumped the bellows, and the sharp fillet knife, thirty-two centimeters long and frightening to hold by the handle—Shin-ae took these knives. Her teeth were chattering together. She was going to kill the man. In one brief instant Shin-ae had sprung back onto the veranda, then down to the yard. "I'm going to kill you! I'm going to kill you!" She stabbed at the man's side with the fillet knife. The man screamed and fell back from the dwarf. The fillet knife could have pierced the man's flesh and dealt him a fatal wound to an internal organ. But luck was on the man's side. Because he had fallen away from the dwarf so quickly, the knife had missed. It had glanced off his side and merely traced a line of crimson down his arm. The man clasped his arm and backpedaled as blood began streaming from the wound. Fear had seized him. When Shin-ae had brandished the knife and shouted "I'm going to kill you! I'm going to kill you!" he realized she had tasted blood. The man shook his fist at Shin-ae, but it was a last, feeble effort that couldn't have deterred her. He whirled about and ran off. Shin-ae latched the gate and the hands still holding the knives dropped limply to her sides. The dwarf had risen partway and was watching. The two of them were silent. Shin-ae thought of chickens inside a prefab coop. She had seen a photo of breeders using artificial lighting to increase the hens' pro-duction. The terrible ordeal those hens go through in their coop—the dwarf and I are undergoing the same sort of thing. But all she could think of was that she and the dwarf, unlike the egg-laying hens, were being used in an experiment—an experiment to see how well they could adapt to a sharp disruption of their biological rhythms and to what extent they developed pathological symptoms. Across the back wall the neighbor woman looked at the dwarf, a bloody mess, and at Shin-ae, her hands with the knives hanging limply at her sides. And the woman across the alley was looking at them through her window. As soon as their eyes met Shin-ae's the women flinched and went back inside.

"Mister?" said Shin-ae. "How are you? Are you all right? Tell me you're all right."

"Yes, I'm all right," said the dwarf.

His bloody mess of a face had swollen suddenly. He forced his split lips into a smile. He had a strong grip on life. Shin-ae was startled—where in that weak body had he hidden the strength to weather such an awful ordeal? Thus far he and his family had been more than equal

to their filthy neighborhood, filthy living quarters, meager diet, terrible diseases, and physical fatigue, as well as all the other ordeals that
had oppressed them in various guises.

Again the dwarf gathered his tools together in the toolbag. If the
two neighbor women hadn't been peeking out at Shin-ae, she would
have burst into tears.

"Mister?" Shin-ae spoke quietly. "We're dwarfs too. Maybe we've
never thought of each other that way, but we're on the same side." She
put her bloody fillet knife beneath the newly lowered faucet.

And now her daughter was startled to see the knife. She didn't know
what had taken place that day. Shin-ae could try to explain, but her
daughter was too young to understand properly. It was a most complicated thing. More complicated than simultaneous equations and the
symbols of the chemical elements—the two most difficult things for
her daughter at school. It was on a different scale altogether.

Shin-ae took the fillet knife from her daughter and set it aside.
"Bring me that bucket, will you?"

"Mom, it's only eleven o'clock," said her daughter. "I said I'd fetch
the water, so you go to bed."

"No, starting tonight we'll be getting our water early."

"Did someone come from the water department?"

"They don't come around except to collect the water bill."

"Well, then what?"

"Just wait a bit."

Shin-ae took a deep breath. She thought of the dwarf's face.

"Mom, what is it?"

"Actually, I had a new faucet put in. Don't need that stupid thing
sticking way up out of the ground. We'll be using that one down there."

"So we'll get a good flow now?"

"What do you think?"

"I don't know."

"The neighbors didn't believe him when he said they'd get their water sooner."

"Who's _he_?"

"Someone."

"Someone good?"

"Yes, someone good."

Again Shin-ae knelt and bent over. In that position she took the bucket from her daughter and placed it beneath the new spout. She was afraid she might tumble over. "Dear God, please . . ." With a trembling hand she turned on the tap.

A gurgling sound coursed up the pipe. She turned the tap all the way on.

She could hear it, the gurgle of water.

And then it was spilling from the pipe into the bucket.

"He was right! Here it is!"

The TVs in the two houses front and back were oblivious to the lengthening night. Her daughter bent down next to her and shouted something. But Shin-ae's ears heard only the sound of water.

Space Travel

ONE BY ONE YUN-HO removed the books from the bookshelf. He couldn't understand it. Why did boys turn into jellyfish at the sight of girls, and why did girls do the same at the sight of boys? When he thought of the girls he had slept with he felt like throwing up. Yun-ho didn't like those girls. And that's probably why he had no memories of a happy ending. The ending was always the same: All he wanted to do was cry. Maybe the girls remembered Yun-ho as someone very weak. But the Yun-ho of the present moment cared not at all.

Every book he opened smelled like mildew. Each volume felt thick and heavy and his arms began to ache. But Yun-ho knew this was only the beginning. The gun might be in the very last of these hundreds of books. Yun-ho moved the ladder and began rummaging through the books on the next shelf. Suddenly Chi-sŏp's face came to mind. Yun-ho had been going astray ever since Chi-sŏp was dismissed. Yun-ho's father didn't realize this.

Yun-ho had liked Chi-sŏp. Chi-sŏp had absolutely nothing: no home, no parents, no brothers, no organization he belonged to, no school, no friends. You might think such a person was free. But Chi-sŏp was not free. There was a reason for this but Yun-ho didn't know it at first. It was Yun-ho's father who had brought such a person home.

He had brought home a beggar—or so Yun-ho and his elder sister had thought. The sight Chi-sŏp had presented emerging from the car was laughable. The heat of the June sun was almost palpable, but the person who emerged from the car wore thick winter clothing. All of it was worn-out—clothing you wouldn't want to be dressed in.

"Telephone!"

"I'm not here."

"It's your sister."

"Tell her I'm not here."

"Come on. She knows you're home. Why can't you just pick up in there?"

There was nothing for Yun-ho to do but come down from the ladder.

"What do you want?"

"How was the test?"

"What do you want to know for?"

"Oh, I'm sure you did fine—college prep exam, after all. Looks like I'll be late. Make up a nice excuse for Father."

"Where are you?"

"So long."

"Who's the jerk you're with?"

"What did you say?"

Yun-ho climbed back up the ladder and resumed his search for the gun.

"Father must be out of his mind," his sister had said. "Where do you suppose he came up with that beggar? That's going to be your home tutor. Don't get too close to him. He probably smells. And watch out for lice. Look at that huge, godawful bag—what do you think is in it?"

"I'll go help him with it."

"Don't you dare."

"I think I like him."

"What!"

"I like him. Father finally brought me a good teacher."

"You're out of your mind. You're both out of your mind."

Yun-ho's sister had had a big say in his father's decision to dismiss

Chi-sŏp. From the very first day she had thought ill of Chi-sŏp. Nothing about him would have appealed to her. He wasn't a handsome man and he wasn't physically attractive. His thoughts, moreover, occupied a high plane, and unless he made them accessible to her level she would be oblivious to them. But from the very beginning he ignored her. She was rather pretty. And physically attractive. Sleek legs, white arms, a swelling bosom, large black eyes—and inside her sheer clothing, a suppleness that would set anyone to thinking. Anyone, that is, but Chi-sŏp.

Not once did Chi-sŏp look at her as a woman. And not once did she look at Chi-sŏp as a man. The important thing was that Yun-ho liked Chi-sŏp. Chi-sŏp never sat at Yun-ho's desk for the purpose of teaching him anything other than what Yun-ho asked. Chi-sŏp read a book called *The World Ten Thousand Years from Now*. Every day he read that book, and it alone. Yun-ho showed little interest in it. The shape of the world ten thousand years in the future had nothing to do with him. His problem was the college entrance exam several months ahead. The problems posed on that exam were difficult. All of the subjects were difficult.

Yun-ho had a reason for needing to get these difficult subjects under control. He had to get himself admitted to one of the social science departments at A University. In the entire country, two hundred fifty thousand students wanted to go to college. The total capacity of all the universities was some sixty thousand. A quick calculation would seem to suggest that the odds were on the order of four to one against you. But the situation, if you looked more closely, was quite different.

Enrollment in the social science departments at A University was limited to five hundred thirty students. The very best students in the land were burning the midnight oil. Yun-ho had to win against odds of five hundred to one. It was a competition his father had wanted. At first it seemed things would turn out fine. After all, Chi-sŏp was there. While Yun-ho studied, Chi-sŏp read *The World Ten Thousand Years from Now*. Yun-ho believed in Chi-sŏp. Chi-sŏp had been expelled during his final year at A University's law school. Yun-ho didn't know the reason.

"Tell me about it."

"Tell you about what?"

"About what happened to you."

"I was giving them my opinion, and someone behind me hit me with a metal pipe, knocked me cold."

"What do you mean?"

At the time, there was too much that Yun-ho didn't know. The Yun-ho of that time, one year earlier, was no different from a child. Chi-sŏp was the grandson of a friend of Yun-ho's grandfather. Both of these grandfathers had passed away. Chi-sŏp's grandfather had lived away from the ancestral home for more than ten years. His life on the outside had been horrible. He had lived on millet gone bad, whatever millet the wind hadn't stolen, and at night he had endured icy cold. His clothing consisted of an army uniform of single-ply cotton dyed with pounded grass. Every day he saw people die. He had killed Japanese soldiers. And what had he to show for more than ten years of hit-and-run fighting in a cold and windy land? Nothing. He had returned to his ancestral home.

"Son!" His mother had called to him. "Son, the military police are coming. They're coming to take you away."

"Mother, just let me stay here."

"All right. I'm worn out myself."

That was the only time he'd been arrested. The first thing they did was force-feed him water. His belly swelled until it looked like a large drum. He felt like he was suffocating. One entire evening they tortured him in all manner of ways. He was a bloody mess. His bones were broken. Water gushed from his mouth when they released him from the torture chamber. They chained his broken legs and put him in a cell. That wasn't the end of it. The guards ganged up and tortured him. They gathered the vermin inside the cell and heaped them on his naked body.

The military police had been different. They had kicked open the gate of the ancestral home and sprayed gunfire as they entered. His wanderings away from home had prevented him from properly instructing his son. Chi-sŏp, the son of that son, didn't know what his grandfather had wanted. Yun-ho liked him.

"I'm a dodo bird," Chi-sŏp had said.

Yun-ho had never heard anything so intriguing. "What kind of bird is that, _hyŏng?_"

"It's a bird that lived on the island of Mauritius in the Indian Ocean. It didn't need to use its wings, so they degenerated. And then it couldn't fly anymore. Every last one of them was captured, and now it's extinct."

Chi-sŏp was not a person to utter a single meaningless word to Yun-ho. When Yun-ho was at school Chi-sŏp preferred to stay in the slum across the sewer creek. From the third-floor loft in Yun-ho's house you could see clusters of squatters' homes above the creek—as well as the smokestack of the brick factory. Later Chi-sŏp had said he'd met beings from outer space over there. Yun-ho had laughed. Chi-sŏp was not the sort to give up easily. He had led Yun-ho outside, saying he would introduce him to these creatures and their families.

A large moon floated above the bank. In several of the homes small children were crying. The strangest smell issued from that neighborhood. Someone was rowing a wooden boat toward the bank. Half a dozen times Yun-ho had to hop over a drunk sprawled underfoot. The dwarf's family lived right beside the bank. Small ripples of water slapped against the edge of their cramped yard. The dwarf sat in the yard cleaning his tools. Pipe cutter, monkey wrench, socket wrench, screwdriver, hammer, faucets, pump valves, a selection of screws, T-joints, U-joints, hacksaw—those were the dwarf's tools. All metal and nothing else.

In the moonlight those tools resembled the dwarf. Beside him one of his sons was fixing a radio. The radio was broken and the son couldn't tune in to his high school correspondence lectures. The dwarf's daughter played a guitar with a broken string next to a flowerbed the size of a pair of outstretched hands. Pansies blossomed there. Everything used by the dwarf and his son and daughter came from the Last Chance Market.

The dwarf's wife worked on dolls in a cottage factory. Her job was to put skirts on the little girl dolls. All day long she made skirts and put them on, a hundred skirts for a hundred dolls, before returning home to cook a late supper. She rinsed one and a half cups of barley rice, put it in the pot, boiled it, and served it with six sliced potatoes on top. The dwarf and his family took their supper sitting on their tiny veranda. They ate their barley rice and potatoes and their withered green peppers dipped in dark soybean paste. Chi-sŏp picked up a piece of paper lying at the edge of the veranda. He gave it to Yun-ho. Slowly, one syllable at a time, Yun-ho read the form, entitled "Condemnation of Hillside Structures in Redevelopment Zone."

The dwarf and his family said not a word. Children continued to cry in the houses. The odd smell was still in the air.

That night Yun-ho didn't study. Chi-sŏp didn't read his book. For the first time he talked about life on the moon. The moon was a pure world, he said, and Earth an impure world. And then Yun-ho told Chi-sŏp what he had learned from a book—that even if humans made the moon habitable, those who settled there would find themselves living in a barren wasteland. The surroundings were monotonous, the daily life wearisome. If you didn't wear a cumbersome spacesuit, you couldn't go outside the base. The slightest tear in that outfit, and you lost your life. The same if you misread your watch. If the watch was wrong you didn't realize you were out of oxygen, and you died. And night lasted for three hundred and fifty-four hours, or some fourteen Earth days. "But . . . " Chi-sŏp had said, shaking his head. At that time, there were so many things Yun-ho didn't know. And so he concerned himself only with scientific facts. Smiling, Chi-sŏp proceeded to talk about astronomical observations in outer space.

Those who work in the observatory to be established on the moon will be happy, he said. To him the moon was a golden world, a world unto itself. The events that took place on Earth were too horrible, he said. According to his book, time on Earth was utterly wasted, oaths and promises were broken, prayers went unanswered. Tears flowed in vain, the spirit was suppressed, hopes went unrealized. The most terrible thing was the suffering people underwent because of their thoughts. Chi-sŏp wanted to talk more about the dodo, but he fell silent. That night Yun-ho dreamed that an alien came up beneath his window and knocked on the pane. And he dreamed that the dwarf climbed the brick factory smokestack and sent a paper airplane flying. In class the next day nothing registered in his mind.

Yun-ho paused atop the ladder. He hadn't seen Chi-sŏp leaving. He *had* seen the chauffeur cleaning the bloodstains from the back seat. He'd seen the housekeeper removing the bloodstains from the tile walkway outside the front door.

"Whore!" he said to himself atop the ladder.

"Good," his sister had said when she saw the water from the faucet washing the blood down the tile walkway. "Good for you. Father came home and got rid of him."

"How come?"

"How come?" his sister had said. "Well, he made a mess of your studies."

"Who did? Where do you get off talking like that?"

"Shut up. You don't know a thing, but you think you're so big. You probably don't even know he was in prison."

"What does that have to do with my studies?"

"Look at this blood."

"That's enough, you whore!"

"Oh!"

"Don't you talk about him anymore. All you think about is screwing some guy—what do you know, chatterbox?"

That year Yun-ho failed the college entrance exam dismally. The social science departments at A University, which Father had so rigidly insisted on, had been unrealistic from the start. After dismissing Chi-sŏp, Father had invited expert tutors to the house to instruct Yun-ho. Each in turn drove up in his car and put in his time with Yun-ho before driving on to the house of the next student. Father thought if he just paid expert tutors in English, mathematics, and Korean two hundred thousand *wŏn* every month, or six hundred thousand altogether, Yun-ho's grades would improve noticeably. This was a departure from the usual thought patterns of the lawyer he was. He kept a pistol hidden in one of his books. His personal secretary had shoved the bleeding Chi-sŏp into the car. No one knew where the driver had let him out. And no one knew what Chi-sŏp was doing at the dwarf's house before the eviction squad had begun demolishing it, starting with the north wall. He had come back bleeding. Even while Yun-ho was under the guidance of the expert tutors he knew he would fail. He was the one who was studying, after all. His hope was the history department at B University. His father had given him an encouraging slap on the back, saying a man shouldn't despair. Failure was the fertilizer for future success, he added.

As Yun-ho listened to the steam hissing from the third-floor loft, he looked out at the snow-covered field. The dwarf's neighborhood had vanished. Yun-ho moved the ladder and began rummaging through the next bookshelf. "Whore!" he said to himself again. He could imagine the mischief his sister was up to just then. The lawyer's handgun was reluctant to present itself. It occurred to Yun-ho that he was no longer a child. He was living the life of an entrance-exam repeater. His father had placed him in a completely new circle: membership by invitation only. Days the group attended a cram school on Sejong Avenue; nights they took special instruction in a spacious tenth-floor penthouse apartment along the banks of the Han River. There was nothing In-gyu didn't know. He approached Yun-ho like a little devil.

"Gonna join?" In-gyu asked.

"Join what?"

"A club where we study animal life. We've got two hundred color slides."

"Animal life? I don't get it."

"Join the club and you'll see, okay?"

"I'll think about it. You ever heard of a dodo bird?"

"Girls'll be there too."

"Never heard of a dodo?"

"Oh, come on. There's no birds where we meet, nothing like that."

In-gyu was the direct opposite of a person like Chi-sŏp. During the Sunday night meetings of the club, he took every opportunity to show off, blabbering in a loud voice. They had no classes on Sunday. No instructors came. To keep informed of their son's progress in his classes, In-gyu's parents flew from Pusan to Seoul twice a month. The housekeeper wasn't aware of the mischief the kids were up to. The girls drank Coke in the living room. The boys went into the room at the far end of the hall. Yun-ho saw one boy open a small box and stick his nose inside. He sniffed for a time, then sprawled out on his back. In-gyu set up the slide projector. He turned it on. The boys held their breath. Inside the box was glue. Another boy snatched the container, held it close, and poked his face inside.

In-gyu hadn't lied. They were color slides, all right. Made in Denmark. Shocking slides. But Yun-ho couldn't watch until the end. He went out to the living room and picked up his bag, and one of the girls got up as well. In the elevator Yun-ho noticed Ŭn-hŭi for the first time. She was the purest and most innocent member of the club.

"I've got it," Yun-ho said.

"Got what?"

"I know why you flunked."

"Tell me."

"An alien came. Stole your answer sheet."

"Oh! Is that so," Ŭn-hŭi said unsmiling. "But why did it steal *my* sheet?"

Yun-ho remained silent as the elevator door opened. And then as Ŭn-hŭi walked toward her car he said, "The alien . . . "

Ŭn-hŭi came to a stop.

" . . . already knew I'd flunked."

Ŭn-hŭi thought for a moment and for the first time flashed a smile. She walked toward her car. Yun-ho wished he could talk with Chi-sŏp about Ŭn-hŭi. Ŭn-hŭi was extremely pretty. Yun-ho realized he went to the cram school, and to the tenth-floor apartment, simply to see Ŭn-hŭi. Otherwise he would have stopped going by now. The instructors at the cram school and the experts who came at night made an enormous amount of money. Every Saturday night, college instructors appeared. They examined this select circle of entrance-exam repeaters on their lessons. If any of them were losing ground they pointed this out and steered them in a new direction. They figured out which areas the professors were particularly interested in, the form their questions took, when this or that question had appeared previously on the exam, and which kinds of questions were likely to appear on the following year's exam. Yun-ho spent a year among them. Chi-sŏp wasn't there. There was only Ŭn-hŭi.

Yun-ho's mind was unsettled. And so he came down from the ladder. He went downstairs.

"Auntie," he called to the housekeeper. "Did Pok-sun go somewhere?"

"Her mother came up from the provinces. She said she'd be back by ten."

"Well, you can go too, Auntie. Don't your children miss you?"

"I'm okay. Maybe next time."

"Why don't you go now? Sister said she'd be late. And I'm not sure if Father will come home late or stay at a hotel. Something important's going on, and he has meetings every day. You saw the news on TV, didn't you?"

"Will you be all right by yourself?"

In-gyu was there, though. In-gyu was a little devil. There was truly nothing he didn't know. On Sunday afternoons he went to a dimly lit drinking place. It was a place that played ear-splitting music. Yun-ho was a problem for In-gyu. And so In-gyu tried to win him over. Like the other kids, In-gyu swayed to the music where they sat. Beneath the table he touched the knee of the girl sitting across from him. The boys and girls ardently rubbed knees. Yun-ho couldn't sit long there. The girl across from Yun-ho offered him some wine. In-gyu drew the girl near and whispered something in her ear. Yun-ho rose. The girl followed him out and linked her arm in his. She snuggled up close to him. Yun-ho slept with her that night. If Chi-sŏp were there, Yun-ho would have talked with him. The dwarf's daughter had played her guitar with the broken string next to the flowerbed where the pansies were blooming, a flowerbed the size of your outstretched hands. In-gyu was pleased with himself. Yun-ho went down a gloomy, unlit alley to a small hotel. When he slept with other girls he used the same hotel. The hallways and stairs were covered with a frayed red carpet. In-gyu thought he had won Yun-ho over.

"I'm scared the alien's going to come back." Ŭn-hŭi was aware of the change in Yun-ho. "Think it'll steal my answer sheet again?"

"Cut it out," Yun-ho had said. "You know what I've been up to, don't you?"

"Mmm."

"You'll do fine."

"Tell me the truth."

"Count these fingers—that's how many girls I've slept with."

"I know."

"You ever hear of a dodo bird? It didn't use its wings. So they de-generated. And then it couldn't fly anymore and now it's extinct. I'm one of those dodo birds. It's too bad, but you are too. We live with trash who take what's important and stab it in the back."

"Answer my question, will you? Do you think the alien's going to steal my answer sheet?"

"I said you'll do fine."

"And what about you?"

"I'm looking for someone. For my _hyŏng_ Chi-sŏp and his friend the dwarf. You don't know my wish, do you?"

"That's right. I don't. I don't know anything."

Yun-ho went back up the ladder and took out books. He was by himself. His mind was settled. He thought about Ŭn-hŭi and he felt heavy inside. When he had told her about what he'd been doing with the girls she'd looked at him with tearful eyes. What he couldn't stand was that In-gyu thought about Ŭn-hŭi at the same time that he was touching other girls. He probably thought about her even when he was watching those color slides. Still, he couldn't do anything with Ŭn-hŭi. He took into account the status of Ŭn-hŭi's father, and the effect on him and his own father if he were to do something stupid with her. If In-gyu hadn't been so completely calculating, Yun-ho might have for-given him. Yun-ho's father knew nothing. From the time he had dis-missed Chi-sŏp, Yun-ho had taken the wrong path. With the college prep exam just a few days away Yun-ho had been given one final test by the experts. No one took this preliminary entrance exam lightly. Because this exam, which qualified a person to enter college, had a bearing on which university a student was qualified to attend. In appli-cations to A University, as elsewhere, the preliminary entrance exam counted as much as thirty percent. It all started the day the students made the standard visit to the exam sites. In-gyu and Yun-ho had been scheduled for the same room. The two of them would be sitting diagonally opposite each other.

"Don't think I'm bad," said In-gyu. This was the first time Yun-ho had seen him talk with a straight face. "I know you've got something going with Ŭn-hŭi."

"So?"

"And you know I like Ŭn-hŭi, too, don't you?"

"So?"

"So you haven't scored yet. And the fact that I like her is no good as far as the two of you are concerned, right?"

"You want an answer to that?"

"I'll get to the point. I back off from Ŭn-hŭi—make a clean break. In return, you help me."

"How?"

"You know the layout. Tomorrow you and I sit kitty-corner. The exam questions are all arranged the same way. Don't cover up your test sheet with your arm. And before you mark your answer sheet, circle the right answer—*ka, na, ta,* or *ra*—on the test sheet. Got it? Just make sure you don't cover up your test sheet with your arm. And that's all the cooperation I'll expect."

Yun-ho had nothing to say. The dwarf's son was fixing the radio. He'd bought it at the Last Chance Market.

The telephone rang. Yun-ho came down from the ladder. He hesitated, then lifted the receiver. It would probably be his father's secretary telling him Father was busy and would spend the night at the hotel. His hunch was off the mark. It was Ŭn-hŭi. Something hot rose from his chest up his throat.

"Hello," said Ŭn-hŭi. "Hello."

Yun-ho replaced the receiver. He slumped down into a chair. More than half of the books remained to be looked through, books his father used to impress people. He'd better find that gun in a hurry, Yun-ho thought. Again the phone rang. Yun-ho ignored it. He shoved the ladder aside. Furiously he took out all the books he could reach. The gun appeared in one of them. That volume had been placed ever so naturally among several other books in the space behind a set of world history books. His father had hollowed out a space with a razor and placed the gun there. It was very small. Yun-ho made sure the chamber was loaded. *I'm going to put an end to this right now.*

He returned the scattered books to their places and turned out the light. As he left for the living room the doorbell rang. Yun-ho stiffened, listening. The sound knew no end. He had to answer it. Yun-ho wanted to cry. Ŭn-hŭi was so pretty. The previous year too it had snowed the day of the entrance exam. The snow had accumulated on her hair and coat. Yun-ho touched the pistol in his pocket.

"I'm giving you five minutes—sit down—then leave," said Yun-ho.

"Is this your room?" Ŭn-hŭi asked. So he doesn't have a mother, she realized with her woman's intuition. She came up to Yun-ho's side as he looked out through the windows. "Don't worry—I'm by myself," she said.

"Your five minutes are up."

"How'd you do on the test?"

"Stop it, Ŭn-hŭi. Will you please leave?"

"The others went to In-gyu's apartment. I knew you wouldn't. And I'm not leaving until you tell me why you're avoiding me."

"Leave."

"I don't want to."

"I'll kill you if you don't."

"Do what you want."

"It's no joke," Yun-ho said, producing the pistol. He leveled it at Ŭn-hŭi's chest.

"So," Ŭn-hŭi said, her voice faint.

"You have no idea," said Yun-ho. "I did what In-gyu wanted."

"What did In-gyu want?"

"You."

"Don't talk about that."

"He said he'd give you up if I helped him with the answers. So today I did it."

Ŭn-hŭi could say nothing for a moment. And then: "Put that gun away. . . . Will you please put that damned gun away?"

Tears gathered in Ŭn-hŭi's eyes. Yun-ho let his arm drop.

"Five minutes are up. Just leave. And don't worry about the alien stealing your answer sheet. You'll do fine. I gave up. In-gyu's not going to college either. I wrote down his name and his registration number on my answer sheet."

"You did! What's going to happen?"

"Why don't you go to KIST and ask the computer?"

"So both of you are going to fail?"

Yun-ho slumped down like an ash heap collapsing. He held out the pistol to Ŭn-hŭi. She took it.

"Shoot me," said Yun-ho. "If you hadn't come looking for me, it'd be all over. So now it's up to you. But don't worry, I won't really be dead. I'm going to the moon, and I'll have a lot to do there. Can't get anything done here. It's like Chi-sŏp *hyŏng*'s book says. Time is utterly wasted, oaths and promises are broken, prayers go unanswered. I have to go there so I can find the things that have disappeared here. All right, I don't want to wait anymore—shoot."

Tears streamed from Yun-ho's eyes. He watched Ŭn-hŭi take aim with the pistol.

"Well, there's one thing I want you to do for me," said Ŭn-hŭi. "If you see the alien, tell it not to steal my answer sheet."

Tears pooled in Ŭn-hŭi's eyes as well. Yun-ho was completely spent.

"Shoot—now," he said again.

Holding the pistol, Ŭn-hŭi unbuttoned her jacket. Then unzipped her dress. She placed the pistol on Yun-ho's desk and dropped her arms, and she was naked. Like a mother she approached Yun-ho and took his teary face in her arms and bosom. Yun-ho didn't know what Chi-sŏp had done that day he had gone to the dwarf's house. The dwarf and his family had had dinner on their plank veranda. They had eaten in silence. Yun-ho wondered what he'd been doing wrong the last two years. He couldn't come up with an answer.

A Little Ball Launched by a Dwarf

1

PEOPLE CALLED FATHER A DWARF. Their perception was correct. Father *was* a dwarf. Sad to say, that was their only correct perception of Father. They were wrong about everything else. On that eternal fact I would bet all that we have—*we* meaning Father, Mother, my brother Yŏng-ho, my sister Yŏng-hŭi, and I. And when I say "all," that includes "the lives of us five." People who live in heaven don't need to think of hell. But the five of us lived in hell and we thought of heaven. There wasn't a single day that we didn't. Because each and every day of our life was insufferable. Our life was a war. And in that war, every day, we were losers. Still, Mother put up with it. But what happened on that particular morning seemed difficult even for her to bear.

"The precinct head brought this," I said.

Mother was sitting at the end of our tiny veranda eating breakfast.

"What is it?" she asked.

"A condemnation notice."

"So, finally," Mother said. "They're telling us the house has to go, aren't they? Well, we knew we'd eventually have to deal with this, just like everything else."

Mother stopped eating. I looked down at her meal tray. Steamed barley with rice, dark soybean paste, a couple of shriveled-up peppers, potato chunks in soy sauce.

Slowly I read her the notice:

Eden District

House number: 444,1   September 10, 197X

TO: Mr. Kim Pul-i, 46-1839 Felicity Precinct, Eden District, Seoul

RE: Condemnation of Hillside Structures in Redevelopment Zone

As listed owner of the following structure, which according to the provisional authorization of new housing developments has been found to lie within the Felicity Zone 3 Redevelopment Area, you are hereby requested, pursuant to article 15 of the Municipal Housing Reconstruction and Redevelopment Act and articles 5 and 42 of the Building Code, to demolish said structure by September 30, 197X. Noncompliance will result in demolition being enforced under the terms of applicable law, in which case you will be liable for the expenses thereof.

Condemned Structure: 46-1839 Felicity Precinct, Eden District, Seoul

Construction: Lot Size: Floor Space:

*****

Chief, Eden District

Mother sat without a word at the end of the veranda. The shadow of the brick factory's tall smokestack angled over our cement wall, covering our tiny yard. The neighbors had come out into the alley and were shouting about something. The precinct head shouldered his way through them and set off toward the bank of the sewer creek. Mother took her unfinished breakfast into the kitchen. There she sat, knees drawn up. She lifted a hand and struck the kitchen floor once, and then her chest.

I went to the precinct office. It was thronged with the people of Felicity Precinct, all loudly expressing their opinions. Perhaps two or three at most were listening; the rest, dozens of them, chattered away practically in unison. But what was the use? Chatter wouldn't solve a problem like this.

A notice had been posted on the bulletin board outside. It concerned such matters as the procedure for occupying an apartment, what to do in case one gave up the right of occupancy, and the resettlement allowance to which one was entitled. The area around the office was like an open-air market. Swirls of residents and apartment brokers rushed this way and that. There I met Father, my younger brother, and my sister. Father sat outside the seal engraver's shop. Yŏng-ho was approaching the bulletin board I'd just left. Yŏng-hŭi stood in front of a black car parked at the entrance to the alley. They had left home early in the morning looking for work, then returned upon hearing about the condemnation notice. Who could work on a day such as this? I walked up to Father and shouldered his toolbag. My brother approached and transferred the bag to his shoulder. I yielded without protest, and in the process I saw Yŏng-hŭi come toward us. Her face was flushed. Several apartment brokers surrounded us offering to buy our occupancy rights. Father was reading a book. This was something we had never seen him do. The cover was wrapped in paper, so I couldn't tell what it was. Yŏng-hŭi bent over and took Father's hand. Father looked up with a blank expression, then rose, brushing off his backside. "Look, a dwarf," said those who had never seen him before.

Mother was using a kitchen knife to pry off the number plate attached to the front gate post of our house. I took the knife and levered out the nails that held the plate to the post. Yŏng-ho seemed to find this disagreeable. Agreeable work, though, was not something we could hope for. Inscribed on the aluminum plate was the number of our unauthorized dwelling, and Mother knew there would be trouble if she didn't remove it for safekeeping.

Mother looked silently at the plate resting in her palm. Yŏng-hŭi took her hand.

"If you all hadn't lost your jobs I wouldn't be so concerned," Mother said. "Twenty days from now—it would take a miracle. All we can do now is deal with things one at a time."

"Are you talking about selling our occupancy rights?" asked Yŏng-hŭi.

"Selling—what are you talking about!" shouted Yŏng-ho.

"Well, it takes money to move into an apartment."

"We're not going to an apartment either."

"Then what are we going to do?"

"We're going to live right here. This is our home."

Yŏng-ho bounded up the stone steps and put Father's toolbag under the veranda.

"Someone was talking about this only a month ago," said Father. He had just finished reading the condemnation notice, which Mother had handed him. "Since the city has built apartments for us, there's nothing more to talk about."

"They weren't built for *us*," Yŏng-ho said.

"We need lots of money to move in, don't we?" asked Yŏng-hŭi. She was standing in front of the pansies in the yard. "We're not leaving. We've got no place to go. Isn't that right, Eldest Brother?" she asked me.

"I'm not going to stand here while some son of a bitch tears down our house," said Yŏng-ho. "No matter who he is."

"Stop it," I said. "The law's on their side."

As Father had said, there was nothing more to talk about.

Yŏng-hŭi, standing where the pansies grew, looked away. She was crying. It didn't take much for her to cry. She had been like that since childhood.

"Don't cry, Yŏng-hŭi," I used to tell her.

"The tears keep coming out."

"Then try to be quiet about it."

"Mmm."

But she couldn't. We were at the grassy place near the bank of the sewer creek and she was crying. I put my hand over her mouth. Yŏng-hŭi smelled like grass. From the alley in the residential area across the sewer creek came the smell of grilled meat. Although I knew what it was, I used to ask Mother anyway.

"Mom, what's that smell?"

Mother walked on without a word.

Again I asked: "What is it, Mom?"

Mother took my hand and walked faster. "It's meat cooking. One of these days we'll have ourselves some."

"When?"

"All right now, hurry along," Mother said. "You study hard, and you can live in a nice house and have meat every day."

"That's a lie!" I said, shoving Mother's hand aside. "Father's a bad man."

Mother came to a dead stop. "What did you say?"

"My father's a bad man."

"You want a spanking? Your father's a good man."

"I want to have clothes with pockets like everyone else."

"You hurry along, now."

"Mom, how come you don't put pockets on our clothes? 'Cause you don't have money or food to put in them, right?"

"One more word about your father and I'll give you a spanking—remember that."

"Father can't even be a bad guy. Bad guys have lots of money and stuff."

"Your father's a good man."

"I know," I said. "You've said it a thousand times. But I don't believe it anymore."

"Mommy," said Yŏng-hŭi. She was standing at the door to the kitchen. "Eldest Brother didn't listen to you. He sneaked out to smell the meat. I stayed right here."

Mother said nothing. I scowled at Yŏng-hŭi.

"Look, Mommy, he wants to hit me because I told you he went out to smell the meat."

Yŏng-hŭi wasn't about to stop crying. I removed my hand from her mouth. It was a mistake to take her to the grassy place. I regretted hitting her. Yŏng-hŭi's cute face was soaked with tears. Back then our clothes didn't have pockets.

Father set the condemnation notice on the edge of the veranda and read his book. We didn't hope for anything from Father. He had put in enough work over the years. And he had suffered enough. Father wasn't the only one to have experienced trouble. His father, his grandfather, his grandfather's father, that father's grandfather, and so on down the line, from one generation to the next—they may have experienced even more trouble than he. At the print shop I once had the opportunity to typeset copy for an unusual document of sale. The setting of one part in particular required me to move my hands fast and hard: "Maidservant Kim Yi-dŏk begot slave Kŭm-dong in the *kyŏngin* year; slave Kŭm-dong's good wife begot slave Kim Kŭm-i in the *chŏngin* year; slave Kŭm-dong's good wife begot slave Tŏk-su in the *kisa* year; slave Kŭm-dong's good wife begot slave Chon-se in the *shinmi* year; slave Kŭm-dong's good wife begot slave Yŏng-sŏk in the *kyeyu* year; slave Kim Kŭm-i's good wife begot slave Ch'ŏl-su in the *pyŏngsul* year; slave Kim Kŭm-i's good wife begot slave Kŭm-san in the *muja* year." At first I didn't realize what I was working with. But by the time I composed the next plate I had an inkling. It was part of a sales document involving slaves. I typeset that book for ten days. During that time I said nothing to Father. Nor did I say anything to Mother. Mother's mother, her grandmother, her grandmother's mother, that mother's grandmother—I knew what kind of work they had done as humble people of the lowest class. And in Mother's case it was no different. Not for a day did she enjoy peace of mind, and the drudgery she performed to pay off her indebtedness was the same. Our ancestors were bound by heredity to a life of physical toil. They could be inherited, bought and sold, given away, and taxed.

One day Mother said to me, "You children are suffering and it's all because of me. It has nothing to do with your father."

She had said this to me for I was the eldest son. It was something she had heard from her mother and now she was passing it on to me. For a millennium our ancestors had left behind these words for their posterity. But I already knew. I knew that Father was the offspring of a hereditary slave.

During the generation of my grandfather's father the slavery system came to an end. At first my paternal great-grandparents knew nothing of it. When finally they learned of their freedom what do you suppose they said? "Please don't send us away." Grandfather was different. He tried to liberate himself from the old ways. Grandfather's elderly master gave him a house and land. But it was to no avail. In terms of ignorance, Grandfather was no improvement upon Great-grandfather. Through Great-grandfather's generation the life experiences of one's forefathers were helpful, but they proved of no help to Grandfather's generation. Grandfather had neither education nor experience to draw on. He lost his house and his land.

"Was Grandfather a dwarf too?" Yŏng-ho once asked.

I gave him a rap on the head.

When Yŏng-ho was somewhat older he said, "Why do we have to hush things up like before? Isn't it kind of ridiculous? I mean, nothing's changed."

I kept silent.

Yŏng-hŭi produced a handkerchief and dabbed at her eyes. Father continued to read his book. Mother was talking with Myŏng-hŭi's mother, who lived in the house in back of ours.

"How much did you sell for?"

"We got a hundred and seventy thousand."

"I guess that's more than the moving allowance City Hall said they'd give us?"

"Twenty thousand more. In any event, you folks won't be able to move into an apartment, either, will you?"

"I should think not!"

"They say it's five hundred eighty thousand if you buy an apartment and three hundred thousand if you lease. And either way you have to pay fifteen thousand a month."

"So everyone's selling their occupancy rights?"

"Yes. And don't you folks wait till the last minute."

Mother wore a pained expression.

"We're ready to leave. We could go tomorrow," Myŏng-hŭi's mother added, "if you folks can give us the money. A couple swings of the ax will take care of our house."

Again tears gathered in Yŏng-hŭi's eyes. She was like that even after she grew up. Girls cry easily. I went to Yŏng-hŭi and she pointed to the cement terrace where our crocks of condiments stood. Written in the cement was "Myŏng-hŭi likes Yŏng-su." It's been there ever since the house was built. Yŏng-hŭi smiled. That was the happiest time for us. Father and Mother had carried home rocks from a ditch. They'd made steps with them and cemented the walls. We were still young and couldn't do hard work. Even so, there was much to do. For several days we didn't go to school. Every day was fun. Several times a day a group of people we had never seen before would tour the neighborhood. That was the only time the young children in their dirty clothes stopped crying. Even the browbeaten dogs of shouting owners stopped barking and retreated. The entire neighborhood grew calm. Suddenly it was so still—what the heck was going on? I was ashamed of the way our neighborhood smelled. They had bowed and greeted Father. Father had to stand on tiptoe to shake hands with them. But that didn't matter to us. In our eyes our dwarf of a father was a giant.

"See that?" I had asked.

Yŏng-ho nodded.

"So did I," Yŏng-hŭi said.

The man who had just bowed and greeted Father said he would put in a bridge over the sewer creek, pave the streets, and renovate the houses in our neighborhood. Taking our cue from the adults, we clapped loudly, very loudly. The next man quoted the previous one's promise to put in a bridge and pave the streets, and said we should put that man to work for the district chief; *he,* on the other hand, promised to do this and that on behalf of the *nation*, and asked for our support. Once again the grown-ups clapped. And once again we followed their lead. Until I myself was grown up I often thought of that incident. My impression of those two was deeply embedded in my mind. I hated them. They were liars. They had such fantastic plans. But plans were not what we needed. A lot of people had already made many plans. But nothing had changed. And even if those people had achieved something, we wouldn't have been affected. What we needed were people who could understand our suffering and take it upon themselves.

"She's one in a million," said Mother.

"Who?" asked Yŏng-ho.

"Myŏng-hŭi's mother. She lent us a hundred and fifty thousand so we can give our renter's deposit back to him."

"Yŏng-hŭi's Mom," said Myŏng-hŭi's mother over the back wall. "Don't take what I said the wrong way."

"I won't," said Mother. "And you can rest assured we'll pay you back."

"You know where that money came from."

"Yes I do. When I think of your Myŏng-hŭi I get all choked up."

"Myŏng-hŭi *ŏnni*," Yŏng-hŭi used to call out. "Come on over! Come on over to our house!"

"You like your new house?"

"Mmm-hmm."

"If you don't get rid of what you wrote on the terrace I'm not coming over."

"I can't."

"Why not?"

"Because the cement's all hard."

"Then I'm not coming over."

I could tell Yŏng-hŭi was crushed. But I saw Myŏng-hŭi anyway. Back then there were woods off to the right of the sewer creek bank. If you sat there you could see the lights from the print shop through the trees. The people there, they worked through the night.

"If you promise me something then I'll let you do it," said Myŏng-hŭi.

"Promise what?" I said.

"That you won't work at that print shop."

"Are you out of your mind? I'm not going to work at a place like that."

"Really? You promise?"

"Yeah. I promise."

"All right. You can feel me, then."

Myŏng-hŭi offered me her chest. It was positively tiny.

"You're the first one," Myŏng-hŭi said. "No one but you has ever felt my chest."

I had my left arm around her shoulders and felt her with my right hand. The curves of her chest were warm.

"Don't tell anyone," she whispered. I could feel her breath beneath my ear.

"I won't."

"And don't tell your brother and sister."

"I'm not going to."

"If you keep it a secret and keep the promise you just made, I'll let you do whatever you want."

"For real?"

"For real."

"Can I feel you somewhere else now?"

Myŏng-hŭi, though, looked like she didn't have any energy. She was always like that with me. Sometimes she just sat there in a daze.

"What's the matter?" I was worried. "Are you sick?"

"No."

"Well, what is it, then?"

"I don't like the food we eat at home."

"How come?"

"I'm sick of it."

"You'll die, then."

"I want to die."

"Myŏng-hŭi, I'm not going to work at that shitty old print shop. I'm going to study and go to work for a big company. I promise."

"I'm hungry," little Myŏng-hŭi said with a smile.

"What would you like to eat?" I asked her.

She took my hands. And as she answered, she counted off on my fingers one by one: "Citrus soda, grapes, instant noodles, pastries, apples, eggs, meat, rice without barley, laver."

She left one finger uncounted. That was all Myŏng-hŭi needed at the time. When she was older she became a tearoom waitress, an express bus conductress, and a caddy. One day she returned home looking pale. This was her farewell. Later Mother said that whenever Myŏng-hŭi came home her stomach was big. Myŏng-hŭi breathed her last at a suicide prevention center, the kind that deals with poisonings. "No, Mommy, no!" she shouted while in the throes of the poison. Grownup Myŏng-hŭi, at her final moment, must have been wandering among the memories of her childhood. The savings account she left behind contained a hundred ninety thousand _wŏn_.

"Here's a hundred fifty thousand _wŏn_," Myŏng-hŭi's mother had said. "The first thing you want to do is let your renters leave."

Mother silently accepted the money. "No one else will move in knowing the house is going to be torn down."

"That's what I mean. Spare yourself all those mean things they're saying. Since they want to leave, let them go."

"But how can I take this money?"

"Myŏng-hŭi _ŏnni_ liked you," Yŏng-hŭi said to me. "You knew that, didn't you?"

"Enough," I said.

Yŏng-hŭi played her guitar. The moon rose above the smokestack of the brick factory. My radio wasn't working; I missed several days of lectures for my high school correspondence course.

I couldn't keep the promise I'd made to Myŏng-hŭi. I dropped out at the beginning of my third year of middle school. I couldn't attend any longer. Mother and Father hoped I'd continue my studies. But they didn't have the wherewithal to support me. Upon close observation Father appeared much older than others his age. Apart from those of us in the family, no one knew this. Father was three feet three inches tall and weighed seventy pounds. Swayed by their preconceptions of these physical defects of Father's, people didn't realize he was old. Father fell into a state of resignation and depression at the realization that he had entered his twilight years. His teeth were going bad and many nights he couldn't sleep. His eyesight weakened and his hair thinned out. His attention span and powers of judgment diminished, not to mention his willpower. Over the course of his life Father had done five kinds of work—selling bonds, sharpening knives, washing windows in high-rises, installing water pumps, and repairing water lines. And then one day he announced he would do something else: He would work for a circus. He brought home a hunchback and they proceeded to discuss a variety of things. First, he could work as an assistant to the hunch-back. The two of them discussed the routine they would perform. At this point Mother protested. We raised objections as well. Father backed down listlessly. The hunchback sat looking at us with a blank expression. He left with tears rolling down his cheeks. From the rear he looked absolutely dismal. Father's dream was shattered. Shoulder-ing his heavy toolbag, Father went out in search of work. It was that evening that it happened.

"Children!" Mother called out to us. "Something's wrong with your father's voice."

"What is it?" I asked him. Father didn't say a thing.

"I'd better go to the drugstore," said Mother. She stepped down into the yard.

"Get me some alum," said Father. It didn't sound like his voice. We could hear his stubby tongue rolling up inside his mouth. Mother came back with some lozenges called Hibitan.

"They didn't have any alum, but this is supposed to be better—you suck on them. Here, will you take them, please?"

Father silently accepted the medicine and put one of the lozenges in his mouth. After this, Father couldn't speak well. His tongue kept curl-ing up inside his mouth. When he slept, he bit his tongue.

"Your father is worn out," Mother said. "Don't depend on him any-more. The three of you need to go to work instead."

Mother cried. She went to work at the print shop bindery. Wear-ing a rubber thimble, she folded printed sheets. I grew fearful. I left to start work as an assistant in the print shop office. I learned later that without sweat you gain nothing. Myŏng-hŭi wouldn't see me. She gave me the cold shoulder. In the space of a few months Yŏng-ho and Yŏng-hŭi dropped out of school as well. We felt more comfortable about that than you might think. No one harmed us. We received unseen protection. Just as aboriginal peoples in South Africa were granted protected status in designated areas, we received protection as a different group. I realized that we could not set foot outside our area. After putting in time as an office helper and then with line spacing, special characters, and type distribution, I did type resetting. Yŏng-ho did printing. I didn't like the idea of both of us working at the same place. Yŏng-ho felt likewise. And so before he started at the print shop he tried doing odd jobs at an ironworks. And he worked at a furniture shop. I went there and saw him at work. I saw little Yŏng-ho standing amid the din and the haze of sawdust and I told him to quit. Although there was an awful din at the print shop as well, there wasn't any sawdust. We worked ourselves to the bone. Our wrists thickened in the print shop. At the time, Yŏng-hŭi worked in a bakeshop located in the corner of a supermarket on the main street. If nothing else, we were grateful that she worked in a clean environment. Yŏng-hŭi wore a sky-blue uniform. Through the bakeshop window Yŏng-ho and I watched her work. She was pretty. People would not have believed Yŏng-hŭi was the daughter of a dwarf. We thought that no matter what, we should study. If we didn't, we'd never be able to leave our area. The world was divided arbitrarily between those who had studied and those who hadn't. Ours was a terribly backward society. It operated exactly the opposite of what we had learned in school. I read any book I could get my hands on. After I moved up from type resetting to typesetting I developed the habit of reading what I was working on. If I felt my little brother and sister needed to read it, I would take the galleys and run off several proofs. Yŏng-ho and Yŏng-hŭi listened carefully to what I said. Eagerly they read the proofs I brought home for them. The truth was, these efforts involved no great sacrifice on my part. I passed the high school qualifying exam and entered the correspondence high school program.

Late one autumn night that year Father took me for a ride in the sewer creek in a small wooden rowboat. He silently plied the oars.

"Come back!" Yŏng-hŭi shouted from the yard. "That boat's not safe!"

Father rowed out into the stream anyway. Yŏng-hŭi's faint outline came into view, beckoning us. Starlight glittered on the surface of the water. The boat was leaking. We had made off with some planks when the church on the hill was built. Yŏng-ho and I had risen late at night and brought them home. It was no loss to the church. Our boat, though, was in bad shape. Yŏng-hŭi worried about Father. I knew how to swim. In the middle of the stream Father took in the oars. The water in the boat was up to our ankles. I removed a shoe and bailed. Father took the shoe from me. He was smiling.

"Yŏng-su," he said. "Remember the hunchback who was here yesterday?"

"When?"

"Yesterday."

I took off my other shoe and bailed with it. Again Father stopped me.

"I don't know what you mean," I said.

"It's no use playing dumb. I know what you're thinking."

"What do you mean?" I asked respectfully.

He was talking about something that had happened three and a half years ago, not yesterday. It was the first time I had ever seen the hunchback. Father, however, continued.

"We used to work together. We did a balancing act on a huge wheel."

"Father, what are you saying? When did you do that?"

"You're the oldest son. If you, the oldest son, won't believe me, then your brother and sister won't."

"I'm sure Mother doesn't know about this, either."

"Son," Father said. "You're the only one who needs to know. Your mother is ill. The hunchback who was here yesterday will come again. Don't stop me. The other work is too hard for me now. How long did you think I could change water lines and install pumps? I can't come down tall buildings on a rope anymore, either. I just can't do it."

"It's all right if you don't work, Father. *We're* working."

"Who told all of you to go to work?" Father said. "All you need to do is go to school. That's your job."

"All right, Father," I said. "Now please give me that shoe."

Father gazed at me, then returned the shoe. I bailed water.

"Yesterday the hunchback was here because he wanted to help me. He'll be here tomorrow too. You say you've never met him? Don't be ridiculous. He and I worked together. Remember? Don't you even think of trying to lord it over me."

"When did you say that man was here?"

"Yesterday."

"Please pass me those oars."

Father gave me the oars. There was nothing I could say. It was three and a half years previous, and not the day before, when we had met the hunchback, but Father wouldn't have believed me had I told him this now. I rowed carefully. The boat had sunk beneath the surface by the time we reached shore. I took Father in my arms and we made our way through the waterweeds. Both of us were soaked. Father was shivering all over. I handed him to Mother. There was no one in this world who was better at nursing Father.

"Something's wrong with Father," I said.

"You shut your mouth!" said Mother. "When is it ever going to sink in? He's worn out, that's why."

That winter Father kept to his room. I retrieved the boat and tied it to a post. The days grew cold and I brought the boat into our yard. That same night the stream froze over.

In the evening Myŏng-hŭi's mother visited once again. "Yŏng-hŭi's Mother," she said, "wait a bit longer. The price they're offering for the occupancy rights keeps going up. It was a hundred and seventy thousand this morning, and now it's jumped to one eighty-five. We were foolish to go ahead and sell—look at what we lost."

"Goodness!"

"Fifteen thousand!"

Mother found the aluminum number plate she had pried off during the day and wrapped it in a piece of paper. This she placed in the wardrobe along with the condemnation notice.

"Yŏng-hŭi," Mother called. "Where did your father go?"

"I don't know."

"Yŏng-ho."

"Father went out a little while ago. He didn't say anything."

"Yŏng-hŭi, where's Eldest Brother?"

"Inside."

"I wonder where he could have gone." Mother's voice had grown anxious. "Children, go find your father."

I was reading the book Father had put down before he left. It was called *The World Ten Thousand Years from Now*. All day long Yŏng-hŭi had sat in front of the pansies playing her guitar with the broken string. It was the guitar we had bought at the Last Chance Market. That's where I had gone to buy a radio for my high school correspondence course lessons, and Yŏng-hŭi had tagged along. I had found a radio in usable condition. Yŏng-hŭi had picked up a guitar lying in the dust and tried it out. She bent over the instrument and strummed it. Her profile, half covered by her long hair, was so pretty. The sound she produced on the guitar was a perfect complement to her. I wouldn't be able to afford the radio now. So I found a cheaper one and gestured toward the guitar Yŏng-hŭi was holding. The radio broke down and one of the guitar strings snapped. Yŏng-hŭi played the guitar, snapped string and all. I didn't know what was on Father's mind. Father had borrowed *The World Ten Thousand Years from Now* from a young man who lived in the residential area across the sewer creek. His name was Chi-sŏp. He lived in a three-story house in that bright, clean residential area. The family had hired Chi-sŏp as a tutor. He and Father were able to communicate with each other. I had overheard Chi-sŏp. We could expect nothing from this world, he had said.

"Why is that?" Father had asked.

"Because the only thing people have are selfish desires," said Chi-sŏp. "There is not a soul who knows what it is to shed tears for others. A land with such people and no others is a dead land."

"I'll say!"

"Haven't you worked your whole life long, sir?"

"Worked? Yes, I have. And I've worked hard. Everyone in the family's worked hard."

"And you've never done anything bad? Never broken the law?"

"No."

"In that case, you must not have prayed. Or else your heart's not in your prayers."

"I've prayed."

"But look at yourself. Isn't it obvious that something's wrong? Haven't you been treated unfairly? Now you must leave this dead land."

"Leave? Where to?"

"To the moon."

"Children!"

Mother's anxious voice was louder. I put down the book and hurried outside. Yŏng-ho and Yŏng-hŭi were looking in the wrong place. I went to the bank of the sewer creek and looked straight up at the sky. The brick factory's tall smokestack loomed near. Father was standing at the very top. Just one step in front of him hung the moon. Father took hold of the lightning rod and reached out with his foot. In that position he sent a paper airplane flying.

2

I lay in the grass near the bank of the sewer creek. I was damp all over with dew. With the slightest movement the dewdrops on the weeds and grass fell onto me. I had been lying there on my stomach all night long. I could see nothing. And then little by little the darkness began to retreat. A lump rose in my throat, a lump of pain at not being able to spend the final night in "our house." The neighborhood was sound asleep. But it was unnecessary for me to wait any longer. The rumor that aliens had taken Yŏng-hŭi away in a flying saucer was ridiculous. From the beginning I had put no stock in it.

"Children!" Mother had said. "We can't just sit here and do nothing."

"What am I supposed to do?" I had said. "I already went looking for her."

Where the barbershop had been torn down I had come across The Lush.

"Don't bother looking for her," he said.

"Did you actually see her?"

"That's what I said."

The Lush had a hiccupping fit and wasn't very coherent.

"Sir, you're the only one who says he's seen Yŏng-hŭi. Could you please give us some details?"

"Your father knows."

"No, he doesn't know, either."

"How could that be? Your father sent out the signal and the flying saucer came."

I needn't have listened any further. But I stood there nonetheless.

"It looks like a huge dish. Creatures came out from the bottom and they led Yŏng-hŭi up inside—just like that. It's called a flying saucer."

The Lush was hit with another fit of hiccupping.

"Speak no more," I said.

"Well, why don't you go look for her?" said The Lush. "Go see where your sister is. No place she could be. I was so thirsty I woke up. No one else would wake up at that hour. They took Yŏng-hŭi and they flew off—just like that. They had big huge heads and little spindly legs."

"Goodbye," I said.

"I'm not going yet," said The Lush. "I'll drink these up and then I'll have to go." He pointed to the six windows and double-panel front gate stacked on the floor of what used to be his home. The day before, he had sold the tiles he'd stripped from his roof, his pump head, and two condiment crocks, and he'd drunk the proceeds. More than two-thirds of the people in our neighborhood had torn down their houses and left.

I rose from the grass. The starlight above had grown faint. Slowly the sky began to brighten. I heard the crying of young children. I re-tied my shoelaces, which weren't loose, then jumped up and down several times. My older brother had emerged from our front gate and was walking along the bank. His shoulders drooped.

"Brace up, Big Brother," I used to tell him.

"Bracing up isn't the answer," he said.

"Well, what about courage?"

At lunchtime he came to see me instead of eating. We hunkered down behind the machine room and talked.

"We don't know how to put it into words, no, but this is a kind of fight," he said. Big Brother had a way with words. "We have to fight just to get the basics. The fight is always a conflict between what's right and what's wrong. Think about which side we're on."

"I know that."

Big Brother had skipped lunch. We were limited to thirty minutes for lunch. We worked in the same factory but led an isolated existence there. Everyone in the factory worked in isolation. The company people recorded our output and evaluated us. Of the thirty minutes we had for lunch, they told us to spend ten minutes eating and the remaining twenty minutes kicking a ball around. We workers went out to the cramped yard and all we did was kick that ball. They kept us at a distance from each other—no socializing—and all we did was drip with sweat. And we didn't have proper rest periods. The factory wanted to keep us in line. We worked into the middle of the night in a stuffy, noisy environment. Of course, it wasn't about to kill us. But our pay, which didn't reflect the horrible working conditions plus our sweat, kept our nerves on edge. And so, although we were still growing, we were stunted in certain ways. Our concerns and the company's goals were perpetually in conflict. The company president frequently used the word _recession_. He and his staff employed this word as a smokescreen for the various forms of oppression they used against us. Otherwise he talked about the wealth we would all enjoy if we worked hard. But the hopes he spoke of held no meaning for us. We were more interested in having properly seasoned side dishes in our cafeteria meals. Things never changed. They only grew worse. Our twice-yearly raises were reduced to one. The night-shift bonus was much reduced. The workforce was reduced. The workload increased, the workday lengthened. The day we workers got paid, we watched our tongues. It was difficult to trust our co-workers. Those who spoke up about the unreasonable treatment were fired before anyone knew it. Meanwhile the plant kept expanding. A rotary printing press appeared, then a paper-folding machine, then an offset rotary press. The company president spoke of the crisis that confronted him. If he lost out in the competition with rival companies he would have no choice but to close down. These were the words we workers feared most. The president and his staff realized that.

Just the thought of it was frightening. If a large plant closed its doors a host of workers would have no place to go. The number of employees that small plants could take on was limited. I wouldn't be able to earn any money and might remain unemployed. I could look for a new place to work but it would take getting used to. It would be a small plant, and so the workplace might be worse, the pay might not go up, and the amount might be much smaller than what we received now. It was an awful thought. The majority of the workers had come to the plant in their youth and spent three or four years here, the precious years when young people should be growing. Except for the skills we acquired, there was nothing here in the way of a foothold for growing up. Our understanding was limited to what we were familiar with. None of us wanted to lose the foothold he'd sweated for. The company people didn't want us to think. Workers worked, and that was it. The great majority of the workers accepted a situation in which change was impossible. And there was no one to awaken them to a single thing. Nor did the adults among us have any experience to pass on. All they saw was that reality moved in the direction opposite of what their hearts thought was right. There was so much that we didn't know. This was good news for the company president. His family had a machine they pushed about the yard to cut the grass. In the yard were well-tended trees that absorbed the bright sunlight and grew fast and thick. The trees were cared for by a tree doctor from the General Tree Clinic. I had once passed by that clinic. "Valued Citizens—Are Your Trees Healthy?" read the sign. And beneath in small lettering: "Detection of Pests ∗ Detection of Blight ∗ Pruning ∗ Maintenance." "We don't have any trees at home, and I'm not healthy," said the young assistant beside me. We laughed so hard we had to clutch our sides. And then I wondered what was so funny. Almost every day the young assistant had a nosebleed.

Brother removed his shirt and placed it over my back. Soon his pant-legs were damp with dew from the grass and weeds.

I tried to explain: "No one's seen Yŏng-hŭi except The Lush. This is where he said the flying saucer landed."

"So you stayed up all night? What did you see?"

"You think I believe him?"

"No."

"I didn't know where to look for her."

"Let's go home."

"Big Brother, why do you think Yŏng-hŭi left?"

"Because of you two," Mother had said. "She left because you're hanging around doing nothing. We have no money, no house. It's all your fault. Other youngsters played it safe and they're still working—why did you two have to get yourselves fired?"

"Yŏng-hŭi always says where she's going. I can't figure it out."

"Probably couldn't stand it any more," Big Brother said.

He produced a woeful expression. My brother had always been a deep thinker. And he knew a lot. If Father weren't a dwarf, my brother could have ended up a scholar. In every spare moment he read books. After he dropped out of school he read even more books. It was for his sake that I gave him printed matter fresh off the press. He patiently read even the most difficult material. And when he came into some money he would shop at a used book store and read those books too. Books gave him everything. My brother frequently wore the expression of a suffering man. He copied things down in a notebook, things I didn't understand. These were some of the writings:

"What is violence? Violence is not just bullets, nightsticks, and fists. It is also neglect of the nursing babies who are starving in the nooks and crannies of our city."

"A nation without dissenters is a disaster. Who is bold enough to try to establish order based on violence?"

"The seventeenth-century Swedish prime minister Axel Oxenstierna said to his son, 'Do you realize how unwisely the world is ruled?' Our situation has not improved all that much since Oxenstierna's time."

"If leaders are well off, then human suffering is forgotten. Accordingly, their use of the word *sacrifice* is utterly hypocritical. I think the exploitation and savagery of the past were forthright in comparison."

"Isn't the capacity to cry in response to the despair of one's neighbors paralyzed or forfeited in the so-called educated people who cry while reading *Hamlet* or listening to Mozart?"

"We have witnessed the passing of generation upon generation, century after century, but to what end? Because we were isolated from the world, we gave it nothing, taught it nothing. We have contributed nothing to human thought. . . . From the thought of others we have adopted only the deceptive exterior and useless trappings."

"To govern is to give people something to do in order that they may accept their society's traditions and remain occupied, and to prevent them from wandering the periphery of an empty, dreary life."

For me, my brother was unknowable. While I read the notebook, he wore the expression of a suffering man. It was the very image of a dignified, suffering man. I managed to suppress a laugh. My brother probably scorned me for my ignorance and foolishness.

"What do you figure on doing with this stuff?" I asked.

"Yŏng-ho," Father used to say. "I want you to read books like your brother."

"It's not a matter of doing something with it," my brother said. "Books help me learn about myself."

"Now I understand," I said sometime later. "You're an idealist."

I felt wonderful saying this. I wanted to let my brother know that I'd grown up like him. I wanted him to know I wasn't like other boys and girls—*I* was mature enough to use difficult words. I studied his suffering idealist's face. My expectations were off the mark. My brother was angry. At the time, I couldn't understand why he had to be angry. I myself admitted I was foolish. We were the children of a dwarf. Shoulders drooping, my brother left. I picked up a pebble and threw it into the sewer creek. Bubbles rose silently from the water. From our yard I lobbed pebbles one after another toward the creek.

"Yŏng-ho," said Mother. "That's enough—go down to the precinct office and see what's going on."

"It doesn't matter if I go or not. An hour ago it was two hundred twenty thousand *wŏn*. You think it's gone up again?"

"Go anyway and find out. Tell them we'll sell for two hundred and fifty."

I picked up another pebble and lobbed it toward the creek. People were milling about in front of the precinct office. There were a few cars. Only two kinds of people were there: people selling their occupancy rights and people buying them. The sellers, their faces anxious, tried to read the brokers' expressions. They were underfed faces, all of them. Those faces smelled of tears. I breathed in that smell, breathed it deep inside me. Someone took my arm. It was Yŏng-hŭi. She looked away; her face had been reddened by the sun. She'd been to Chamshil. The current price at the realty offices near where the apartments were going up was also two hundred twenty thousand, she said. I felt there was no use holding out any longer.

"Brother," she said. "Tell Mother we should sell. Before the price drops. Tell her."

"I'll buy," said a woman. "I'm not a real estate agent. I'll be occupying the apartment myself. Will you be able to transfer the title?"

"Of course," I said. "We have the number plate."

"What does this number plate of yours look like?"

"It's a small aluminum plate. It's marked 'unauthorized structure' and there's a number."

"Then what is this 'No Plate' business? Whatever it is, it's cheaper."

"'No Plate' just means a house without a number plate. Years ago when the city surveyed all the squatter houses some of them were left out by mistake, some of them were found to be on private land, and some were lost in the paperwork."

The woman was perspiring. She dabbed at herself with a handkerchief and indicated the bulletin board. Posted there was a title transfer form for unauthorized structures. Written below it was a list of the necessary supporting documents. "Title transfer form, one copy; notarized impression of buyer's registered seal, one copy; duplicate of sales contract, one copy; guarantor's affidavit, one copy," the woman read.

"Just a copy of the sales contract should do it," I said. "And we can write in a purchase date that's a month or two before the date of the condemnation notice."

"Is that going to get us in trouble?"

"No, ma'am, because the title will be transferred to you. And you'll be the occupant of the apartment."

"Isn't that against the law?" The woman stood stiffly, dabbing at her perspiration.

"You could ask the people in the precinct office who take care of housing matters," I said. "Ask them why they're handling something illegal."

"Two hundred twenty thousand is too expensive. Could you lower it ten thousand?"

"Ma'am," I said. "Our house is about to be torn down. If we were to rebuild it, we would need one million three hundred thousand *wŏn*. This was the house our father worked his whole life to build. Our price for that house is two hundred twenty thousand. If we subtract the hundred and fifty thousand deposit we owe our renters, that leaves us with seventy thousand."

"So you're saying two hundred ten thousand won't work?"

I said nothing. The woman turned away. Yŏng-hŭi punched me in the back with her small fist. A short time later she punched me again. She was wearing blue jeans. They looked good on her. Without looking at Yŏng-hŭi's face I turned and walked away.

"Wait before you sell," said a man in a car. "I'll buy."

"For how much?"

"How much are you asking?"

"Two hundred fifty thousand *wŏn*."

"Fine. I'll come around this evening. And if any of your neighbors are selling, tell them to hold out and wait for me."

"Wait a bit longer," Father had said. "There are people who speak the truth and then get buried. I think that's happening to you kids."

Big Brother and I had stood on the concrete bridge above the sewer creek. Father had sat with his legs between the railings, drinking. I had to wait until Father finished. At the far end of the bridge was The Lush, passed out and snoring. Father's capacity was less than a quarter of his. That night Father drank half of The Lush's capacity. It grew late and the neighbors turned off their lights and went to bed. Two houses remained lit—The Lush's and ours. I was afraid Father would drink himself to death that night. Big Brother had not taken Father's bottle away from him. I tried to imagine the day Father closed his eyes for the last time. Death was the end of everything. The minister at the church on the hill was different. He spoke of human nobility, suffering, and salvation. He said humans commenced a different life after they died, but this I couldn't understand. There had been no nobility to Father, no salvation. Only suffering. I had once seen the slave sale document that my brother had typeset. Surely it was not Father alone who had suffered. Father and Mother hoped that all of us children would start a new life. But we had already lost our first battle.

I tried to imagine the day I closed my eyes for the last time. I didn't even measure up to Father. Father, his father, his grandfather, his grandfather's father, that father's grandfather—all of them were the product of their time. I felt that my body had become smaller than Father's. When I closed my eyes for the last time I'd be nothing more than a small clown.

Nobody gave us anything to do. People prevented us from entering the plant. The president and his staff stood at the window of the conference room looking out at us. They had deprived us of our work.

"So, why don't we talk it over again?" Father had said. "You're saying you two are the only ones left? All of you stopped work together and decided to negotiate with the president, but the others betrayed you and you were the only two left. Is that what you're saying?"

"Father, haven't you had enough?" I said.

"Well done." Again Father tilted his bottle and drank. "You did well and those youngsters did well."

"We're going home."

"All right, go ahead. And send your mother out."

"That won't be necessary." It was Mother. She had almost tripped over The Lush. "This is wonderful! The two of you together can't take proper care of your father?"

"Easy now." Father tossed his empty bottle beneath the bridge.

"The boys were splendid today. They met with the president. Told him that if the company was to do well, they'd need to cut a few of their own throats. And not to force the workers to do anything he wouldn't want forced upon himself. Boys, you think your mom understands? Hmm?"

"Father, that's not how it happened," I said. "We couldn't meet anyone. Our plans leaked out and we got fired—that's the size of it."

"It amounts to the same thing!" Father said in a loud voice. "If you'd met with the president that's what you would have said. Right? Answer me."

"Yes," I answered in a small voice.

"Hear that?" he said to Mother. "Did you hear that?"

"No need to worry," Mother said. "The boys are first-rate skilled workers now. They can get a paying job at any factory they go to."

"You don't know what you're talking about."

"I don't? Well, I think it would be good if the boys moved to a different factory."

"It won't work. All the factories know by now. They're all the same—no factory will take the boys. You don't realize what these boys did today."

"That's enough. The way you carry on, a person would think they committed treason or something."

"What?"

"Let's go."

Big Brother strode across the bridge. At the far end he hoisted the comatose Lush on his back. He tottered off and managed not to fall. Brother hadn't eaten right for several days. And he hadn't slept well. His tongue had developed cold sores and he'd lost his appetite. At night he felt wide awake and couldn't sleep. And now all of this was beginning to show. Brother lowered The Lush to the floor of his veranda. The Lush's young daughter appeared rubbing her eyes and laid her father out on his back. We emerged from the alley and took a deep gulp of the night air. There was Mother, carrying Father on her back. My brother turned away, pressing his hands to his head.

The workers, as they usually did, had gone out to the cramped yard to kick the ball around. They made no attempt to turn their heads in our direction. After twenty minutes, dripping with sweat, they surged back inside the plant.

"What the hell!" my brother had mumbled to himself.

"I hope you don't change your mind this evening," said the man in the car.

"If it's two hundred fifty thousand *wŏn*, then no problem," I said.

That night the man in the car bought up the occupancy rights of all the neighbors who still had them. He bought them all up at two hundred fifty thousand apiece; other brokers had paid two hundred twenty thousand. Again that night Yŏng-hŭi sat in front of the pansies playing her guitar. She picked two of the pansies and stuck one in the guitar and the other in her hair. She didn't budge, merely played the guitar. The man offered Father a cigarette.

"It's two hundred fifty thousand—we're clear on that?" Mother asked.

An older man who had accompanied the man in the car opened a black briefcase and displayed the money. He sat down on the veranda and filled out a sales contract. Mother went inside and reappeared with an envelope of documents and a personal seal. Father wrote his name—Kim Pul-i—in Chinese on the seller's line and affixed his seal. The older man didn't realize the meaning of Father's name: *kŭmppuri*, reflecting the desire of poor parents for a son to become wealthy. He had no way of knowing the connotation of painful longing in that name. One by one Mother handed over the items she had wrapped so carefully: the number plate with its knife scratches; the condemnation notice, which had caused Mother to put down her spoon and chopsticks and pound her chest three times; two copies of the notarized impression of Father's registered seal, used for the first time, to dispose of their house dirt cheap; a title transfer form, with Father's name entered; and two copies of the family register, containing the names and ages of the powerless members of our family. Yŏng-hŭi, sitting in front of the pansies at the side of the yard, hung her head. The man held out the money. Mother shook her head, retreated, and sat. Father accepted the money. He held it exactly three seconds, then handed it to Mother. Mother received it with both hands.

The next morning Myŏng-hŭi's mother had her house torn down. Mother repaid her the one hundred fifty thousand *wŏn*. The two wives silently held each other's hand. A moving truck threaded its way into the narrow alley and loaded Myŏng-hŭi's family's belongings. Myŏng-hŭi's mother wiped away her tears with the hem of her skirt.

"Isn't it funny!" she said with a great sigh. "The thing that makes us close makes a time like this so difficult."

These words were pepper in our eyes. The moving truck went past our house. Father lifted his right hand halfway, then lowered it. In his left hand was Chi-sŏp's book. It had been soiled by the grime from Father's hand. In Father and Chi-sŏp we seemed to see two people who had flown off beyond the atmosphere. In a single day they made several round trips to the moon.

"Life is too hard," Father had said. "So I decided to go to the moon and work at an observatory. My job is to keep an eye on the telescope lens. Since there's no dust on the moon, there's no need to clean the lens or anything like that. But they still need someone to keep an eye on it."

"Father, do you really think something like that's possible?" I asked.

"What have you learned up to now?" Father said. "Three centuries have gone by since Newton came out with his laws. You've learned about them, right? Ever since grade school. And you talk like someone who knows nothing about the fundamental laws of the universe."

"So, did someone say he'd take you to the moon?"

"Chi-sŏp wrote a letter to the Johnson Space Center in Houston. He'll get an answer from Mr. Ross, who's in charge there. It can probably be arranged in the future—I'll go with the astronauts."

"Would you please give that book back to Chi-sŏp?" I asked. "And don't believe what he says—he's crazy."

"Look at these pictures. That's Francis Bacon, and that's Robert

Goddard. The people of their time called them lunatics too. And do you know what achievements these lunatics left us with?"

"No, I don't."

"Dead learning—that's what you got at school."

"Anyway, would you please give him back the book?"

"All of you are hoping I'll have troubles on this earth till the end and die all withered up, aren't you? Hoping I'll be beaten down by hard work, struggle to the end, and breathe my last. No?"

"Think whatever you like."

"Don't any of you want to learn something from Chi-sŏp?"

"What the hell are we supposed to learn from him?"

"I'll show you. I'm going to talk to Chi-sŏp, and by the time Mr. Ross' letter arrives, I'll show you how to launch an iron ball."

"Couldn't find her?"

"No."

"Then where have you been all night?"

I picked up another pebble and lobbed it toward the sewer creek. Mother was exhausted too and could speak of nothing else. Big Brother ushered Mother inside the gate of our house. It was a quiet morning. Over a hundred houses had been torn down and only a few were left. If Yŏng-hŭi hadn't gone off, we too would have left the previous day. There was no other reason for us to miss the demolition deadline.

Our last days in Felicity Precinct were a nightmare. We wandered in search of Yŏng-hŭi. No one had seen her. Yŏng-hŭi had left home without a bag. All she had taken were the guitar with the broken string and the two pansies. I lobbed a slightly larger pebble. No sound this time either. The ripples pushed out among the waterweeds. Chi-sŏp was walking straight toward me; he'd just passed the lot where the barbershop had stood. In his hand was beef. Father met him at the gate, took his hand, and led him into the yard. Father handed the beef to Mother in the kitchen. The kitchen grew smoky. My brother was hunkered down in front of the fuel box fanning the fire. He stood up, wiped away tears, and fed wood into the fuel box. Mother emerged from the kitchen and wiped her tears. For several days now we had been splitting the wood from Myŏng-hŭi's house and using it for fuel. Brother split the doorjamb from Myŏng-hŭi's house, fed the fuel box, and came outside. He smelled of smoke. Father had a hacking cough. Father and Chi-sŏp said nothing. Chi-sŏp read the book he had lent Father. Father had said Chi-sŏp was in prison. According to Father, he had gone to prison without doing anything wrong. Chi-sŏp sat on the edge of the veranda reading the book. My brother and I stood beside the cement wall looking out. All the houses had been torn down and we had a direct view of the precinct office. Beyond it we could see bright, clean houses. To the right of those houses was a main street with a supermarket. The bakeshop where Yŏng-hŭi had worked was visible. From where we had stood outside the bakeshop window she looked truly pretty. No one would have believed she was the daughter of a dwarf. We had looked for Yŏng-hŭi as long as we could but hadn't found her.

I could smell beef soup boiling on the stove. And grilled beef. Mother set down the meal table and wiped it with a dishcloth. People were standing in front of the precinct office. People with sledgehammers. They crossed the empty lots where the houses had been torn down and came toward us. I locked the front gate. Mother set the table. My brother then took it out to the veranda. He worried about me. Needless worries. I would have remained calm even if they were to bring their sledgehammers down on my head. Father began eating first. Then Chi-sŏp beside him. Mother, sitting at the end of the veranda, drank soup. My brother and I soaked our cooked rice in our soup. There was knocking at the gate. We remained where we were and ate. Where was Yŏng-hŭi at this moment? What kind of meal was she eating? We didn't know. Resting on our meal table was all the time that had passed in our family, ever since the days of our first ancestors. If you took that time and cut it with a knifeblade, from every opening there would flow blood and tears, hollow laughter, and a hacking cough. The people who had been knocking at the gate surrounded the house. They smashed our cement walls. Holes appeared and then the walls came down. Dust rose. Mother turned toward us. In silence we continued to eat. Father placed slices of grilled beef on top of the rice in our bowls. They stood examining us through the haze of the cement dust. They didn't enter, waiting until we had finished our meal. Mother went into the kitchen and returned with scorched-rice broth. Father and Chi-sŏp drank. When the broth was gone Mother picked up the meal table. I stepped down into the yard and opened the front gate. Mother brought the meal table out to the yard. Brother followed with the cloth bundles containing our quilts and clothing. The people with the sledgehammers inspected us silently from across the ruins of the walls. One by one we hauled out the things Mother had packed. Mother went into the kitchen and came out with the bamboo rice strainer, kitchen knives, and cutting board. Father emerged with his bag of tools over his shoulder. Standing before the people with sledge-hammers was a man holding not a sledgehammer but paper and pen. His eyes met Father's. Father indicated the house with his free hand, then turned away. The people with sledgehammers began pounding at the house. They swarmed at the house and knocked it down. Mother sat with her back to the house, hearing but not seeing it collapse. They struck at the north-facing wall and the roof came down. The roof came down and dust rose. The men retreated, then swarmed at the remaining walls. It seemed so easy and then it was over. They put down their sledgehammers and cleaned their sweaty faces. The man with the paper wrote something down. Chi-sŏp handed the book to Father. He approached the man.

"What have you done just now?" he asked respectfully.

It took the man a few seconds to understand. "You had until the thirtieth to demolish the house, correct? The deadline passed. We carried out the demolition according to the law. So there."

As the man was about to turn away Chi-sŏp hastened to speak. "Sir, do you understand what you have ordered to be done? It could be a thousand years, but for convenience' sake we'll say five hundred. What you have just done, sir, is tear down a house that stood for five hundred years. Not five years—five hundred years."

"Five hundred years? What the hell are you talking about?"

"You don't know?" Chi-sŏp countered.

"Move!"

"You trapped them. You or your superiors. You must have known that over a hundred families settled here? And you trapped those people, didn't you? Go on, tell them—tell them I hit you."

Unbelieving, the man neglected to turn away. Chi-sŏp's fist landed flush in the man's face. The man crouched, burying his face in his hands. Blood flowed between his fingers. As he crouched, Chi-sŏp hit him once more. The man sprawled forward limply. We had had no time to intervene. Nor had the people with the sledgehammers. Too late, they surged forward and fell upon Chi-sŏp. Together several of them hit, butted, stomped him. It was time for my brother and me to step forward. But Father took us by the arm and drew us aside.

"Stay out of it," he said. "You two need to find someone who can speak up for us."

My brother and I watched, Father detaining us. The end came quickly and simply. The man rose and Chi-sŏp lay sprawled on the ground as if dead. The people stood Chi-sŏp up. Mother broke into sobs. Chi-sŏp's face was covered with blood. It streamed from his head down his face. They led Chi-sŏp away. They went the way they had come, straight across the empty lots. They could be seen passing the precinct office, heading toward the main street. Father turned to us and gave the book to my brother. Father walked off toward them. His small shadow followed him. I could no longer bear up. Sleep overcame me. I retrieved a section of our front gate and lay down on it. Feeling the sun on my back, I slowly drifted off to sleep. Except for Chi-sŏp and the people in our family, the whole world was strange. I take that back. Even Father and Chi-sŏp were a bit strange. As I lay in the sunshine I had a dream. Yŏng-hŭi was throwing the two pansies into wastewater from a factory.

3

The owl in the clock on the living room wall hooted four times. I'd never been up this late. Compared with this one night, the seventeen years I'd lived till then seemed so long. But seventeen years was nothing compared with the time lived by our ancestors, a period once calculated by Eldest Brother. And the time lived by our ancestors was

nothing compared with . . . ? Well, Father had said he would go to the
moon and work at an observatory. From the moon even Coma Berenices is distinctly visible. According to Chi-sŏp's book, that nebular
constellation is five billion light-years away. I can't even compare my
seventeen years to five billion years. Even a thousand years might be
just a few grains of sand in comparison. To me, five billion years is an
eternity. I have no idea what eternity feels like. If it has some connection with death, though, then maybe through death I can begin to understand it.

When I think of death a scene comes to mind: a desert horizon.
Around nightfall the wind gets sandy. At the end of the line described
by the horizon I stand naked. My legs are slightly spread, my arms
drawn close to me. My head is lowered halfway and my hair covers my
chest. If I close my eyes and count to ten my outline fades and disap-
pears. All that remains is the windy gray horizon. This is death as I
know it. Isn't such a death something like eternity? Our life is gray-
ness. Not until I left our house could I observe it from the outside.
Our gray-coated house and our gray-coated family were revealed to
me in miniature. The people in our family ate with their foreheads
touching, talked with their foreheads touching. They spoke softly and
I couldn't understand them. Mother, reduced to a size even smaller
than Father's, stopped on her way into the kitchen and looked up at the
sky. Even the sky was gray. I hadn't run away from home dreaming of
my own independence. Leaving home didn't mean I was free. From the
outside I could look at our house. It was horrible. Like my two older
brothers, I had dropped out of school. Just before that, I had read these
words in our supplementary reader: "Water, water, every where, Nor
any drop to drink." The Ancient Mariner had lost his boat and was
afloat on the sea. With water all around him he was thirsty. From the
outside I watched our miniature house and the miniature people of my
family, all enveloped in gray, and I thought of the Ancient Mariner. I
was the same as he.

I got out of bed. The bed trembled but no matter. He was fast asleep.
Just to be sure, I opened the bottle again and shook some of the drug
onto the handkerchief. I gently covered his mouth and nose with the

handkerchief and silently counted to ten. I thought back to the beginning. He had stood next to me while the older man wrote out the sales contract. And he had stood next to me while Father signed the contract and stamped it with his seal. He had noticed me running up to the precinct office the day the condemnation notice arrived. He had left my side when Mother handed over the items she had wrapped so carefully. As he turned away his right hand brushed against my chest. Mother received the money with both hands. Nobody saw me leave. I choked back my rising tears. I sneaked out to the alley beside the sewer creek and went to the precinct office. Not a soul remained from the mass of people there during the day. His car was parked in front of the bulletin board. I stood in front of the car and waited for him. He appeared, surrounded by his men, and was speaking to them in a loud voice. He stiffened when he saw me. The older man handed him the black briefcase. He sent his men away and approached me.

"Waiting for me?" he asked.

I nodded.

"How come?"

"Is ours in there too?" I asked, indicating the black briefcase.

"It better be."

"I came to get it."

"And then what?"

I had no answer.

"What's on your mind? I have to go."

"That's our house," I managed to say.

He looked down at me.

"Not any more," he said. "I bought it—paid money for it."

He produced a key and unlocked the car. After setting the black briefcase inside, he got in. I knocked on the window with the palm of my hand. He opened the door on the other side. Not until I climbed in did I realize I'd left home with the guitar. He took the guitar and placed it in the back seat for me. He turned the car around in front of the precinct office and we left. I sank down, burying myself in the seat.

"Sit up," he said. We had left Felicity Precinct and were on the way out of Eden District. As he drove he took a look at my face. We arrived at a red light and he took the flower from my hair and sniffed it. Then he stuck the small blossom in his upper-left jacket pocket.

"We live in Yŏngdong," he said. "I'll let you off a little farther along, and you can go back home."

"I don't want to," I said. "I don't have a home to go back to anymore."

"What are you going to do, then? Steal the briefcase?"

"I haven't decided."

"Fine," he said. "In the meantime I'll give you a job. But you'll have to listen to me. If you don't, then out you go. Fact is, you're pretty—thought so the first time I saw you. But there's one thing you have to remember: Never say no to me, no matter what. If you can do that, I'm willing to give you more money than anyone else I've hired. Think it over and decide."

There was nothing to think over. Eldest Brother said it had taken a thousand years to build our house. I hadn't really understood what he meant by that. Exaggeration, of course, entered into what Eldest Brother said. But he wasn't lying. When I turned seventeen Mother quietly tried to teach me a woman's traditional duties toward kin and family. Chastity she emphasized till she was blue in the face. She couldn't forgive me if I so much as thought about a man at night. She would have strangled herself if she'd known the kind of life I'd led since leaving home. He treated me kindly. The very first thing he did was have some clothes tailored for me. Several outfits, all at once. I felt obligated to pretty myself up for him. His office, like his apartment, was in Yŏngdong. In the office I cut clippings on residential housing from the newspaper and pasted them in an album. I did the same thing every day. If there weren't any articles on residential housing I killed time reading other articles. His advertisements appeared in the paper every day: "Everyone's interested in Chamshil. Call now for free consultation on Chamshil apartments. Ŭna, a real estate agent you can depend on—Ŭna Realty." Advertisements for residential complexes also appeared: "New Ch'ŏnho Bridge, Chamshil area, fast-growing location along First Kangnam Way. Bargain-priced units for your dream home. Don't miss this opportunity—Ŭna Home Realty." He was a ruthless man. Twenty-nine years of age, he was capable of anything. The number of apartment occupancy rights he'd bought in our neighborhood seemed like a lot to me—but for him it wasn't. He had practically cornered the market on occupancy rights in the redevelopment zones. He had also tucked away a fair amount of land in the Yŏngdong area.

His family was wealthy. What he was doing now, he had told me, was only a warmup. He was destined for greater things in his father's company. After returning to the apartment at night he would call home. At the other end of the line sat his father. He reported to his father what he had done and asked his advice. He practically stood at attention when he telephoned him. After the call he examined item by item the ledgers kept by his employees. For four hundred fifty thousand *wŏn* each he sold the apartment rights he had bought in our neighborhood—and not a penny less. It was unthinkable. I had assumed he would get ten or twenty thousand *wŏn* more than what he had paid. While he sat in the living room working, the housekeeper set out his meal and waited for him to come to the table. The housekeeper had been sent by his mother. He paid her extra not to inform his family about his arrangement with me. After I moved in, the housekeeper would leave for the night. Per our agreement, I never said no to him. No one could say no to him. I was living with a person who occupied a world completely different from mine. He and I were different from the day we were born. Mother said that my first cry was a scream. Perhaps my first breath was hot as hellfire. I was undernourished in my mother's womb; his birth was a thing of warmth. My first breath was the pain of acid flowing over a wound; his was comfortable and sweet. We grew up differently as well. Many choices were open to him. I remember nothing but what was given to my two brothers and me. Mother had dressed us in clothes without pockets. He got stronger as he grew, but we were the opposite—we got weaker. He wanted me. Wanted me, then wanted me again. I slept in the nude every night. I dreamed every night. In the dream my brothers had found jobs at a different factory and had left for work. Father made several trips a day to the moon and back. Half asleep, I would hear Mother's words: "Yŏng-hŭi, what are you doing now that you've left home?"

And then I would answer: "Our apartment occupancy rights are in his strongbox. I put them at the very bottom. They haven't been sold yet. I'll get them back before he sells them. I learned the combination."

"Who told you to do something like that? Get up and get your clothes on—right now."

"I can't, Mom."

"We've decided to go to Sŏngnam. Get up—quick."

"I can't."

"The naked body of one of your great-grandmother's younger sisters plugged up the local reservoir. Do you know why? Because she shared her master's bed. Her mistress had her beaten to death."

"Mom, I'm different."

"You're the same."

"Different."

"The same."

"I'm different!"

"You're going to go to hell because of that. A young thing and you like it!"

"That's right. I like it."

"You go to hell!"

I squirmed and opened my eyes. It was the middle of the night. He was fast asleep and wouldn't awaken. My body smelled of his semen. He liked me. Young me. Liked me absolutely. And so I could liberate myself from guilty thoughts.

I took what was ours from the strongbox. In the strongbox was money along with a pistol and a knife. I took the money and the knife as well. I imagined Father curled up at the foot of the observatory on the moon. Maybe he had already seen Coma Berenices, five billion light-years away. To me, five billion years was an eternity. Not much I can say about eternity. As far as I was concerned, one night was too long. I removed the handkerchief from his face and recapped the bottle. Thank heaven for that drug! It had anesthetized my suffering body that first night and put me to sleep. And so I hadn't been able to see his expression that first time. I opened my handbag and looked inside. Everything was there. I got dressed. My mind was a blur. I opened the door and went out to the living room. I didn't look back at him. Nothing else of mine remained in the apartment. The clothes I had on the day I left home, the shoes with the worn-down heels, the guitar with the broken string that Eldest Brother had given me—all were long gone. I took a deep breath and opened the apartment door. Outside, I pushed the door shut. It locked automatically.

Daybreak was still distant. I waited for a taxi in front of the apartment building, caught one. The driver turned on the headlights and sped down the empty streets of Yŏngdong. We started across the Third Han River Bridge and I asked the driver to stop. I opened the door and climbed out, and the refreshing air wakened my foggy mind. I rested my arms against the railing and looked down at the surface of the Han and the milky light now reflected on the flowing water. The driver likewise climbed out and leaned against the railing. He watched me as he lit a cigarette. The sky began to brighten. All during the winter, when Father had lain in bed, Mother had gone to work. I realized now that these were the dawn colors that had greeted Mother when she left the house. I heard the screech of a boat dredging for gravel. I got back in the taxi and after taking the Namsan Tunnel we sped through downtown. The sinners were still asleep. No mercy to be found on these streets. I got out at Paradise District. I passed some time walking its streets and alleys. Finally I went to a tearoom and ordered a hot drink. As I drank I produced the sales documents Father had stamped with his seal and tore them up. When we were young this entire area was vegetable patches. I finished my drink and walked along the asphalt road that had covered those gardens. No need to wander any longer. I went straight to the precinct office. First thing in the morning and it was crowded. One of the clerks in the Construction Section glanced at me as I took my place at the end of the line. He stopped what he was doing and gave me a piercing look.

"Isn't that the dwarf's daughter?"

The whispering of the employees reached me. I stood tall, awaiting my turn. I heard documents being stamped, number plates dropping into a container, laughter. I produced the number plate for our house. I felt the scratches from Mother's kitchen knife against my fingertips. My turn came.

"What's up?" the Construction Section clerk asked. "Do you know your family moved?"

"Yes," I said. "I need a proof-of-demolition certificate."

"A proof-of-demolition certificate? What for?" He produced a puzzled expression. "You sold your right of occupancy, didn't you? With that gone, what do you need this other for?"

"The man in the sedan bought it," said the man next to him.

I stood quietly for a few seconds. "Which side are you on, mister?" I said. "We're the ones who ought to be moving into an apartment."

"I can't argue with that."

The clerk looked at the man next to him. They shrugged.

"Do you have the papers?" the clerk asked me.

"What papers?" said the man next to him. "As long as she has the notification letter and the number plate we don't have anything to say in the matter."

"Here they are," I said.

I handed him the number plate and condemnation notice. The two of them compared these with the ledger. The second man tossed the number plate into a large receptacle. Inside were many other number plates. Our number plate dropped onto the others with a faint tinny click. The clerk handed me a form.

With a trembling hand I filled in Father's name, citizen's registration number, and date of birth and the date of origin of our squatter home. I couldn't write straight. I'm weaker, I thought, that's why. As my eldest brother had said, I've been a crybaby ever since I was young. Tears blurred my vision and I paused before finishing. I pushed the proof-of-demolition form in front of the clerk:

Number 458	Verification of Demolition of Unauthorized Structure	_Effective_ immediately
	Applicant Name: Kim Pul-i	
	Resident registration number: 123456-123456	
	Date of birth: 1929/3/11	

Address: 46-1839 Felicity Precinct, Eden
District, Seoul

Legal address: 276 Felicity Village, Felicity Town-
ship, Eden County, Kyŏnggi Province

Location of condemned structure: 46-1839 Felicity
Precinct, Eden District, Seoul

Classification: *owner-occupied* (O) *rental* (   )

Demolition date: 197X/X/X

Unauthorized structure in existence since:
196X/5/8

Use
Application for occupancy of apartment

Verification of the above hereby requested: 197X/10/7

Applicant: Kim Pul-i

Verified: 197X/10/7

Chief, Felicity Precinct 1, Eden District

"I don't know the demolition date," I said.

The clerk fixed me with a stare. "Where have you been?"

I said nothing.

He wrote in the date: October 1.

"And you don't know where they moved, right?"

"Right."

"You haven't heard anything?"

Now it was my legs that felt rubbery. I propped myself up against
the edge of the desk. The second man prodded the clerk. Using a
small seal, the clerk stamped the form next to the word "Verified" and
passed it behind him to the section chief. Holding a hand to my head,
I left the line. I felt a faint fever throughout my body. The section chief
rose and beckoned me. He stamped his official seal above the words
"Chief, Felicity Precinct 1." Before handing it to me, he took me to the

window. He indicated a neighborhood below a grape patch, across the main street.

"Third house from the upper end," he said. "Ask for the missus there. Mrs. Yun Shin-ae. She knew your father very well. She came here several times a day—looking for you."

"I've met her," I said. "I need to drop by the District Office and then go to Housing Affairs. When I'm done there I'll go see her."

"The missus will tell you everything," said the section chief. "She's a very nice missus."

"Thank you."

I said goodbye and left. The office employees were watching me as I talked with the chief. They wanted to say something to me. I couldn't have remained there a moment longer.

I went to the main street and caught a taxi. We passed the super-market and the bakeshop came into sight. Other girls were doing the work I used to do. If I took a look I could see our neighborhood at a glance. I steadied myself. I couldn't bring myself to take that look. My business at the District Office went smoothly. I went to the Housing Section, turned in my proof-of-demolition, and applied for apartment occupancy. Descending the steps to the entrance, I was hit with dizzi-ness. I felt like I'd been away from home for years.

He'd made me even weaker. Since leaving home I hadn't had a peaceful night's sleep. I was undernourished not only in my mother's womb but after I was born. The table at which we ate together was al-ways loaded with food. But its nourishment didn't last. It was more than just the mental pressure. He offered me tasty food and then pro-ceeded to exploit the calories it contained. Staying up all that last night had its effect too. My only thought was to lie down somewhere, any-where. I had to take care of my business and go see Shin-ae. She would send me to my family.

The taxi retraced the route I had taken at dawn. After emerg-ing from the Namsan Tunnel I crossed the Third Han River Bridge. His apartment building, standing in an open field, came into sight. I opened my handbag and felt his knife inside. At the top of the ivory handle was a small metal attachment the size of a bead. Press it and the blade shot out. I had the taxi stop in front of the Housing Affairs office. Numerous people were walking toward the entrance. I hurriedly worked my way among them. And then I was carried forward. Carried by the people to the plaza in front of the building. The white building reflected the sunlight, dazzling my eyes. It was like a banquet day—awnings and all. I found the place with the application forms and stood in line. My turn came and the clerk asked to see my receipt from the District Office. He then handed me an application form. I left the line and ran my eyes through the section concerning the leasing of apartments. Among the regulations listed was this one: "Applicant and occupant must be one and the same and cannot offer a third party the right to sublease or to lease as security for an obligation." A dead issue. On the part of the application form containing that provision I jotted down Father's name, address, and citizen's ID number. Again my hand shook. My legs grew rubbery and I felt like squatting down. After filling out the form I got back in line. In that line there was no one from a redevelopment zone but me. Even so, the clerk at the desk at the head of the line asked everyone the same question: "You bought it, didn't you?"

He asked, knowing full well the answer. But his question did not bring a quick response from anyone.

"You bought it, didn't you?" this clerk asked me as well.

"Yes, I bought it!"

That's what I would have answered if only I hadn't felt sick. He was an unfriendly man in a bad mood. I was sick. I said nothing. This clerk stapled together my application form, the receipt from the District Office, and the copy of our family register. He stamped the top of each page with his receipt seal. I took the papers, turned to leave, then made myself small. I went to the far side of the line and surveyed the area directly in front of the building. There he was, standing in front of his car. Standing there strong in body. I waited for him to leave, making my weak body small. I thought I just might kill him if I encountered him. The thought of dying had probably never crossed his mind. What did he know about human suffering? About despair? He'd never heard the rattling of an empty rice bowl, never heard the clatter of hands and feet, knees, teeth that couldn't bear the cold. Naked I'd received him whenever he had wanted, and he'd never heard the moans I'd swallowed. He was one of those who branded people with red-hot iron. I opened the briefcase and felt the knife. There he was, waving. A man emerged from the building. He shook hands with the man and together they climbed into his car. The car made its way alongside the people and left the plaza. Again tears oozed from my eyes. What he had was too much.

I followed people into the Business Section. Again I fell into line. I felt my forehead and waited my turn.

"Aren't you feeling well?" the clerk asked when my turn came.

"No, I'm all right," I said as I handed him my papers.

He verified the documents, jotted an application number on my receipt, and told me to go to the Accounting Section and pay. A woman found some water and gave it to me. I drank the water. The people in the Accounting Section asked nothing. They counted the money, stamped a receipt, and gave it to me.

"It's all over," I said.

The people looked at me.

I wonder if they knew.

I was done at the Housing Affairs building and I left. I made it to Shin-ae's house without collapsing on the street. As I pressed the buzzer at the front gate I looked at our neighborhood. Our house, the neighbors' houses, all the other houses—they were nowhere to be seen. The bank of the sewer creek was gone, the brick factory smokestack was gone, the hillside path was gone. No trace there of the dwarf, the dwarf's wife, the dwarf's two sons, and the dwarf's daughter. Only a broad clearing. Calling to her daughter, Shin-ae took me in her arms. I couldn't even produce a proper how-are-you. Shin-ae had once tended to Father like this when he was injured, and had helped him up. She and her daughter carried me inside and lay me down. While she undid my blouse her daughter brought a washcloth. She treated me as Mother would have. She wiped my face with the washcloth, wiped my hands and feet, then covered me up with a fluffy quilt.

"Thank you, ma'am." I was barely able to open my eyes.

"Now don't you say another word," she said. "We're bringing the doctor over. Let's not talk anymore today."

"I'm all right," I said. My eyelids dropped shut. "It's just that I haven't been able to sleep. And now I'm sleepy."

"Go to sleep, then. And sweet dreams."

"I got back what they took from us."

"Good for you!"

"Paperwork and all."

"Good for you."

"You know where they moved, don't you?"

"Of course."

"I saw the section chief." I wasn't sure if I was asleep or awake as I said this. "He said you'd tell me everything."

"Is that all he said?"

"Did something happen?"

"Go to sleep. We can talk later."

"I don't think I can go to sleep until I've heard."

I opened my eyes again. The daughter went out to the veranda. Presently I heard the front gate close. She had left for the clinic to fetch the doctor.

"Your family were beside themselves trying to find you," she said. "From this window you can see where your mother was waiting, there where the house was torn down. The main thing was that your father went missing. Your family was moving to Sŏngnam, but your father wasn't here. Well, what's the use of dragging it out? Your father's passed on. They found out the day they brought down the smokestack to the brick factory. The demolition people discovered your father— he'd fallen inside it."

The thing was, I couldn't get up. I was lying on my side, eyes closed, like a wounded insect. I couldn't breathe. I pounded my chest. Father was standing in front of our torn-down house. Father was short. Mother took Father on her back when he was injured, turned toward the alley, and entered it. Blood streamed from Father. I called out to my brothers. My brothers came running. We stood in the yard looking up at the sky. Overhead a black iron ball traced a straight line across the sky. Father, standing on top of the brick factory smokestack, waved at us. Mother set down the meal tray at the end of our plank veranda. I heard the doctor come in through the front gate. Shin-ae took my hand. *Ahhhhhh!* The wail rose slowly in my throat.

"Yŏng-hŭi, don't cry," Eldest Brother had said. "For God's sake don't cry. Someone will hear you."

I couldn't stop crying.

"Doesn't it make you mad, Eldest Brother?"

"Stop it, I said."

"I want you to kill those devils who call Father a dwarf."

"Yes, I'm going to kill them."

"You promise?"

"Yes, I promise."

"Promise."

On the Footbridge

SHIN-AE COULDN'T GET a grip on herself. Here she was in the heart of the city and all around her as far as the eye could see were people, buildings, vehicles. Exhaust fumes, body odors, the stench of burning rubber issued from the streets. It was difficult even to stop for a moment and glance about. The sidewalks overflowed with people, the roadways with vehicles. There was no place to linger. No place to pause a few seconds to try and boost her low spirits.

She was on her way to the hospital. Her younger brother was there. Not yet forty and he didn't eat right and couldn't sleep. All of his doctors were internal specialists. Something was wrong with his stomach and he couldn't digest food. But despite his sessions with the doctors, there was no real improvement in his condition. His weight had dropped from a hundred and thirty-nine pounds to a hundred and twelve. Shin-ae's husband had taken him to a psychiatrist. The doctors who had seen him had urged hospitalization. Fortunately, one of the doctors had been a college classmate of his and knew him well. Shin-ae put her mind to rest knowing her brother had met a doctor he could trust.

His physical condition improved dramatically.

Shin-ae climbed the steep steps of a footbridge. Partway across she stopped, moved to the side, and clutched the railing to escape the flow of people. The building where her brother's friend had gone to work was visible. This was his closest friend. Shin-ae was all too familiar with the temperaments of these two. Their temperaments were remarkably alike. When Shin-ae was young the idols she worshiped were the protagonists of a story about opposition to one man's despotism. It was the same with her brother when he grew up, despite the ten-year difference in their ages. His generation had not had a happy time of it in college. The slightest stir, and the universities shut down. And so, though it was an old story to Shin-ae, her brother's generation hadn't had the experience of being in a dim classroom during the last class of the day and watching the professor stride off after citing the tax system as one of the sparks of the French Revolution. By good fortune her brother and his friend had read books in his tiny back room— including books the other students would have found bothersome— and debated each other while drawing endlessly on cigarettes.

For these two, the society in which they lived was a monstrosity. It was a monster that wielded terrible power at its pleasure. Her brother and his friend saw themselves as oil floating on water. Oil does not mix with water. But such a comparison is not really apt. What was truly awful was the fact that the two of them stumbled along inside this great monstrosity even though they didn't accept it.

It was in the afternoon and Shin-ae's brother was sitting outside Citizens Hall on a bench where the bronze statue of Admiral Yi Sun-shin was visible. He sat on the fourth bench waiting for his friend. Across from the benches were fifteen public telephone booths. These fifteen booths, with their aluminum frames and polyethylene doors, were numbered 703 to 717. Shin-ae's brother entered number 712 and called his friend.

"Are you going to be a while?" he asked.

His friend said nothing for several seconds.

"Something wrong?"

"I'm coming—can you wait a little longer?"

"Hey, if you can't leave work now then take your time. If you're busy we can always meet later."

"Just stay put. I ought to see you today."

"I'll wait, then."

"Do that." His friend hung up.

Shin-ae's brother emerged from number 712. In spite of himself he looked at the bronze statue of Admiral Yi Sun-shin propping up the oppressive sky of this stifling city. Quickly he looked away. Cunning posterity was torturing the admiral by setting him there in the midst of traffic exhaust. Shin-ae's brother returned to the fourth bench and waited.

His friend was carried in on the Saturday afternoon tide of humanity. He sat down beside Shin-ae's brother. At a glance you would think they were strangers. There was a time, back when they were in college, that they had adopted this posture. They had sat like strangers on a bench outside the faculty center. It was the time when demonstrations—the only way the students could express their views—first became subject to suppression by a well-trained organization and the new machinery of oppression. Some of us have conveniently forgotten, but, yes, there was such a period, a period we lived through. The lips of those who held opposing views were sealed. At the time, Shin-ae's brother and his friend frequently met with like-minded students to talk. They had decided to write down their thoughts and print them in the school newspaper. Shin-ae's brother and his friend did the writing. But the copy they had stayed up all night to write was returned to them by the editor himself. To print such crap in a newspaper, he told them, was a terrible crime. And even if he did run it for them, it would cause them great pain. This man was a professor.

He got straight to the point: "What in God's name do you guys want? What is it you want? Tell me."

"Did you read what we wrote?"

"Silence!" The editor pounded on his desk. "I know, you're going to stir up more trouble. Just when we have a semblance of order, you start in again."

"That's incorrect," the brother's friend said.

"Incorrect?"

"Incorrect."

"How so?"

"There has to be an ending in order to start again."

"Now look here," the editor said, unexpectedly lowering his voice. "What have you cooked up this time?"

The two young people looked at each other, a bit confused by the subdued tone.

Hearing no response, the grown-up shouted again: "Chaos!" His voice was very loud now. "All you want is chaos. You yourselves are locking the gates to this university."

"That's true," said Shin-ae's brother.

The professor could only stare at him.

"We tried to close the gates so they couldn't get in."

"That's not what I meant."

"We can't post guards."

"Get out!" the professor shouted.

"Please give us our copy," the brother's friend said.

"No way. Not until you tell me your motive for writing this crap."

"We thought we should make it known that we have an opposing viewpoint," said the friend.

"And you?" the professor asked the brother.

"The same."

"No," the professor said, indicating the copy. "It's subversive. And you knew that when you wrote it, didn't you?"

"What kind of writing is _non_-subversive?"

"You knew it, didn't you?"

"We have learned that a country in which we cannot voice an opposing viewpoint is a disaster."

"Who said you couldn't voice an opposing viewpoint?"

"You know the answer to that, sir."

The professor fell silent for a moment. Then he thrust the copy at them, saying, "We can talk and talk but it won't solve a thing. We're not the ones who plan and carry things out. The people who _do_ are different. Since you want this copy, I'll give it back to you. But you shouldn't resent me for keeping it out of print; instead you ought to be thankful. Print this and nothing would come of it. Here, take it."

"Let's go," the friend said.

Outside, Shin-ae's brother and his friend sadly reread their essay, which was riddled with colored pencil marks where their thoughts had been crossed out. Shin-ae had read it over. It was nothing remarkable. Several times she had laughed inwardly. Her brother and his friend had tried to pour out everything they knew in less than twenty manuscript pages. Their argument was not readily apparent. Even so, the editor had struck out line after line with his colored pencil. "An unseen power is blocking peaceful change"—this passage had been scored so forcefully that several pages had been ripped. The ferocity issuing from the editor's fingertips was palpable. Suppressing a terrible anger, Shin-ae's brother and his friend hurried to the women students' center.

The pair borrowed the women student association's mimeograph and stayed up all night at Shin-ae's house, working in the basement room beneath the veranda as if on a holy mission. Under the light bulb in the corner where the coal briquettes were piled they worked the roller of the mimeograph. The next morning they left without eating. Each of them carried a stack of the newspapers they'd mimeographed. These they distributed among the students. The students recoiled and scurried away.

"Hey!"

The pair hadn't seen the editor approach.

He told them: "I was hoping you two would get rid of that copy yourselves. And now you're stabbing me in the back. I won't say anything else. But you have to realize that kids think differently now. How many of them will actually read this stilted, boring, mimeo stuff? Think they'll follow you like they did in the last demonstration? Look, do you see any students coming up to you for this ditto-machine stuff? Pick it up and go back to class. Read the situation. The exams that got postponed because of the last demonstration are tomorrow. If you're going to fight, you need someone to fight against. Who the hell are you two fighting? The sunlight? The moonlight? Shadows maybe?"

"No," the brother's friend said.

"I didn't think so," the editor said.

"It's ourselves," Shin-ae's brother said.

The editor smiled. "Let's leave it at that. All right? Then look around and see who your neighbors are."

These were most assuredly the words of a hypocrite. But there was something the editor did see correctly: Even the students who shared the same thoughts as this pair, and who met them frequently to talk, no longer sided with them. Shin-ae smiled in spite of herself when she thought of the two of them as they had been then. Youngsters who had once shouted slogans had since gone into the army. New laws had been passed. The young ones had begun playing poker on campus. They had finally discovered the fun of card games. Shin-ae's brother and his friend were in the wrong place at the wrong time. It seemed only the two of them were left. They couldn't even talk about their hopes.

The editor's observation was correct. But it wasn't right. After listening to his hypocritical words that morning, Shin-ae's brother and his friend sat without speaking on the bench outside the faculty center. Under their arms were tucked the newspapers they'd run off on the mimeograph the previous night. As Shin-ae saw it, the two of them were wounded.

They could not get up from the bench. Quickly, very quickly, Shin-ae's brother and his friend had to make a decision about the society in which they lived. The two of them were hungry and sleepy. Still, they thought about their times, their society, and their role. Shin-ae's brother and his friend had been so serious then.

"This much is clear," the friend finally said. "Everybody's joining one side."

"How come?" Shin-ae's brother asked.

"That's what we have to understand. And as they join that side they get paralyzed."

"That's it—paralysis," said Shin-ae's brother. He agreed with his friend. His voice grew softer, his eyes distant.

"Here comes The Bat," said his friend.

That was what he called the editor. The editor's grandfather had worked on behalf of the Japanese when they ruled Korea as their colony. The editor's father had done similar work. Even now you can go to the library and read in an old newspaper a piece he wrote called "Yi Ki-bung, the Man." The editor was talking with a student. This was a student who had abandoned the pair some time before. Shin-ae's brother and his friend had realized too late that the two of them were the only ones left. Their friends with the unusually loud voices had gone in the army, all of them. Shin-ae's brother and his friend sat silently. At a glance you would think they were strangers.

It was exactly the same now as they sat on the bench where the bronze statue of Admiral Yi Sun-shin was visible. At first, they didn't speak. The Saturday afternoon tide of humanity swept past Shin-ae's brother and his friend. All of the phone booths across from the bench were occupied. The two of them were utterly depressed. There was nothing they could take delight in. They still believed that a lot of people were afflicted with some terminal illness.

That day the friend spoke after a considerable silence.

"I'm being threatened and tempted." His expression had hardened. When he looked up, his face seemed desperately serious.

"How come?"

"The Bat."

"The Bat?"

"Don't tell me you forgot."

"Isn't he still at the university?" Shin-ae's brother sounded alarmed.

"He's threatening me."

"Where?"

"Check the newspaper. He's a big shot."

"Shit!"

Several people waiting at the phone booths turned to look at them. Seeing that nothing had happened, they turned back.

"Actually, it's not surprising," said Shin-ae's brother. His face was becoming more like his friend's. "It's just like him."

"For sure."

"How is he threatening you, then?"

"He said he's going to put me in a position next to him."

The friend's voice was gloomy. Shin-ae's brother had nothing to say. His friend spoke.

"I felt like a complete idiot when he called me. Even the department head was surprised; he said, 'Well, what are you waiting for?' And I went into his office. I must have been the envy of the whole place. But when I was right in front of him in his office with the red carpet, I tried to close off my mind. All I could think of was that this number one big shot, this mister sky-high, was a hypocrite, an opportunist, someone's lackey who had walked all over us. He was smiling and— get this—he actually shook my hand. 'I know this is ancient history,' he says, 'but I've taken you for a fine young man ever since I was at the university—though of course I was well aware of your weak points. But that's all in the past. Starting next week I want you in the office next door helping me.' See? I do that, and he'll pull me up the ladder."

For the slightest instant an expression came over his face that Shin-ae's brother had never seen. "In short, he's asking me to join his side," said the friend.

"He's thinking how much you're worth to him if he can use you." Now it was Shin-ae's brother speaking. "Any reason why a person who made life so difficult for us at school would change once he gets outside?"

"Nope."

"What do you suppose he wants from you?"

"Loyalty. Maybe he thinks I've got what he doesn't have."

"I don't get it," Shin-ae's brother said. "After all this time you feel *tempted* by what he says? Why? It's funny to hear you call it 'threatening,' but doesn't it sound *really* strange to call it 'temptation'? If you feel it's tempting, then who have *you* been all this time? I know this is ancient history. But nobody forced us to march and shout, nobody forced us to hide, nobody forced us to stay up all night with the mimeograph, right? You wrote that the previous generation wasn't guilty of setting forth glittering, hypocritical hopes that confused people's minds in order to cover up their corruption and the unjust distribution of wealth. You wrote that no matter how well a society turns out, for the sake of the next generation it must never lose the voice of criticism and dissent. You've always said there's one thing we really ought to be ashamed of and it isn't poverty. I just don't get it. This temptation you speak of—what the hell is it?"

But it was growing late. The Saturday afternoon tide of humanity gradually swelled. Shin-ae's brother felt stifled as he sat there. He hadn't known. He had believed in his friend.

"It's strange," his friend said in a weighty tone. "My thoughts have never really flowered. I feel like they're withering away."

"That's no good." Shin-ae's brother sprang to his feet. "We shouldn't have started talking at a place like this. Let's go somewhere else."

"Remember how I used to talk about paralysis and all that?"

"Sure. And you were right."

"There were people who said I couldn't possibly be right."

"We need a biochemical product that will work on everyone. We'll have to make one."

"It just makes me nervous, though. I can't bear it. I was getting threats from my co-workers even before The Bat arrived. The thing that worries me is that I'll have to behave myself in front of these people. Personally that's my biggest worry."

To Shin-ae, the two of them were still children at that time. That day, the two of them lost themselves in the tide of humanity and descended into a pedestrian underpass. Extricating themselves, they entered Mugyo-dong. There they drank. Drank until they could drink no more. Shin-ae's brother couldn't collect his wits. There were a lot of people. Drinking places were the only spots not occupied by their enemies—their last oasis.

"I can't forgive," the friend said. "Drop dead, all of you! Dragged along, paralyzed, can't see an inch in front of you!"

In Shin-ae's view, her brother and his friend had the same innate temperament. But, she thought as she held the railing of the footbridge, who had killed her brother's friend?

Her brother's friend had changed. At first her brother said his friend had knuckled under from exhaustion. But for a long time he hadn't seen his friend. And even if they were to meet, they had little to talk about now. His friend worked next door to the man who had given them their first wound. He had decided to make no effort to find his lost hopes. He lived in a large house with air conditioning and central heating, a house that lacked for nothing. It looked like one version of paradise. His friend's paradise was always warm. He had hung expensive paintings there. He would soon have a car for his wife and children.

But Shin-ae omitted the word _happiness_ from these thoughts. Children age and die so soon, Shin-ae thought as she descended the footbridge steps. They die paralyzed. Her brother's friend, true to his words at the drinking place, hadn't forgiven himself.

Shin-ae found her brother asleep in his hospital bed. As the nurse left she put a finger to her lips. A photo lay beside her brother's head. His wife had placed it there. In the photo his children were smiling. Little beings, smiling innocently, who weakened people more than anything else.

Orbital Rotation

YUN-HO SPENT his third year quietly. December of the second year had been nothing but trouble, as had the following January. If not for his father, those two months would have passed uneventfully as well. His father had tried to uncover the reason for Yun-ho's failure in the college prep exam. Yun-ho had said nothing. His score the first year had been 267. The cutoff point that year was 196. His father didn't know why Yun-ho, having passed by 71 points, proceeded to fail the exam the following year. When he finally found out, he turned pale. He tried to interpret his son's failure as a form of rebellion. Yun-ho pitied his father for thinking that way. He made no attempt to avoid the beating. His father was angry and he beat his son with a steel cable. For the last few months his father had been looking through old lawbooks from other countries and underlining. Yun-ho knew what his father was doing. The cable with its four strands cleaved the air and coiled about Yun-ho. His older sister had wept aloud. If the secretary hadn't informed him of the time, the lawyer might very well have left his son's body with deep wounds. He stopped the beating and went to the hotel. He and his colleagues held important meetings at the hotel. Yun-ho's sister removed his clothes. His underwear had cut deep into his flesh and was soaked with blood. Night and day for four days Yun-ho bore the pain.

The fault lay with his father. From the outset he had tried to raise Yun-ho as a member of a completely different class. His superiority complex prodded Yun-ho toward the social science departments at A University. Finally, after two months had passed, Yun-ho's father asked him what he intended to do. Yun-ho said, as he had in the beginning, that he would study history at B University. Because his grades and test scores as they now stood were sufficient to admit him to B University, he would hot take courses at a cram school and wouldn't consider private tutoring. The thought of cram school courses and private tutors made him want to throw up. It was then that his father's expectations collapsed. Calmly his father backed off. He was not angry. He must have thought there was no need to burn the remnants of his shattered dream.

Yun-ho had managed to deflect his father's requests and expectations, and now he was free. During March and April of that third year he read a booklet called _The Worker's Handbook_. Among its contents were such things as the Labor Standards Act and its enforcement ordinance, the Labor Safety Regulations, the Trade Union Act and its enforcement ordinance, the Labor Dispute Mediation Act and its enforcement ordinance, the Labor Committee Act and its enforcement ordinance, the Emergency Act for national defense, the Ŭngang Textile Collective Agreement, the Ŭngang Textile Labor/Management Committee Regulations, and the Ŭngang Textile Branch Management By-laws. Yun-ho read this booklet in the neighborhood to which he had just moved. It was a bright, spotless neighborhood. When his father had first said he would sell the three-story family home in Felicity Precinct and move to a single-story dwelling in the wooded foothills of Pugak Mountain, his sister had stamped her feet and voiced her displeasure. But then she had visited the house with the secretary, and after that she had awaited the day they would move. The neighborhood was fenced off. There was a guardpost at the entrance where security people stopped vehicles and checked the identity of all who entered. Yun-ho had the feeling of entering a different world. The streets were clean, the houses picturesque. No one went about this settlement of fine homes on foot.

Spring brought fragrances that filled the neighborhood. Double cherry blossoms, climbing roses, lilacs, yulan trees, mountain rhododendrons, viburnum, redbuds, and whatnot came into bloom. Bees buzzed about. Sounds from the past could not be heard in this neighborhood. What Yun-ho saw after a rain was lovely beyond words. He often heard there the sound of a small spirit that was shrinking. But he lived on, stifling himself. There was no better book than *The Worker's Handbook.*

"What's that book?"

"Hmm?"

"The book."

"It's not a book."

"Well, what is it, then?"

With April gone, the girl next door struck up a conversation. She was leaning against her red car, her eyes boring into Yun-ho. Yun-ho didn't say a word in reply. Girls were all alike. Just like the cram school courses and the private tutors, the thought of them made him feel like throwing up. When it came to sleeping with girls, he had no memories of a happy ending. He had only wanted to cry. But then this girl from next door had swept up to Yun-ho and snatched the booklet. She read the title, and Yun-ho watched as she read the table of contents. Kyŏng-ae was now seventeen, and in the second of her three years of high school. She scanned the contents, then turned to the first section and read the gothic headings one after another: Observance of Working Conditions, Equal Treatment, Prohibition of Violence, Elimination of Intermediary Exploitation, and Guarantee of the Exercise of Civil Rights. She was blushing when she returned *The Worker's Handbook.*

Yun-ho couldn't understand why she had blushed. She was wearing a dazzling white sweater and dazzling white pants. Her grandfather was dying, though Yun-ho didn't know this at the time. Kyŏng-ae's clothes clung to her body. The next time they saw each other she wore a dress. She had come to his house.

"Our cell is meeting," she said with no preliminaries.

"Your what?" Yun-ho asked.

"Cell."

"What's a cell?"

"C-E-L-L—like in 'cell technique,' you know?"

"Yeah, I know." Yun-ho looked into Kyŏng-ae's face. "But why the visit?"

"To invite you?"

"Me? How come?"

"Because our discussion topic is teenage workers."

"You figured me wrong. Not much I can say about that."

"Where did that _Worker's Handbook_ come from?"

"I got it at Ŭngang."

"And you met some workers there—right?"

This time it was Kyŏng-ae peering intently at Yun-ho's face. If only he had turned his face away he could have avoided it. Yun-ho found himself being drawn to this seventeen-year-old girl. At that moment Kyŏng-ae's grandfather was dying. Kyŏng-ae's grandfather was very wealthy. But in spite of that great wealth he heaved one last great breath and closed his eyes. The cord of his life was easily snapped. The neighborhood was awash with the thick fragrance of flowers. Automobiles arrived bearing large wreaths on their roofs. There were too many wreaths to count precisely. Yun-ho's sister couldn't stand the fulsome fragrance and shut the windows tight. All the flower shops in Seoul must have run out of flowers, she said.

That night Yun-ho's father and his lawyer friends drank at the bar in his basement. They had dropped by Kyŏng-ae's house. None of them would have been able to shake hands with Kyŏng-ae's grandfather. Yun-ho studied English. He also studied mathematics, and hated every minute of it. By and by he went to the window and saw Kyŏng-ae's house beyond the lawn and the climbing roses. Kyŏng-ae, wearing black, emerged from the house. The girl touched the withering flowers on the wreaths. Her grandfather's body had begun to reek by now, he thought. But when they met the following day Kyŏng-ae shook her head, saying his body would never decompose. After the girl ushered

Yun-ho into her red car she talked about what the morticians had done all the previous night. They were amazingly skillful.

"I don't get it," Kyŏng-ae said. "I know I'll die someday. And I'll be buried in the ground. And after I've turned into dirt Grandfather will be lying there in his coffin just the way he is now."

"Your grandfather's a king."

"An autocrat."

"Didn't you cry?"

"Why should I have to cry? Nobody else did. Right now the grown-ups are squabbling."

"How come?"

"They've got their eyes on Grandfather's position."

"Where are we going?"

"To the Student Center."

When they arrived some girls were standing in front of the gift shop that sold sacred items. They surrounded Kyŏng-ae and took her hand. The boys were in the rec room inside the Student Center waiting for the girls. As the girls went inside, one boy was making a telephone call, one was at a candy machine searching his pockets for coins, and one had opened his schoolbag and was making sure he had his candles, his Bible, a text titled *Conversations on Belief,* the cup he would use, and other items he had brought for the occasion. The boys' general affairs representative arrived with the key to the basement chapel. The others followed him downstairs. Above the entrance to the building Yun-ho read "Freedom, Justice, Peace"; on the wall above the rec room registration area he read in Latin "Pax Romana." Kyŏng-ae guided him.

They descended twenty steps and a wooden cross came into sight. Yun-ho watched as Kyŏng-ae approached the wall to the left, dipped her fingers in holy water, and made the sign of the cross. Kyŏng-ae recited a prayer: "Lord, with this holy water please cleanse me of my sins, bid Satan be gone, and remove from my mind all evil thoughts." That day the students in their basement chapel held a thirty-minute discussion on the subject of teenage workers. Yun-ho sat quietly, listening. Each time his eyes met Kyŏng-ae's she gave him a smile. Beyond the students' shoulders could be seen an alcove that held a holy statue and, within the marble altar, a ciborium. Crimson electric light filtered through the half-open curtains. The students' voices rose. Fervently they gave voice to their thoughts. The students were clutching at shadows. And then they called on Yun-ho.

"*Oppa!*" Kyŏng-ae called out to him. The others laughed.

"Our adviser couldn't come," said the president, "and so we've brought our *sŏnbae* Han Yun-ho. We'll ask him to speak now."

"I've just realized why your adviser couldn't come," said Yun-ho. "He must have had nothing to say."

The students laughed.

"He must have been awfully embarrassed."

Again the students laughed.

"And I feel ashamed of myself. But I'm suprised that none of you do."

"Why is that?" asked a girl.

"You've taken teenage workers as your theme," Yun-ho said, "and talked for thirty minutes or so. You talked as if you were knowledgeable, but you aren't. There isn't one person in our country who can talk about teenage workers without feeling guilty. And that includes me. When I lived in Felicity Precinct I was introduced to a dwarf. I got to know him. That man had nothing but trouble all his life, and then he passed away. That man's sons and daughter work in a factory zone. The work they do is complicated and tiring. Their young friends don't know how to express themselves and they wouldn't know how to react to humane treatment. The work they do at their workplace stunts their growth. Every day an enormous production plan looms over them. The workers operate machines. The young workers fit the rhythm of their daily lives to machines. Thoughts, feelings—they're lost to the machines. Remember what you studied at school? The force of a falling object becomes mechanical energy, and the force of a wound spring, and so on. Well, these workers are the same: They're used for mechanical energy. And so, you may be able to talk about teenage workers—about *work, duty, natural rights;* I cannot. And you may suggest that we help them; I cannot. Your feelings are of no help to them. I saw what the young companions of the dwarf's son and daughter experienced, and I felt something. In the year 197X, Korea is full of criminals. There is not one person who is not a criminal."

Before Yun-ho finished he heard a guitar. One of the boys had gone to the corner and started playing.

"Please continue," said a girl to Yun-ho.

"Very quietly," said another girl to the boy.

It was sad music. The sound of the guitar made Yun-ho think of the stars in the Milky Way. Yun-ho thought about the movement of tiny stars. Kyŏng-ae, not saying a word, observed Yun-ho and no one else. In conclusion Yun-ho gave a few concrete examples of what the sons and daughter of the dead dwarf had experienced at the factories. The dwarf's older son had worked with a drill at an automobile assembly plant. His younger son had done polishing work. His daughter had gone to work at a textile plant, where she tended a weaving machine. The older son was unable to work now. The students, though, failed to understand Yun-ho's words as they should have. To win over the students and make them understand, Yun-ho would have to have read *The Worker's Handbook* to them from start to finish, would have had to cite examples of how human beings had been treated in the workplace, would have had to explain the workplace in concrete terms, describe in detail the light from the sky there, talk about where they ate and slept, talk about the power imbalance between employer and employee and how this affected the distribution of power, bring to light the history of the labor movement, and describe the expressions on the faces of the young workers as they rose from uncomfortable beds after dreaming a dream of their ancestral home. Yun-ho gave up trying and finished his talk.

The students wanted to move on to the next activity. Among the boys were several impatient ones who clearly had decided at the outset not to listen to Yun-ho.

Kyŏng-ae approached and apologized for them. "Don't let it bother you," she said. "The others like you. Can I get you something to drink?"

"It's all right," said Yun-ho. "I'd better get going."

"Why?"

"I don't fit in here."

"You don't want to disappoint the ones who like you."

"Nobody like that here."

"Yes there is!"

"I feel like I'm suffocating here. I want to leave."

"You said we're all criminals. And so we all live in jails, right?"

The boys had risen and stepped back behind the chairs. The girls took seats in every other chair. Two of them put some slips of folded paper in a container made of aluminum foil and mixed them up. The boys chose from this.

"Your partner's the guest," said a girl.

"You're my partner," said Kyŏng-ae.

"Who decided on teenage workers?" Yun-ho asked.

"Why?"

"I can't forgive whoever did it."

"I'm in mourning."

"I'd sooner forgive someone for selling his own freedom."

"Grandfather's body won't decompose. Tomorrow's the funeral. I'm in mourning. You shouldn't do anything to me."

Yun-ho saw an image of the Virgin Mary next to the alcove. The boys unfolded the slips of paper and located their partners. The girls looked at the boys who had sat down beside them. Some of the students were satisfied, some were disappointed. The students began setting a table with the things they had brought: rainbow rice cake, hamburgers, cookies, and fruit, along with milk and Coca-Cola. One student plugged in a coffeepot to the left of the door.

The students' preparations were complete. They had succeeded in sneaking in a portable stereo and records. The guitar had posed no problem. It had long been accepted as a necessary part of these co-ed meetings. The girls lit candles. The boys turned off the lights. The students sat around the table and consumed what was arranged there. They couldn't have been happier.

"Playing house," said Kyŏng-ae. "I'm sorry. But you shouldn't leave early."

"Why are you going for me?" Yun-ho asked Kyŏng-ae, who had drawn close to him.

"Because I like you," Kyŏng-ae said in an undertone. "If the subject had been freedom, I couldn't have talked with you."

"So all this business about poor working kids was just an excuse."

"That was a great talk you gave. You opened my eyes today."

"All that business about poor working kids and now even your God is debased."

"Don't say that." Kyŏng-ae scowled.

"Quiet, everyone," a girl said. "Okay—all set?"

A boy played the guitar. He was the boy who had set Yun-ho to thinking about the movement of tiny stars. As he played he sang, ". . . the wind knows . . . " Yun-ho watched this boy's partner reposition the candles while drinking Coca-Cola. Once again the impatient ones among the boys wanted to move on to the next activity. One of them left. The students sang together.

"Can you hear us?" someone called out.

The boy who had left reappeared. "Nope," he said while locking the door.

"Get the stereo going."

"Time for dancing already?"

"Hold on," said the general secretary for the boys. "First the games."

"You play too," said Kyŏng-ae.

"I'll just watch," said Yun-ho.

"Wait and see. You'll get involved."

The students moved the table toward the wall. Yun-ho saw the fourteen stations of the cross on the wall opposite. A game began. From the boys and girls came loud shouts and loud laughter. The boys removed their jackets. A few girls had begun to perspire and they too liberated themselves from their jackets. When it came time for the countdown game, Kyŏng-ae returned to Yun-ho and sat beside him. She placed her small hand between his. The boys placed their partners' hand between theirs. The boys and girls closed their eyes. Yun-ho watched as the game leader instructed everyone to count exactly to fifteen and stand up, then extinguished two of the candles. Of the remaining three candles, one cast a faint light on Kyŏng-ae's face. The boys began to stand up. Some stood early, some stood late. The short span of fifteen seconds gave rise to many miscalculations. The group leader asked each pair in which the boy's timing was far off to stand on one of the small chairs. This proved impossible, and down they came. Some girls pushed their partner off. Unless the partners embraced, they couldn't turn in a circle on the small chair. A boy extinguished one of the candles. Two girls shielded the last two candles with their hands. Yun-ho heard people climbing onto the chairs.

"Come on up," Kyŏng-ae said.

"You can't order me," said Yun-ho.

"Then you order me, just this once."

"No reason to."

"Think of something."

"I'm going to lay you out on the torture rack."

Kyŏng-ae silently held out her hand. Yun-ho took it and climbed onto the chair. Kyŏng-ae took his hands, placed them in the small of her back, and linked them together. Then she circled his back with her arms and embraced him. As she felt Yun-ho's arms tighten about her she lifted her feet from the chair. The two of them turned about on the chair in a small orbit. Others fell over along with their chair.

"All right," Kyŏng-ae whispered.

Yun-ho released her.

"You were fantastic!" a girl said to Kyŏng-ae in an undertone. Her partner put out one of the two remaining candles. Someone else turned on the stereo. As the boys and girls listened to the music they began talking, partner to partner. This was the time they had all been waiting for. The remaining candle cast its light against a single wall and the ceiling. The boys and girls dared not put out this last candle. As the record turned, a woman's voice sang: "One summer day two goldfish fought in a pond; the body of one rose to the surface and turned foul; the water too turned foul and nothing could live there." Yun-ho sat with his back to the wall. For a time Kyŏng-ae didn't look up. The sensation of Yun-ho's arms tightening about her was with her still. The morticians were amazingly skillful. But there was nothing they could do about her dead grandfather's sensory organs. Kyŏng-ae's grandfather was a man who had lived his life in the thrall of basic physical sensation. Yun-ho had Kyŏng-ae look up, then reminded her of his promise.

"What are you going to do with me?" she asked.

"Lay you out on the rack and torture you," he said.

"For what?"

"Time for you to spill out your crimes."

"Fine, do what you want," Kyŏng-ae said.

Yun-ho stood her up and said, "Take off your clothes."

"You're crazy," Kyŏng-ae laughed.

The others turned off the stereo. They surrounded Yun-ho and Kyŏng-ae. Yun-ho grabbed the neck of Kyŏng-ae's dress. The same hand suddenly swept down, and Kyŏng-ae shrieked, covering her face. The others laughed. Kyŏng-ae imagined her clothes being ripped open to reveal her nude body. Momentarily ashamed, she bit her lip. Yun-ho pretended to tie her hands together. The torturer intended to hang the naked prisoner from a vertical rack. "I've committed no crime," Kyŏng-ae said. The girls laughed. Yun-ho stood her up on a chair and had her raise her arms. She gave the appearance of being roped to the rack. "I'll let you hang there till you confess," said Yun-ho. To the others this looked like the start of something tedious. And so they turned the stereo back on and resumed their conversations. Kyŏng-ae's head drooped. In that position she slumped toward Yun-ho. He took her in his arms and lay her on the floor. Kyŏng-ae thought of the wreaths standing in front of her house. The flowers were withering. After the torturer had positioned Kyŏng-ae squarely he tied her arms and then her legs together and then secured them to posts. Yun-ho pretended to turn the posts.

"Scream," said Yun-ho. "Your tendons and flesh are being ripped apart."

"I don't feel a thing," said Kyŏng-ae. "I didn't like standing up there, so I pretended to faint. I'm completely comfortable now."

"I'm going to make you tell the truth."

Yun-ho tightened the four invisible posts three turns each. He couldn't be sure, for there were no specific records, but he imagined the torture chambers in the underground prisons of yesteryear full of screams at that moment. Lips had contorted, flesh had ripped, blood had flowed. Yun-ho rested a hand on Kyŏng-ae's chest.

"Your heart is going to burst," Yun-ho said quietly. "If you don't confess, I'll give the posts another turn."

"I'm comfortable," said Kyŏng-ae. "Nothing for me to confess."

"All that business about the poor working kids."

"I don't want to hear it."

"You come to me with all that business about the poor working kids."

"I said I don't want to hear it."

"Keep talking."

"I don't know who this dwarf man is."

"What about Ŭngang Textile?"

"I knew it," said Kyŏng-ae. "It was Grandfather's company."

"What did your grandfather have?"

"Lots of companies, lots of factories, a beautiful island, a farm outside the city, a big house with a swimming pool, a bar downstairs, and an escalator, lots of machines, lots of cars, lots of cows—"

"Enough. Now let's hear about your crimes."

"I'm a criminal," said Kyŏng-ae. "I've committed lots of crimes. But the funny thing is, I can't tell you what any of them are."

"Because your entire lifestyle is a crime." Again Yun-ho turned the imaginary posts.

"It hurts," Kyŏng-ae said for the first time. "That really does make me feel like my heart is going to explode."

"Talk about your crimes, I said."

"I liked it when your family moved in next door. I liked you from the beginning. I think about you when I'm in bed. That's my crime."

"Your bed's always warm, isn't it? What was the temperature in your room last winter, when it was so cold that fifty-year-old oak trees split their bark?"

"I don't know."

"You wore short-sleeve shirts even in winter, didn't you? And you could have a bath in your own bathtub anytime you wanted, couldn't you? You've never woken up cold and hungry, have you? But you know what happened when the dwarf man's daughter went to work at the Ŭngang Textile factory?"

"No."

"In the cafeteria she lived on 'rice' that was actually more barley than rice, kimchi that had gone off, and soup made from dried radish leaves and stems. The temperature in her dormitory room was twenty-seven degrees. And while she was eating that lousy food and trying to catch some sleep in that awful bed, do you know what kind of treatment she was getting?"

"No."

"She—a human being—was treated like a cheap piece of machinery."

"I don't know what you're talking about," Kyŏng-ae said feebly.

"You'll find out." Yun-ho started to get up.

"No!"

"It's not a crime for a seventeen-year-old girl to think about the boy next door," said the torturer.

"I didn't know," said Kyŏng-ae.

"And *that's* your crime," said Yun-ho. "It's the crime of everyone who doesn't know. Your grandfather wielded terrible power, just as he wanted. Never before have so many people worked under the tyrannical demands of one person. Your grandfather disregarded every article of law. Forced labor, restrictions on mental and physical freedom, bonuses and wages, termination, retirement bonus, minimum wage, working hours, nighttime and holiday work, paid vacation, underage employment. And besides his illegal activities that violated these legal provisions, he suppressed labor union activity, threatened to close down the workplace, and committed other violations too numerous to mention. I saw a book that the dwarf man's daughter was reading. Written in it are the things your grandfather said—things like 'Now is the time to accumulate, not the time to distribute.' And then your grandfather died. Who did he share with? When? How? Of all the things he should have given to the dead dwarf's son and daughter and their young co-workers, he gave nothing. And you didn't know that, did you? Because you didn't know, you spent your school vacations on your grandfather's beautiful private island, you rode in a red car, your dining table always had meat and fresh vegetables, in your warm bed you thought about a boy, and to get close to that boy you fed him that line about the poor working kids, didn't you? Now you've got to free yourself from your crime. Until now the dwarf man's sons and daughter and all their young co-workers have been sacrificed for the likes of you. From now on it's your turn to be sacrificed for them. Understand? You tell that to the grown-ups when you get home."

Kyŏng-ae, though, said nothing. Yun-ho observed her. She was retching. She turned her face to the side and threw up what she had eaten. Yun-ho took out his handerchief and cradled the side of her head, then released her from the four invisible stakes. The others were dancing.

The others had been waiting for a long time. Heat issued from their bodies. Yun-ho helped Kyŏng-ae to the area beneath the candle. A girl made her some coffee. As Kyŏng-ae drank it she looked at Yun-ho and smiled. The torturer's shoulders now drooped and he shook his head. Kyŏng-ae remained seated while the others danced. Later she leaned back against the wall and wrote something. Before she left the basement chapel that day Kyŏng-ae prayed: "Saint Thomas Aquinas, I ask you to pray for us!"

Yun-ho spent that third year quietly. His father spoke no more about the social science departments at A University. He really had backed off unconditionally. It was raining by the time Yun-ho returned with Kyŏng-ae to their neighborhood. The withering flowers stood out in the rain. Kyŏng-ae's grandfather was not a man born to meet with a happy death.

Yun-ho watched Kyŏng-ae start to enter her house, then run back into the rain. She handed him a piece of paper and turned away. The driver of her red car rushed out from the house with an umbrella. Yun-ho read the epitaph Kyŏng-ae had written for her grandfather.

"Here sleeps a terrible miser who was easily angered. He died because of his lust for money and power. He was a man who lived his entire life without a single friend. Although he praised himself for great achievements in developing our nation's economy, he made not one substantial contribution to the life of our people. Not a single person wept when he died."

The following day Kyŏng-ae, dressed in black, attended her grandfather's funeral. Kyŏng-ae was still young. The same with Yun-ho. Yun-ho, though, told himself that upon his entrance to college he would marry her. During the course of that third year Yun-ho thought often about the goals they should set for themselves. Such things as love, respect, ethics, freedom, justice, and ideals.

City of Machines

JULY AND AUGUST WERE extraordinarily hot and humid. The
papers were full of articles calling it the worst heat in thirty years.
The entire country was tinder dry. But Yun-ho had nothing to worry
about. His father had installed an air conditioner and it spewed out
cold air without the slightest sound. One day this city of Ŭngang had
suddenly loomed huge in Yun-ho's mind; if not for that he would
have been content to prepare for the examination in his pleasant surroundings. The city of Ŭngang left a gloomy outline in Yun-ho's mind.
The sons and daughter of the dead dwarf worked there. To Yun-ho,
Ŭngang was merely one part of the surface of a small planet. The dead
dwarf's children survived in this part of the dark surface by perform-
ing sweaty labor at a work site of machines. It was easy for them to
find work. Not because they possessed superior job skills but because
those machines could not operate without people's help. Already the
dwarf's children had undergone numerous trials. But they were not
noteworthy in this respect, for they belonged to a group with a mini-
mal standard of living.

The dead dwarf had used tools of metal. In his last years the
toolbag on his shoulder had carried a pipe cutter, monkey wrench,
socket wrench, screwdriver, hammer, faucets, pump valves, T-joints,

U-joints, screws, and hacksaw. A most peculiar smell came from the neighborhood where the dwarf's family lived.

Yun-ho had visited the dwarf's house, leapfrogging some half a dozen drunks sprawled underfoot. The dwarf's wife had rinsed, readied, and boiled barley and had peeled potatoes. To Yun-ho, going to college was the number one problem. Before failing the entrance exam he had never thought about inequality. He understood the English word *poverty* only as a current-affairs term. In his mind *poverty* was connected with the English words *population* and *pollution,* and he memorized them as the three P's. Such were the things taught in the public schools, at the cram schools, and in study groups, and such were the things that stifled the pupils. The dwarf had sat in his yard by the bank of the sewer creek tending to his tools. Yun-ho saw his death as the end of an era. Even when Yun-ho had slept with girls he had thought of the dwarf's death. The girls didn't like this.

"Please," said one girl. "Would you please not talk about the midget?"

"Why not?"

"He reminds me of a worm."

"He was a human being, not a worm."

"Whatever."

The girl lay naked.

"*You're* the one who's a worm," Yun-ho had said.

Ŭn-hŭi was different. She sat silently for a time. She was a very pretty girl.

"It's strange," Ŭn-hŭi said. "I can't describe what I'm thinking about."

"And what are you thinking about?"

"It's hard to explain. Everybody deserves a chance, but they took his chance away." Ŭn-hŭi spoke carefully. She was the purest and most innocent of the circle of first-time entrance-exam repeaters.

The year that Yun-ho became a second-time entrance-exam repeater, Ŭn-hŭi started college. Her first impression of college was not especially favorable. She would visit Yun-ho, sit without saying a word, then leave. The one thing those first few months of college had given Ŭn-hŭi was freedom. It was the peculiar freedom of leaving home in time for class and, from that moment on, not having to accept parental interference. Her driver dropped Ŭn-hŭi off in an alley where the main entrance to the university was in sight some two hundred yards off, then returned home. When the other students saw Ŭn-hŭi they thought immediately of her father. By Yun-ho's moral standards, Ŭn-hŭi's father was not a person deserving of respect. The other students were not even comfortable talking about the weather in front of Ŭn-hŭi. They were on their guard with her; they felt vulnerable in her presence. Ŭn-hŭi's father's role as a lawyer was even more important than Yun-ho's father's role. And so the students' reaction was well founded. The lawyers held their meetings in absolute secrecy. When Yun-ho talked of the dwarf's children, Ŭn-hŭi had listened in rapt attention.

Yun-ho had an influence on Ŭn-hŭi. She too thought of Ŭngang as being chock full of dark machines.

"It's because of you," Ŭn-hŭi said. "You've got me in your clutches."

"Wrong," said Yun-ho. "I haven't forced you into anything."

"No, it's not force. It's just that you want."

"Me? Want what?"

"You want me."

But in this respect Ŭn-hŭi was the same.

"What have I done to you?" Yun-ho asked.

"It's not that," said Ŭn-hŭi. "It's just that I can't do it with other boys."

"I can do it with other girls."

"That's what you said. And that's why I cried. I don't like it if it's not you."

And Yun-ho knew that. Still he had gone to the small hotel and slept with other girls.

A frayed red carpet covered the floors of this hotel in the gloomy, unlit alley. Yun-ho always felt depressed after sleeping with a girl. The depression reached deep inside him. The act felt infinitely foolish—

even called into question the very meaning of his existence. It seemed as foolish as the body before his eyes. Yun-ho should have been quicker to give his love to Ŭn-hŭi.

That summer Yun-ho made up his mind to love Ŭn-hŭi. Ŭn-hŭi thought that perhaps Yun-ho would become a labor activist or a social activist. She certainly did not think of him simply as someone who had to take the entrance exam a third time. And so the image of Ŭngang, where the dead dwarf's children worked, loomed large in her mind, as it did in Yun-ho's. When Yun-ho thought of Ŭngang, he sensed his own shriveled self.

Ŭngang is large, its inner workings complex. When Ŭngang people speak of their city, one of the things you might not immediately understand is their use of the word *claustrophobic.* Located not far from Seoul on a peninsula on the West Sea, Ŭngang has the ocean on three sides.

When the tide is in, the first thing the people of Ŭngang discover is the motion of the ocean's surface. That surface, rising and falling twice a day, makes you feel as if the whole of Ŭngang moves according to the gravitational pull of everything beyond the earth. In area Ŭngang is seventy-six square miles, in population 810,000. Compared with the major cities of our country, it is large in area and the population is about right for its size. Still, you have to wonder why Ŭngang people use the word *claustrophobic.* Is it a matter of their temperament? Or is it the profound skepticism, invisible to outsiders, that has spread throughout their lives? Social control does not enter into this view. No one there would speak out in dissatisfaction about restraints on individual action as a means to maintain order. You might think that a genuine social scientist could give an adequate account of the society's realities, structure, temper, and changes. But few people fulfill their responsibilities, a characteristic of our times. In a sense, Ŭngang is a forsaken city.

Office of education, city hall, police department, tax office, courthouse, prosecutor's office, port authority, customshouse, chamber of commerce and industry, cultural center, correctional facility, churches, factories, labor unions—these and more are there. The workers can quickly get used to their factory jobs, but it is not such a simple matter for them to understand what people actually do in these institutions, organizations, and assemblies. The people of Ŭngang see Seoul people filling the docks and leaving for the islands. The Seoul people go to the islands to dig the clams and catch the crabs that they lack at home. How foolish they are, the Ŭngang people think. The Seoul people aren't interested in seeing the oil slicks. The wind is blowing from the ocean toward the land. In Ŭngang there can be nothing more important than the wind. The Ŭngang people realized that too late.

In school the children learn the history of Ŭngang. Opened to the outside world in 1883, it developed into an international treaty port and an industrial city. Ŭngang's industrial zone has thriving sectors in metals, ceramics, chemicals, petroleum, shipbuilding, wood products, plate glass, textiles, electronics, motor vehicles, and steel, and Ŭngang is singled out in the textbooks as the leading producer of plate glass in Korea. And although high tide can differ from low by almost thirty feet, the installation of floodgates has eliminated any inconvenience.

Downtown is a place of ups and downs with its many hills, and since the hills in the heart of the city spread east and west, the urban district is divided into north and south. The industrial zone is to the north. Black smoke rises from countless smokestacks; inside the factories machines are turning. This is where the workers work. And this is where the dead dwarf's children are working. Mixed with the air they breathe are toxic gases, sooty smoke, and dust particles. All the factories, in proportion to the amount of manufactured goods they produce, spew wastewater and sludge in various shades of brown into the waterways. Wastewater from the factories upstream is reused by factories downstream, is again spewed out, and flows on down to the sea. Ŭngang's inner harbor is a basin collecting polluted seawater. Life in the vicinity of the factories is slowly dying.

Flowers bloom in Ŭngang as elsewhere, but spring there is a season when the cold, dry northwest winds give way to the monsoon from the southeast. High pressure over the ocean gives rise to these seasonal southeast winds that usher in the summer heat.

The typhoons that arrive from summer through early autumn blow through Ŭngang and into the interior. The cold, dry seasonal winds from the northwest usher in winter.

With winter's arrival snow falls in Ŭngang as elsewhere, but the factory workers can't see it fall and accumulate. The waterways don't freeze over no matter how cold it gets, and snow amasses only in the residential areas.

In Ŭngang the prevailing winds are onshore during the day and offshore at night. These winds carry the toxic gases and sooty smoke from the factory zone either to the ocean or inland. One night in May, however, the people of Ŭngang realized the wind had suddenly shifted. There was no wind blowing toward the ocean or toward the interior. Instead there was a calm above the factory zone followed by a wind blowing directly toward the residential area. This wind followed the contours of the downtown hills and crossed into the residential area, where it settled and spread out. Small children who had just fallen asleep were the very first to know the wind had shifted. The adults saw that the children were suddenly having trouble breathing.

The adults rushed to the hospital, children in their arms, but then they too had trouble breathing because of the stench in the air. Their eyes smarted, their throats grew hot. Those who could not bear it ran out onto the streets. Fog settled over downtown and the residential areas; streetlights could no longer be seen. Chaos broke out and public order collapsed in an instant. Thieves and thugs seized this unimaginable opportunity and ran wild. The residential areas emptied out, their occupants fleeing for the highway that led toward the heart of the nation. All this happened in the space of three hours, from nine o'clock to midnight, but the people of Ŭngang shuddered at the exposure of their helplessness in the face of a great terror. In this short period the Ŭngang people experienced the full spectrum of anxiety. Although no one could have expressed it, they realized they were living under ecological conditions without precedent in the history of Ŭngang. The next day they told themselves they had better try to solve the problem. But before long they ran up against a massive wall and ultimately they made a listless retreat. The prime movers of Ŭngang were in Seoul. The people of Ŭngang thought they could hold public meetings or even demonstrate if need be. They were left with mouths agape when they realized too late that this was impossible.

Yun-ho was forever thinking about how his father was involved in something terrible.

The many factories, the people who managed them, and the people who directed those managers, all were in Seoul. To run the factory machines they used only the minimum energy required by the laws of physics, and with a fraction of this energy they measured and announced the level of pollution in Ŭngang. Before the people of Ŭngang go to bed they check the wind direction. From the factory zone where the dwarf's children work, the wind sweeps the toxic gases and sooty smoke inland or toward the ocean. The Ŭngang people think no further. They don't think about the laborers in this factory zone where upwards of one hundred thousand tons of wastewater a day are sent flowing to the sea. As long as the air doesn't hang over the factory area and then blow toward the residential area, these people do not awaken from their deep sleep. Nor do they need to know that there are four labor supervisors in the Ŭngang central district office of the Labor Bureau. These four supervisors oversee more than a thousand places of business. One person is responsible not for two hundred and fifty workers but for two hundred and fifty places of business.

It is there that the dwarf's children work and live. When he first arrived, the dwarf's elder son thought that his life there could get no worse. His first night in Ŭngang he had spent in the office of the workers' church, he had told Yun-ho. There he saw a survey the workers had filled out for the people at the church:

1. Motive for seeking work

   a. Poverty: 58.1%
   b. Family discord: 15.1
   c. Aspiration for city life: 12.4
   d. Friend's urging: 11.7
   e. Other: 2.7

2. Desired workplace requisite

   a. High pay: 8.4%
   b. Humane treatment: 71.6
   c. Opportunity to learn job skills: 19.1
   d. Other: 0.9

3. Level of work-related fatigue

   a. Always: 59.8%
   b. Sometimes: 33.8
   c. Seldom: 5.7
   d. Never: 0.7

4. Do you think the Labor Union executives are company agents?

   a. Yes, most are: 39.1%
   b. Yes, to a slight extent: 28.3
   c. Not at all: 19.2
   d. Don't know: 13.4

5. Do you think that anyone in our country who works hard, consumes wisely, and saves can live well?

   a. Yes: 41.3%
   b. To an extent: 21.5
   c. Only with difficulty: 33.5
   d. Impossible: 3.8

His eyes kept returning to several of these figures: the 58.1 percent who mentioned poverty, the 71.6 percent who mentioned humane treatment, the 59.8 percent who were always fatigued, the 39.1 percent who thought almost all the Labor Union executives were company agents, the 33.5 percent who considered it somewhat difficult to live well, and the 3.8 percent who thought it impossible to live well. The dwarf's elder son thought about the despair, antipathy, and alienation of the handful of those who had responded "impossible."

"I knew then that I had to do more than just work," the dwarf's elder son had said later.

"Why was that?" asked Yun-ho.

"You shouldn't have to ask. The day I went to work at Ŭngang Motors seven people on the assembly line were kicked out."

"Kicked out? You mean they were fired? Did they do something wrong?"

"No."

"There's no labor union—is that it?"

"No, there's a union."

"Then it's possible to get fired without cause? Didn't the union officials do anything?"

"They work for management."

"What kind of a labor union is that?"

"It's a labor union."

"He's going to have more unhappiness." This was Ŭn-hŭi talking.

"Do *you* think you're happy?" said Yun-ho. "He needs something to work for, just like anyone else."

"You're right!" Ŭn-hŭi exclaimed.

There was just one thing Ŭn-hŭi wanted that summer. Yun-ho knew what that was. And he knew what the dwarf's elder son wanted as well. There was nothing Yun-ho could do for the dwarf's children, though. The machines that operated in the factories were things of precision, but society was full of peculiar habits, surveillance, inefficiencies, and dangers. To the dwarf's elder son, everything looked black, like the steam engines you see in photographs.

The dwarf's younger son went to work for Ŭngang Electronics, where his first job was to load and carry castings on a metal handcart. For three months he worked as a trainee. When he began tŏ do polishing work, one of the union officials handed him a piece of paper.

"He didn't join the union," Yun-ho said.

"He won't be happy either," said Ŭn-hŭi.

"He started reading books so he'd know what demands to present to management. He spoke with the workers he trusted and told them to drop out of the union."

"What's he going to do?"

"His dream is a new union."

"Where does his sister work?"

"Ŭngang Textile."

"How's Yŏng-hŭi?" When Yun-ho asked the dwarf's elder son about his sister, the son shook his head.

"She's not working," he said. "She got a dismissal notice from the company."

"What's the reason?"

"They say she wouldn't listen to her immediate superior. But I'm not worrying. The young people in the union are onto it and they're doing a good job."

That was the first time Yun-ho had seen the dwarf's elder son smile. Yun-ho couldn't talk long with him. The dwarf's elder son was busy. He still didn't know that the economic life of our country is essentially controlled by dozens of people who don't appear in the public eye. They run large factories and load their products onto sixty-thousand-ton freighters docked at Ŭngang's inner harbor.

"It won't work," the dwarf's elder son had said later. "There's nothing we can do."

"Who's 'we'?"

"Me, my brother, and my sister, and the people who work for Ŭngang."

"Aren't you expecting too much all of a sudden?" Yun-ho asked.

"You wouldn't understand," the dwarf's elder son had said without meeting Yun-ho's gaze.

The American air conditioner his father had installed certainly did spew out cold air, and it did so without a sound. July and August of that year were extraordinarily hot. The machines in Ŭngang's factory zone kept running that summer. There was too much Yun-ho didn't know. The dwarf's elder son had wept countless times after starting work at Ŭngang. He'd been threatened countless times, subjected to violence, hospitalized, even been taken into custody. His face was unrecognizably drawn. His eyes alone looked extraordinarily large. His ideals tormented him.

"My dream is something very simple," he said weakly.

"I know," said Yun-ho.

He observed Yun-ho quietly before speaking again. "We haven't been able to hold the general meeting or the union rep meeting that we scheduled. Everything's one-sided. Nothing goes according to the law. All we do is lose. I've lost face with the people I work with. And the only thing I've given them is more trouble."

"I'm sure they understand you."

"What about you?"

"I understand you."

"Then you have to help me."

"How?"

The dwarf's elder son rested his hand on Yun-ho's back.

"Take me to your house. I won't budge from your room. When I see my opportunity I'll leave."

"What the hell are you going to do?"

"I've got to see him."

"See who?"

"The man who runs the Ŭngang Group. Your next-door neighbor."

"What are you going to say when you see him?"

The dwarf's eldest son let his hand drop from Yun-ho's back. "Nothing," he said. "I'm going to kill him."

"You're out of your mind!" Yun-ho shouted. "You don't solve anything by killing people. You've lost your mind."

"Fine," he said in a soft voice. "I don't need anyone's help. I'll do it myself, under my own power."

"You're killing *yourself.* Who in God's name are you going to die for?"

"No one."

"Well, then?"

"Let's not talk anymore."

"If you want to see him, go to Brazil," Yun-ho said, suppressing his anger. "He's taking some time off with his youngest daughter; she's seventeen. Go to the resort area in Santos and shout his name."

"I'll have to wait till he gets back," said the dwarf's eldest son. "I've got to kill him." And then he turned away.

There was nothing Yun-ho could do to help the dwarf's elder son. There was one person alone that Yun-ho could help and that was Ŭn-hŭi. Ŭn-hŭi wanted Yun-ho. She would visit him, sit without saying a word, then return home. Yun-ho took Ŭn-hŭi to the hotel in the gloomy, unlit alley. The hotel with the frayed red carpet.

Yun-ho placed his index finger against Ŭn-hŭi's lips. Ŭn-hŭi spread her fingers, placed them over her eyes, and looked through them at Yun-ho. When he took Ŭn-hŭi in his arms her dress made a rustling sound as it rumpled up. Naked, Ŭn-hŭi covered Yun-ho's face with her hands, then brought it to her bosom. Yun-ho tightened his arms about her and Ŭn-hŭi breathed in deeply. But it was no use. For Yun-ho had run up against a fundamental moral issue. "That's why we have to put an end to this now," he mumbled. As Yun-ho held Ŭn-hŭi in his arms there arose in his mind an image of Ŭngang chock full of dark machines.

We'll form an organization—he can't do it all by himself, thought Yun-ho as he left the hotel that day.

The Cost of Living for a Family of Ŭngang Laborers

I DIDN'T WANT TO LISTEN any more. Yŏng-hŭi was talking about the town of Lilliput near Lake Hastro in Germany. I wasn't catching all the details, but I could tell it was a sad story. When she thought about our departed father, tears always appeared. Lilliput is an international town of dwarfs. Dwarfs from various countries have gathered there to live. Recently the world's shortest man, a Turk whose height is thirty-one inches, moved there. The dwarf population of Lilliput steadily increases. In places other than Lilliput dwarfs live lives of inconvenience and danger because the scale of everything is too large.

For dwarfs there is no place as safe as the town of Lilliput. The necessities of daily life, not to mention the houses and furniture, are made to size for dwarfs. There is nothing there to endanger the life of a dwarf—no suppression, no fear, no discrimination, no violence. The town of Lilliput has no dictators. No one to parcel out small shares of power to his followers, no one to draft cruel laws. There is no large industry, no factories, no managers. The dwarfs who have gathered there from various countries have reduced the world to their scale. They have exercised the vote. They have disregarded anything that smacks of nationality. They all participated eagerly in the vote and chose Marianne Char as town manager. This woman's height is thirty-nine inches. Through their collective power and their ardent wish for an autonomous community they established a town of dwarfs. Yŏng-hŭi sounded excited. I thought of the dwarfs there as revolutionaries. They don't worry about the sons and daughters who will be born there. They were miserable in the places where the giants lived.

Currently the dwarfs of Lilliput are debating such issues as medical care suited to their needs, social psychological problems, and financial matters. There are several points still to be resolved, but Marianne Char, the town manager, has said, "We are very happy."

Yŏng-hŭi wrote the word *happiness*. She thought of our departed father. I saw tears gather in Yŏng-hŭi's eyes. Father should have lived in a place like Lilliput. There would have been nobody to say, "Look at the midget." If Father had lived near Lake Hastro he wouldn't have died before his time. "Murdered Father"—that's what Yŏng-ho had said. I hadn't been able to prevent him from saying it. When I thought about the deep, pitch-black interior of the brick factory smokestack, I felt a choking sensation. Father's stature was small but his suffering was great. Father's height was forty-six inches, his weight seventy pounds. I often dreamed of Father during my early days at Ŭngang. In the dream Father looked no more than twenty inches tall. Tiny Father was dragging a huge spoon. A copper spoon coated with blue tarnish. From above his head the blazing sun beat down. The copper spoon was too heavy for Father. Exhausted, he put down the spoon, which was taller than he, and rested. And then he climbed into the spoon and lay down. Lay down in the copper spoon, which had grown hot in the blazing sun, and went to sleep. I lifted the end of the spoon and shook Father. He didn't open his eyes. Father was shrinking in the copper spoon. Crying, I took Father's copper spoon and shook it.

Mother said to me, "There's nothing to worry about." She ran her fingers through my hair. "Don't think about being the man of the family. And then you won't have that dream. Whatever you do, don't think about all the heavy responsibilities you have now that Father has passed on."

"The thought of being the man of the family has never entered my mind," I said.

"Oh yes it has," Mother said. "It's something you yourself aren't aware of. Those thoughts are there, somewhere inside you."

As Mother had said, those thoughts were there, in a corner of my mind.

"You're the eldest son, my boy," Father had always said. "If anything should happen to me, you're the pillar of the family."

"Yŏng-su," Mother had said, "I can still work, and Yŏng-ho and Yŏng-hŭi are all grown up. We'll trust in your decisions and we'll follow you."

The city of Ŭngang was utterly different from the town of Lilliput. This pained Yŏng-hŭi. It was a land where all living things suffered. We had come to Ŭngang in order to live. In Ŭngang we had resumed our daily routine, which had ceased for a time after Father passed on. I used to think there was nothing as abstract as life. It was neither tangible nor visible. It was something Father had given to us. To use the terminology of a biology book from my middle school days, Father had reproduced something identical to himself, propagated his race, and passed on. According to Mother, Father had passed on to a different circle of life. Father's body was reduced to half a handful of ash in the crematorium. Mother did not want to believe it, even when she received that half a handful of ash. She didn't believe that the dead disappeared completely. We scattered that half-handful of ash over the flowing water. Yŏng-ho and I wiped away tears with our fists.

"All done with your homework?" Father had asked.

"No." Using my ruler, I drew a pointed triangle.

"Do your homework."

"This *is* my homework."

Father peered at what I had drawn.

"It's the food pyramid," I explained.

"What use is it?"

"It explains the food chain."

"Explain it to me, then."

"These green plants way down at the bottom are at level one. The animals that eat those plants are at level two, the small meat-eaters that eat those animals are at level three, and the large meat-eating animals up above are at level four."

"Yŏng-ho," said Father, "can you explain this as well as your brother?"

"No, I can't," Yŏng-ho had said. "Not the way Brother did. We're down at the bottom. For us, there's nothing to catch for food. But above us there are three levels of things that want to eat us."

"Father needs to rest!" Mother had said. "He's been working too hard all these years. Now he can have a good rest."

"Mother, you're the one who should rest," I said.

Mother set afloat the white paper wrapping that had held the half-handful of ash. We sat beside the water and watched the water flow. Father disappeared. The breeze blew. The sun felt warm. Several birds flew past Mother. I saw a hillside worn away by a mudslide. Yŏng-ho and I stopped crying almost simultaneously. Father's death transformed our daily life. When we moved to Ŭngang we started worrying about everything, even our breathing. At first we took extremely feeble breaths, as if we were desiccated beans.

Yŏng-ho went to work first—at Ŭngang Electronics Plant One. Yŏng-hŭi went to work at the Ŭngang Textile Plant. Once I was sure these two younger siblings of mine had gotten their jobs I went to work at Ŭngang Motors. All three of us started out as trainees in Ŭngang Group factories. We began working at jobs completely different from what our departed Father had done. Each of us was merely one among numerous workers operating machines inside huge factories. And there again we were trainees not yet familiar with the job skills. Even in that group we belonged to the lowest class. In any event, now that we were working in those big factories we were able to find housing not far away. Consistent with our social standing, we lived in a slum. The work we did was unskilled labor. Yŏng-ho loaded and carried castings on a metal handcart. Yŏng-hŭi, still in training, cleaned the central corridor leading to the workrooms. I delivered small parts to the people on the automobile assembly line. A single automobile

was made of an incalculable number of parts. The workers who were
senior to me worked hard. Those on the assembly line regarded me as
just another machine. To the factory manager the workers were one
big machine.

The peculiar thing was, I would have stopped working there sooner
had I not thought about the progress, the revolutions, in technology.
The first few days I was fascinated by the extraordinary technology.
The foundry, the forging room, the heat treatment room, the sheet
metal room, the welding room, the machine-tool room, the finishing
room, the paint room—I was taken on a tour of each of these and
others, then placed at my assembly line. The heat and colors of the
foundry where the cylinder blocks were manufactured excited me. But
the place where I really wanted to work was the machine-tool room. I
wanted to learn lathe work. An automatic lathe at work seemed a very
fine thing. The lathe I saw was making the screw pattern in tire valve
stems. A stem spun around on an axis, and the bite cut a pretty little
spiral in its surface. As I stood watching the lathe, machine oil from
the shaft flowed down into an oil pan. To me it looked like perspiration. While the lathe workers monitored the speed of the bite they pat-
ted the new trainees on the shoulder. I left the machine-tool shop determined to work with a lathe myself.

Yŏng-ho's case was similar. He wanted to do polishing work. He
would talk to me about the polishing machines. Polishing was another job that demanded great precision. Yŏng-ho held his breath in
the presence of mechanics who continually operated within a margin
of error of five-thousandths of a millimeter. Father was powerless. He
couldn't even send his two sons to technical school. Father was tortured by his times. A dwarf father could not overcome economic torture. If we had graduated from technical school we would have done
skilled work from the beginning. I was fortunate. Within a month I
was given a hand drill that resembled a pistol. When I thought about
the automatic lathe, I had to laugh. Mother was delighted, though.
She believed that as a mechanic on an assembly line I had been given
the opportunity to take part in the production of a fine automobile. I
didn't explain to her the work I did. I drilled holes in car trunks. Af-

ter I drilled the holes my job was to set Phillips head screws in them. I used two tools and both were shaped like pistols. With one I drilled the holes and with the other I placed the screws and rubber washers. The workers senior to me called me the Two-Gun Kid. For the first time I felt yoked to machines. For the son of a dwarf this was an extraordinary experience. I was both driven and confined by the ceaseless work of the assembly line. Machines determined the pace of the work. Jammed from the waist up inside the trunk of a car, I had to perform my two job assignments simultaneously. When I touched the drill to the sheet of iron in the trunk my small tool recoiled with a bang. Every time I drilled a hole it shook me from the waist up. I worked with a mouthful of screws and washers. No sooner did I drill a hole than I took these parts from my mouth and positioned them.

Every day the lunchtime buzzer saved me. A moment longer, and I would have collapsed. The Two-Gun Kid wasn't able to finish his lunch. Cold sores sprouted on my tongue; my mouth stank of rubber and metal. I rinsed my mouth out with water but the stink remained. I stood in line in the vast cafeteria and had my tray loaded, but whenever I started to eat my hands trembled. I ate about half my soup of dried radish leaves and pike mackerel. And I couldn't eat more than half my rice. Before me sat a bowl of crumbly rice that seemed to have more barley mixed in with it by the day. To go with the soup and rice we had only a few pieces of bland, colorless kimchi. Even if a good lunch had been available I couldn't have eaten it. The toolroom helper waited for me to finish eating. Our food ration was never enough for him. When I pushed my leftovers to him he smiled. I spent the remainder of the mealtime on the roof of the plant. From up there you could see the ocean: the filthy ocean. Ŭngang's inner harbor is a receptacle for polluted seawater. A single small cleaning boat belonging to the Port Authority removed floating matter from the harbor waters. The plant that produced oxidized steel spewed out toxic gases. Those gases floated past where I sat. Enveloped by those gases, I calmed my trembling body's nerves.

Also visible from the roof was the textile plant where Yŏng-hŭi worked. Yŏng-hŭi now wore a blue work smock and a white work cap.

She worked in the Weaving Section of the Production Department. The trainee badge remained on her cap, but the work she did was no different from a regular worker's. In one minute Yŏng-hŭi half-walked, half-ran a hundred and twenty paces. The noise from the weaving machines was terrible. When one of those looms broke down, it either died or worked unpredictably. If it died, Yŏng-hŭi brought it back to life; if it acted strangely, she disconnected the raw silk thread, reconnected it, and then the loom ran normally. Yŏng-hŭi was given fifteen minutes, maximum, for lunch. Those who worked in the Weaving Section took turns running one at a time for their lunch and back. Meanwhile the foreman would look after their loom. When her turn came Yŏng-hŭi too entrusted her loom to the foreman and ran down the central corridor to the cafeteria. The lunch she ate was the same as mine. Pressed by time, Yŏng-hŭi ate in a hurry. She ate in great haste, then hurried back to her work site to half-walk, half-run among the weaving machines. In one hour Yŏng-hŭi walked seven thousand two hundred paces.

The temperature in the workroom was a hundred and two degrees. The heat pouring from the weaving machines always exceeded her body temperature. The hottest temperature during Ŭngang's humid summer is ninety-five degrees. The terrible noise of the weaving machines has no counterpart. Sound is measured in decibels. Under normal conditions the noise level is zero decibels; at fifty decibels conversation is impossible. The noise level in Yŏng-hŭi's workroom was more than ninety decibels. The noise generated by the combined operation of the weaving machines assaulted the slight, sweat-soaked body of Yŏng-hŭi. Yŏng-hŭi woke up crying at night. She cried without Mother knowing it. But Yŏng-hŭi was still young and couldn't think about what kept her in bondage. One day she went to her union office and obtained a copy of *The Worker's Handbook*. When she finished work she went to the workers' church. The church was in the northern part of the industrial zone. The minister wore dirty clothes. Severely nearsighted, he saw the young workers through fish-eye lenses. Yŏng-hŭi squeezed among the workers, sat down, and sang:

The rising sun, our artery,
Tolling the dawn, turning the earth.
Eternal builders, producing without rest,
Oh, we are workers.

Yŏng-hŭi sang this song at home, too, in the softest voice. Yŏng-ho and I silently observed this transformation in her.

Mother always worried that her two sons would get mixed up in something dangerous. She had undergone too much trouble when we lived in Felicity Precinct in Seoul. She couldn't forget the suffering her two sons had experienced when they were fired from their factories. Father had been sitting on the cement bridge drinking.

"Today the boys did something the other boys couldn't do," Father had said while he drank. "They told the president not to force the workers to do anything he wouldn't want forced upon himself."

"No need to worry," said Mother. "The boys can get a paying job at any factory they like."

"You don't know what you're talking about," Father said. "All the factories know by now. There's no factory that will take the boys. You don't realize what these boys did today."

"That's enough!" Mother said impatiently. "Did the boys do something wrong? The way you carry on, a person would think they committed treason or something. The criminals are *those* people."

Mother was right. And Father was well aware of that. But the people who suffered were us. Mother hoped the same thing wouldn't happen to us again.

Yŏng-ho and I decided to do what Mother told us. Mother didn't worry about Yŏng-hŭi. She didn't worry even when Yŏng-hŭi and other union members banded together after the disappearance of the steward. She didn't worry even when Yŏng-hŭi went around with bundles of printed matter containing passages attacking management. The problem lay with me. I couldn't keep the promise I'd made with Yŏng-ho to do what Mother said.

The day I received my second paycheck I went to my union office to see the steward. "This is my pay envelope," I said.

"What about it?" the steward asked. He looked about forty.

"The last two months I've been working nine and a half hours a day."

"And?"

"They didn't pay me for the extra hour and a half."

"Are you the only one?"

"No."

"Well, that's that," the steward said as he smoked a cigarette. "Why don't you run along now."

"Sir," I said. "Would you please look at the laws that govern union locals? According to article nine, section two, I have the right to request protection from unfair labor/management practices."

"And what might these unfair management practices be?"

"Nonpayment for overtime is a violation of article forty-six of the Basic Labor Law. And article twenty-nine, in the Collective Agreement, says that according to the Basic Labor Law the base rate plus fifty percent is to be paid for anything more than eight hours of continuous work."

"I'm so grateful to you," said the steward. "No one has ever brought that up with me. Is that all you wanted to say?"

"I'm working as a regular now. I work with a hand drill but I'm a regular."

"And?"

"I received a helper's pay."

"Anything else?"

"The company has violated article twenty-seven of the Basic Labor Law and article twenty-one of the Collective Agreement."

"You mean firing without cause?"

"On the assembly line alone seven people were fired without good reason."

"Impossible!" The steward drummed his fingers against the edge of his desk. "Firing without cause—it can't be."

"But it's happened. And if the union fails to act, it will keep on happening."

"We'll get an official explanation from the company."

"And," I continued, "this is an article I clipped from the newspaper."

"I saw that article too." The steward sat up as he said this. "The one quoting the chairman as saying he'll set aside two billion *wŏn* a year for social welfare, right? Every year he'll donate a large sum of money to the unfortunate. He probably has a foundation and a management team for it already. Now that seems like a fine thing to do."

"But there's something you should remind the company of at the labor/management meeting."

"And what's that?"

"That money belongs to the union members."

"How so?"

"None of us is paid according to his work. The pay is too low. And the money that's been cut from the amount I deserve is included in that two billion *wŏn*."

"Good point."

"I don't understand how he can take money that rightfully belongs to the workers and say he's going to spend it on other people."

"You're right. They're cheating us."

"The union should keep track of that money and make sure it's returned to the members."

"Yes, it should," said the steward. "And what else do you have to say?"

"That's all."

Three more days I worked as the Two-Gun Kid at Ŭngang Motors. During those three days I had a difficult time at work; I had nosebleeds in bed at night. Things kept happening to my small tools. The drill got stuck and the bit was chipped. I rushed to the workroom for a replacement drill but it happened again.

The workroom helper who used to smile whenever I pushed him the remains of my meal no longer smiled. My foreman loomed threateningly close. I couldn't keep up the relentless work pace demanded by the machines. Steadying my trembling body, I stared at the machines. Work went by me untouched. Even the work I was barely able to finish was marked unsatisfactory by the head inspector. Work that had gone well suddenly became too much for me. During those three days I came to realize the intrigue that went on in this society. Those who were well off tried to undermine the efforts of poor people to combine forces. The union steward was a company man. He did nothing for the workers.

I left Ŭngang Motors just before my name would have been added to the roster of fired workers. Nor did my name appear on the blacklist. I moved to Ŭngang Textile. There I did odd jobs. Mother didn't say a word. Nor did Yŏng-ho. Yŏng-hŭi related my story to a man from the union's General Council whom she met at the workers' church. During this time I saw Mother's budget book:

soybean sprouts	50 _wŏn_
Japanese soy sauce	120
salted mackerel	150
Unification wheat	3800
T-shirt for Yŏng-hŭi	900
visit neighbor child in auto accident	230
shrimp relish	50
room rent	15,000
retirement party for Yŏng-ho's co-worker	500
old woman who lost her way home	140
payment for night watchman	50
subsidy rice	6100
spending money for Yŏng-su	450
aspirin	100
cabbage for making kimchi	220
potatoes and chicken gizzards	110
toothache remedy	120
pike mackerel	180
salt	100
coal briquettes	2320
wheat flour	3820
visit from Yŏng-hŭi's friend at work	380
radio repair	500

needy neighbors	150
bean curd	80

Mother's budget book was crammed with such items. I thought about the money we needed to survive in Ŭngang. Not our living expenses, but just the amount we needed to stay alive. My brother and sister and I were working ourselves to death in the factories. The money we got didn't begin to match our production. That year the minimum cost of living for an urban laborer with a family of four was 83,480 *wŏn*. The total income from my brother and sister and me, as verified by Mother, was 80,231 *wŏn*. But after we took out the insurance premiums, mandatory savings, mutual-aid society payment, union dues, welfare payment, and the money we spent in the cafeteria, Mother actually ended up with no more than 62,351 *wŏn*. To earn this money we worked ourselves to death, and Mother was in a perpetual state of anxiety.

right-side molar	1500
left-side molar	1500

I closed the budget book. If Mother hadn't had those two molars pulled, we might have had almost three thousand *wŏn* for movies and such—if we went by the budget book, that is. Ultimately I decided to pay close attention to the story Yŏng-hŭi was telling. This kind of thing couldn't possibly happen in the town of Lilliput. And so I began to think of another Lilliput.

The Fault Lies with God as Well

I LONGED FOR A WORLD of utter simplicity. Simpler even
than the world Father dreamed of. To go to the moon and work at an
observatory—that was Father's dream. If he had realized that dream
he would have been able to see Coma Berenices, a constellation five
billion light-years away. But poor Father passed on without achieving
anything. His body was reduced to half a handful of ash in the crematorium, and Yŏng-ho and I, standing beside the water, wept at the
sight of Mother scattering it. That was the instant when our dwarf father disappeared into something inanimate. He began suffering the
instant he was born. Just because Father was small was no reason for
the life allotted him to have been so small. Through death Father had
rid himself of the suffering that was larger than his body. Father could
not feed his children well. And he couldn't send us all the way through
school. There was nothing in our home that could be called new. We
never got enough nourishment. We experienced symptoms of abnor-
mality arising from malnutrition. Protein deficiency gave us anemia,
edema, diarrhea. Father worked hard. He worked hard but forfeited
a life of human decency. And so in his last years Father harbored a
grudge against his times. Among the various characteristics of Father's times was this one: Rights were not acknowledged; duties alone

were enforced. Father sought economic and social rights, his injuries didn't heal, and he fell into the smokestack of a brick factory.

Father was a warm man, though. He held out hope for love. The world Father dreamed of was a world that provided work for all—a world where people were fed and clothed in return for their work, where everyone sent all their children through school and loved their neighbor. The ruling class in that world would not lead extravagant lives, Father had said. Because they would have the right to learn about human suffering. No one would lead a life of extravagance. Those who accumulated excessive wealth would be officially recognized as having lost their love for others, and the homes of these loveless families would be screened off from sunshine, blocked from breezes, cut off from electricity, and disconnected from water lines. Flowers and trees do not grow in the yards of such homes. Neither bees nor butterflies fly there. In the world of Father's dreams the only thing that was enforced was love. People would work with love, raise their children with love. Love would make the rain fall, love would lead to equilibrium, love would make the wind blow and make it come to rest, even on the small stems of buttercups. But not even the world Father longed for was an ideal society. The problem lay in having to pass laws for punishing the loveless. If such a world had to have laws, then it was no different from this world. In the world I longed for, everyone would be able to live according to the free exercise of reason. In the world of Father's dreams, they passed laws. I did away with those laws. My idea was to use education as a means for everyone to possess a noble love.

Father gave me the foundation that is love. And I, like Father, held out hope for love. But this city of Ŭngang, where our family of four had moved, was nothing like the ideal city of my mind. There we endured. We hadn't gone to Ŭngang seeking a pleasant living environment. With my own eyes I could see that living things near the factories of Ŭngang were slowly dying. When I passed by Ŭngang Manufacturing and the synthetic-rubber plant I kept my eyes to the ground. When I crossed the small stream that hugged the factory I held my breath. There in plain sight was black wastewater and sludge. The laborers walked to the plant early in the morning. Out they trudged in the evening. Sleep is plastered to the faces of those who work the graveyard shift at factories that operate round the clock. To stay awake, those workers take stimulants. In England the situation seems to have been horrid. I read once that children who worked in the Rotherham factory were whipped so they would stay awake. I also read that this Rotherham factory was actually one of the more humane ones. At the Leighton factory the children would fight one another for a bowl of porridge. And there were sexual assaults. The foreman was terrible. He tied workers by the wrist to their machine. There were instances where he took a file to a worker's teeth. Workers at the Leighton factory worked almost naked, even in winter. Fourteen hours of work a day was the norm. The factory owner prohibited workers from having watches. The single clock at the factory kept the workers going till late at night. Those workers and their families lived in slums near the factory. The workers drank cheap but potent alcohol. Their only source of comfort was the Gospel, which told them they would go to heaven when they died. And there were those who used opium to escape the wretchedness of their lives—used it even with their children. Meanwhile the factory owner and his family lived in a clean house on a clean street with shops. They wore nice clothes and ate tasty food. They had a villa outside the city. The holy father prayed for them. When the workers of England could be patient no more they attacked the factories. The first things they destroyed were the machines. In the ironworks of France the workers sang to the pounding of their hammers. The songs were cries of despair.

In comparison with such conditions, those of us at Ŭngang worked in an ideal environment. There was no factory owner who beat the workers, no foreman to file down our teeth. There was no need for us workers to fight over a bowl of gruel. And none of us injected opium. I suffered on account of my love. Father too must have suffered because of that love. The factory owners in England and France had never suffered. But to think now of the events of a hundred and sixty years earlier in those two countries was laughable.

"The important thing is the present." This was Yŏng-ho speaking.

"Eldest Brother," Yŏng-hǔi asked, "which side are we closer to?"

"What?"

"Are we closer to the situation a hundred and sixty years ago or the situation today?"

What could I say? Yŏng-hǔi knew nothing about the history of machine technology.

"Brother," Yŏng-ho once said when he was little. "Yŏng-hǔi doesn't know a thing."

"What about you, Big Brother?" she asked him.

"I *know*."

"I'll learn too when I go to middle school."

"You can learn now—the Industrial Revolution's in the fifth grade book."

"There's going to be compulsory schooling through ninth grade."

"Don't get your hopes up," Father had said. "But even if there isn't, we'll work it out for you to go to middle school."

"Really, Dad?"

"Really. I promise."

"The wind is doing strange things today," Mother said. "The smoke from the factory's giving me a headache."

"Better run the laundry through again," said Yŏng-hǔi. "The kids who work in that factory are in terrible health."

"Yŏng-hǔi, will you please not waste that pencil?" Mother had said. "Then we can send you to middle school."

"I'm only using the one that Big Brother threw away."

"Use it down to the point. We're not rich, you know."

The rain was over. It was evening, and the cicadas sang in the acacia bushes. Father was coming up to the yard, dragging the boat he had tethered to the bank of the sewer creek.

Yŏng-hǔi, who now worked the night shift, waited for my answer.

"Don't you have a ruler?" I said with a smile.

"Nope, so I can't measure."

"Wild horses are running away with the world," said Yŏng-ho. "So no one can say for sure."

"Right now their descendants drive to work at their factories," said

Yŏng-hŭi. "In those countries the union people and the managers meet on equal terms for talks on labor/management issues."

"What happened to the steward of your local?"

"I don't know," said Yŏng-hŭi. "I think the company people dragged him off somewhere."

"You're going to be late," Mother said. "I wish you wouldn't take those pills that keep you awake. And don't even think about getting Eldest Brother mixed up in your union business. Just let him do his job."

"All right."

But at Ŭngang I couldn't just "do my job." My brother, sister, and I worked ourselves to the bone in the factories, but after we paid our room rent, ate our food, nothing was left. Once again the money we had sweated to earn had all gone to subsistence expenses. And we weren't the only ones. All the workers of Ŭngang lived the same way. We ate poor food, wore poor clothing, and lived in poor health in a dirty home in a dirty neighborhood in a polluted environment. The neighborhood children dressed in dirty clothes and played in dirty alleys. They were abandoned children. I thought about the symptoms of disease that would appear in the children living near the factories as they grew up. When the Ŭngang industrial zone came under a trough of low pressure, the toxic gases spewed out by the various factories hung over the ground, polluting the air.

After arriving in Ŭngang Mother had constant headaches. She also had frequent breathing difficulties, coughing, and nausea. Yŏng-hŭi had hearing problems. The noise in the Weaving Section and the work site was torture for her. At the time, I was working as an assistant mechanic in the Maintenance Department. The instant I first saw Yŏng-hŭi on the night shift I wanted to die. She couldn't keep her eyes open. Eyes shut, she was walking backward among the weaving machines. The temperature inside the workplace at night was a hundred and two. The Ŭngang Textile machines never stopped. Yŏng-hŭi's blue work smock was soaked through with sweat. While Yŏng-hŭi was dozing several looms came to a complete stop. The foreman came up to Yŏng-hŭi and jabbed her in the arm. She snapped to and revived the looms. A spot of crimson blood appeared on the arm of her smock. It was three in the morning. The hardest time was from two until five in the morning, Yŏng-hŭi had said, averting her round, teary eyes. At the far end of her field of vision her oldest brother was working as an assistant mechanic. I oiled the machines that the mechanics serviced and I kept track of the tools. My work uniform was stained with sweat and oil.

I had a desire to effect a revolution—starting in the minds of the people who worked in Ŭngang. I wanted them to long for the same joys, the peace, the justice, the happiness that other people enjoyed. I wanted them to understand that they were not the ones who ought to feel intimidated. Yŏng-hŭi spent many hours observing me. Every day I stood before the office bulletin board. Posted there was the list of those who had retired or been fired or suspended. I would stand in front of the bulletin board feeling smaller than Father. "Look at the midget," people had said. When Father crossed the street, cars would honk. People laughed at the sight of Father. Yŏng-ho had said he would make a land mine and bury it in the path of those people. "Eldest Brother," Yŏng-hŭi had said, "I want you to kill those devils who call Father a midget." Her lips quivered with the vast hatred that lay inside her. In my dreams I used to hear the explosions of mines Yŏng-ho had buried. The cars of those people were swept up in flames. Inside the burning cars they screamed. At Ŭngang I heard the same screaming I had heard in my dreams. This was when the tempering tank at the aluminum electrode factory blew up. The tank was connected with the blast furnace of the casting factory, and the instant it blew up, pillars of deep-red flame shot far into the sky. Quenching water, metal chunks, bricks, fragments of slate collected and then dropped from the sky. The nearby factories sustained damage, too, their roofs flying off or their walls collapsing. We ran over to find the body parts of workers flung every which way in the vicinity of the factory. It was a small factory, but for one instant it produced the loudest noise in Ŭngang. The workers who had managed to survive slumped onto the shoulders of their co-workers and screamed.

I attended the memorial service for the victims at the workers' church in the northern part of the factory zone. Yŏng-hŭi was packed among the laborers, praying. The minister, severely nearsighted, saw these young people through fish-eye lenses. The minister removed his glasses and closed his eyes. I saw the minister and the young people praying. Saw the tears streaming from their closed eyes. And from Mother's eyes as well. Mother lifted the hem of her soiled skirt and wiped her tears. A young man who went to work at the aluminum electrode factory lived with his young bride in rooms rented from our neighbors. He was there when the tempering tank exploded. His young body flew off without a trace. He worked for thirteen hundred *wŏn* a day. The young bereaved bride hanged herself. She was pregnant, Mother said. Curled up in her stomach was yet one more life, one that made Mother cry. I suffered because of the love I had inherited from Father. We lived in a loveless world. Educated people made us suffer. They sat at their desks thinking only of ways to make machines operate at low cost. These people would mix sand with our food if they needed to. These were people who drilled holes in the bottom of the wastewater holding tank and let the sludge run into the ocean instead of passing through the filtration plant. Yŏng-hŭi said the company people had dragged the steward of her union local off somewhere. On one really bleak day they fired upwards of thirty people en masse.

They acted as if they were in a completely different boat from ours. They made more than ten times as much money as we did. In the evening they returned to their happy families in their clean homes far from the industrial area. They lived in warm houses. They didn't know. Management didn't know that the young workers, though they didn't demonstrate when they were anxious to have something, were sprouting into something utterly new. None of the management people tried to see, so none of them knew of this change. If pressed to explain, I would call it a kind of power—a power that is completely skeptical of authority.

I went often to the workers' church to read. The books I needed the minister located for me. The minister emphasized that fear was our greatest enemy. He needn't have mentioned that. I already knew it. I also knew that the ministers at regular churches made use of fear. The minister at the workers' church was different. He too was a man who had suffered on account of love. He took me to a meeting of the Social Studies Group. The union steward didn't return to the plant. A copy of his letter of resignation was posted on the bulletin board, and that was that. The Ŭngang Textile labor union local was quietly foundering. I'll bet management was satisfied. They summoned the union reps to a general meeting and had the vice-steward made steward. Inside the plant all was quiet. The machines operated nonstop, round the clock, the fired workers didn't raise a commotion, and the workers, driven mercilessly by those responsible for production, continued to work obediently. The plant manager was a director. At the directors' meetings at headquarters in Seoul he would thrust out his shoulders and sit down. The senior director praised him. All the shareholders praised him, and even the head of the Ŭngang Group acknowledged his ability. They still held to the illusion that they were creating a paradise. Even if they were to establish this paradise, I thought, it would be theirs and not ours. The key to the gate would never be given to us. They would abandon us beside a rotting garbage heap outside. They would leave with their families in their heated cars, their air-conditioned cars, and discover us alongside the highways leading out of the city. "How filthy!" their wives would say. "Lazy failures!" they would say. They didn't consider the fact that they didn't pay us a fair wage for the work we did.

Yŏng-hŭi brought the new union steward to see me. When she was vice-steward, she had worked with Yŏng-hŭi in the Weaving Department. She too had taken amphetamines on the night shift and then sleeping pills when working the day shift. I explained what we would have to do in the future and how hard it would be. She was an intelligent, pretty girl. This girl, Yŏng-i, was quick to understand what I was saying. She knew more than I did about labor law. She was just too young to organize her thoughts and feelings. All I had to do was show her the way out of that confusion. Every day I saw Yŏng-i. We gathered information, discussed it, found the right way to put it in words, made notes. Yŏng-hŭi would bring Yŏng-i to our house. Mother liked Yŏng-i. To keep our discussions private, we didn't go to the workers' church. When we saw each other at the plant we acted like strangers. Yŏng-hŭi reported to me something the minister had said: I would make an excellent leader. Yŏng-i believed those words. Although Mother felt uneasy, she decided that she could no longer hold me back. Item by item I wrote down what Yŏng-i, as a labor rep, would say to our employers. Yŏng-i convened a meeting of the local's General Council and had four members elected to it. She presented the names of the council members to the company and in return received the roster of management's members and reps. The plant manager sent a large pot of flowers to the local office. The head of the Production Department explained its significance—a wish for a conference on behalf of industrial peace and economic benefits for labor. They believed that the union had lost power. As on any other day, on the bulletin board outside the office they posted the names of those who had been fired or suspended. The young people who had finished the night shift and those on the afternoon shift gathered in front of the conference room and, all alike, waved to the union reps. The employers' reps waved in the direction of the workers. Yŏng-i entered the conference room with the small notebook she and I had prepared in the course of our discussions and study. Yŏng-i wore a white dress and white shoes. She was pretty. Yŏng-hŭi pinned a corsage with a dark purple flower to Yŏng-i's bosom. The young people broke into laughter. The people from management whistled. Yŏng-i didn't laugh.

As one of the five observers on labor's side, I entered the conference room in my oil-stained work uniform. The employers' reps must have laughed at the sight of this incongruous assistant mechanic from Maintenance. They sat across from us, five paces away. I sat in a low chair in the corner and watched. At first the atmosphere was very cordial. The participants drank cold beverages beneath the fan. I drank as well. I was extremely careful, but in the end my glass, used for entertaining plant guests, was smeared with oil. Some twenty minutes passed, and the atmosphere changed.

Employer 3: "We believe we have a good understanding of the particulars concerning improved productivity voiced by our respected assistant plant manager and Production Department head. Since the two sides are writing up the minutes of this meeting, it would be good to make them available to each and every member of the workforce."

Laborer 3: "Here I would like to say a few words about a pin."

Employer 2: "A pin?"

Laborer 3: "Yes, the sharp end of a bobby pin. The respected head of the Production Department will know what I'm talking about."

Employer 4: "What's this all about? Speak up, Yŏng-i."

Laborer 1: "Under the circumstances I have no comment."

Employer 4: "How come?"

Laborer 1: "We are here today as representatives of fifteen hundred laborers."

Employer 3: "Right. And so?"

Laborer 1: "We are using polite speech but the respected assistant plant manager and department head are using plain speech."

Employer 1: "Our mistake."

Employer 3: "What about the minutes? Please correct the first part."

Laborer 1: "Since the respected department head will know the story about the bobby pin better than I, I would like to hear it directly from him."

Employer 4: "I tell you, this is news to me."

Employer 3: "Once more, please—polite speech this time."

Employer 4: "All right. With all due respect, I have absolutely no idea what this bobby pin business is all about."

Employer 2: "Bobby pin?"

Mother: Don't forget a bobby pin, Yŏng-hŭi.

Yŏng-hŭi: Why, Mom?

Mother: If one of your seams comes apart, you'll have to fasten it with the pin.

Laborer 3: "This bobby pin is making the workers cry."

Yŏng-hŭi: If any kid calls Dad a midget, I'll poke him with this.

Mother: Yŏng-hŭi, please. He'll bleed.

Yŏng-hŭi: I'll poke him anyway.

Laborer 3: "It happens when we're on the night shift. By two or three in the morning no one can keep their eyes open. Sometimes we're asleep on our feet. And then the foreman pokes us in the arm with a bobby pin."

Employer 4: "That's nonsense."

Laborer 4: "We're not insects, you know."

Employer 5: "Come on, you two."

Laborer 5: "The foreman holds it near the end. Then he jabs the tip in our arm. It pierces the flesh and jolts us awake so maybe we can do a better job of watching our looms. But during the past month I've seen quite a few union members on the night shift running off between the looms crying."

Laborer 4: "I'd like to know the relationship between bobby pins and improved productivity."

Employer 4: "None whatsoever."

Laborer 2: "You knew about the bobby pins, didn't you?"

Employer 4: "Really, now, this is absurd. Do you think we would simply stand by and allow something like that to happen? If some foreman is using a bobby pin, it's his own sadistic nature—the company has nothing to do with it."

Laborer 1: "In any event, please conduct an investigation."

Employer 1: "Department head, please conduct an investigation. If the allegations are true, please take the necessary corrective measures."

Laborer 1: "This is the bobby pin that was used in the Weaving Section. I know production is important. But I can't have our union members crying and running off between the looms at a time of night when everyone else is asleep in bed."

Employer 1: "The union steward is right. We are civilized people living in a civilized society. If you find something backward happening here, it would be a shameful affair."

Employer 2: "As all of you will know by now, we at this plant do not force you laborers—either through violence, threats, imprisonment, et cetera, or through illegal restrictions on your physical or intellectual freedom—to perform work against your own free will. Even if you create an incident during the course of your work, we do not engage in aggressive behavior."

Laborer 1: "I should offer a dissenting opinion. But since there are other items on our agenda I'll let that pass."

Employer 2: "No, no. Speak up."

Laborer 1: "With all due respect, you said you don't do those things. But they're prohibited to begin with. We have other matters to discuss, so I won't offer my opinion now. There are many instances, though, where prohibitions are no longer being observed."

Employer 5: "If we're going to do everything according to the letter of the law, then most of the machines in Ŭngang will have to shut down."

Employer 4: "And if the machines are shut down they get rusty. And the plants will have to close down. And if that happens, all of you lose your jobs."

Employer 1: "That's a little far-fetched. There are some problems with what you two gentlemen are saying."

Employer 2: "Perhaps we should strike the two gentlemen's remarks from the minutes."

Employer 1: "Yes, please strike them out."

Boy 1: Leave them out.

Boy 2: How come?

Boy 1: We don't play with the midget's boys.

Yŏng-ho: Big Brother.

Me: Easy, Yŏng-ho.

Yŏng-ho: Don't say no to me. I'm going to kill this asshole.

Boy 1: Hey! This guy hit me!

Yŏng-ho: I'm going to kill you! I'm going to kill you!

Me: Leave him alone, Yŏng-ho. Yŏng-ho! Yŏng-ho!

Boy 3: Here comes the midget!

Boy 4: Here comes the midget!

Laborer 2: "What about our plant?"

Employer 2: "What do you mean?"

Employer 1: "For our part, labor/management harmony and industrial peace are necessary. We can't have our talks going off on a tangent."

Laborer 1: "We work hard. We even try to make the machines run faster. But we laborers cannot live a life worthy of human beings. We've been thinking about the work we do in the plants, our cost of living, and our pay. Contrary to the remarks offered by the respected assistant plant manager, we've come to the conclusion that we are backward people living in a backward society. We think that if we are to make the machines run any faster, then we should live a life worthy of human beings."

Employer 1: "This is so far-fetched it's frightening. If you think about it, we're laborers like you. We work and earn money too."

Laborer 1: "We're only the same in the sense that we both receive a pay envelope. But the envelope we receive isn't thick like the one you get. The one we get is absurdly thin. We are here today to let you know we cannot accept that thin envelope indefinitely."

Employer 2: "You put it so well, it all sounds convincing. But may I ask one thing?"

Laborer 1: "Yes."

Employer 2: "Where did you get the money to dress yourself up so nicely? If the envelope is so thin, then where do you get the money to eat and buy clothing and shoes?"

Laborer 1: "I live alone. My parents are no longer alive and I have no younger brothers or sisters to pay tuition for. I don't eat a lot and I'm not in the habit of snacking. When I'm not working I'm tired and all I do is sleep. And I always remind myself to keep my clothes clean so I can wear them for a long time. I bought these clothes and shoes with money I saved up. Because I'm now representing the employees I wanted to look neat. In order to dress up like this I spent more money than a grade three laborer is paid in a month."

Employer 1: "Anyway, what are your demands?"

Laborer 1: "A twenty-five percent pay raise, a two hundred percent bonus, and unconditional rehiring of workers fired without cause—that's all."

Employer 5: "Listen to these kids!"

Employer 4: "There's no need to talk further. Behind the scenes there are subversive elements manipulating these kids."

Yŏng-hŭi: Mom, Eldest Brother broke a window in the big house down there.

Mother: I know. Father went over.

Yŏng-hŭi: The boy who lives there was teasing Father, calling him a midget. So why did Father go over?

Mother: When you children do something wrong, Father has to take responsibility.

Yŏng-hŭi: Until when?

Mother: Until you children are grown-up.

Employer 1: "In the future, if there's some incident, all of you will have to take responsibility."

Mother: And when you're grown-up you'll have to take responsibility yourselves for what you do.

Employer 2: "Your pay was increased last February and we are paying you according to that adjustment. As for a bonus, we paid one at the end of last year."

Laborer 1: "That was a unilateral increase on your part. And the 'bonus' that was paid, you can't attach the name bonus to it, it was so small. It was no more than a month's overtime pay."

Employer 2: "You get paid for overtime, don't you? Go see the people at headquarters—they work overtime until nine or ten at night and you don't hear a peep out of them."

Laborer 1: "They're educated people. You can't compare them with us. We have completely different expectations. They don't stand in line to receive a thin envelope like we do. And they also get a six hundred percent yearly bonus. It's their problem if they don't get the overtime pay they're entitled to. It's not up to us to correct their mistakes."

Employer 5: "This won't do."

Employer 1: "Union Steward, I'll bet you believe the relationship between employers and laborers is completely adversarial."

Laborer 1: "Here at Ŭngang, now, yes."

Employer 1: "That's a mistaken perception. If business goes well, then the people who benefit are you laborers."

Laborer 1: "It shouldn't be a matter of benefits just for the workers. Both labor and management should benefit. This is our goal. Now the situation is too unfair. When it's fair, then we can achieve industrial peace."

Employer 5: "Now cut that out!"

Employer 3: "Calm down now."

Employer 5: "What does that girl know?"

Employer 1: "Please sit down."

Employer 5: "I don't understand why you let that girl ramble on about industrial peace and all."

Employer 3: "Please sit down."

Employer 1: "Let me repeat: You all have the wrong idea. You think that when the company profits, the entire profit is divided among a few people—that's a very dangerous idea. Business profits are returned to society. They're distributed fairly for employee wages, shareholder dividends, and reinvestment in the business itself."

Laborer 1: "With all respect, I knew you'd say something like that."

Employer 1: "If you've got something to say, then speak right up."

Laborer 1: "How is it possible to pile up shameful profits by not paying employees a fair wage—and then returning those profits to society? And what's the use of sharing those profits with shareholders? And what's the use of accumulating those bloody profits? We believe that such a business should not be allowed to expand. To be precise, as long as you run the machines without paying us a wage that enables us to live like human beings, it's not a profit. It should be called something else. I just read in the newspaper that our respected CEO plans to donate two billion *wŏn* a year for the needy. And I saw a photo of our respected CEO smiling for the reporters. This would never have happened if the profits had been fairly distributed in the first place. It's deceitful for a business to demand a one-way sacrifice from the laborers at several factories—eat, sleep, work, and nothing else, then leave when you get a dismissal notice—and then suddenly offer to donate something to society. It's nothing but a smokescreen to avoid public criticism. We've got a list of the directors of the social welfare foundation established by our respected CEO. We held out hope for those gentlemen. But our expectations were shattered. Those gentlemen have absolutely no idea of our physical, economic, and mental suffering. If those gentlemen were truly fine individuals, they would have said that the money to be donated by our respected chairman should first be divided among poor laborers and that other funds would be donated to society."

Employer 5: "Listen to her. I'll never forgive her for this."

Employer 3: "Will you *please* settle down?"

Employer 1: "Union Steward, give us that notebook. And let's adjourn."

Laborer 1: "When will you give us the company's response to our demands?"

Employer 1: "You can forget about that. We have nothing to give to people who look at everything so pessimistically. I don't understand how you can deny the progress we've made."

Laborer 1: "That's not the case. We're the ones who work on the front lines of industry. All we're saying is that the benefits should be returned to us as well. Why do *we* have to suffer on behalf of a healthy economy?"

Employer 1: "Time will solve everything."

Laborer 1: "The laborers have already waited a long time."

Employer 5: "These kids ought to be jailed or something."

Employer 3: "Would you *please* sit down and be quiet?"

Employer 1: "No, he's right. The kids on the night shift and afternoon shift are crowding around outside. Obviously these kids are stirring up the union members and are going to carry out some organized activities. These kids have already broken the law."

Laborer 1: "No. They're here because they're wondering what's happening. And even if there should be some incident, that's the only thing we've done wrong. But the employers are different. Once in a while we make one mistake—in comparison, the employers are breaking ten articles of law a day."

Employer 1: "Please shut the door."

Employer 2: "If you'd be good enough to shut both doors. Don't let these kids out."

Father: Don't let Yŏng-su out for the time being.
Mother: All right.
Yŏng-hŭi: What did Eldest Brother do wrong? It's the fault of the boy in that family.
Father: What did the boy do wrong?
Yŏng-hŭi: He was making fun of you, calling you a midget.
Father: That boy didn't throw a rock and break our window. He didn't do anything wrong. Your father *is* a midget.

And so for three days I couldn't go out and play. I took a sewing needle from Mother's spool and made a fishhook out of it. I heated it in a flame and made the end of it curve just right. I braided two strands of thread, coated it with wax, and attached the hook to the end. The day Mother said I could go out, I ran up the hill behind our house. I broke off a long bush-clover branch and made a fishing pole out of it. Again that year we had a drought. Every day Father went out to work on pumps. The water level in the sewer creek went down noticeably. I went down the bank to the creek and fished. The small fish that I hooked flopped around in the shade of the brick factory smokestack. This, then, was the one and only time I heard from Father's own lips that he was a dwarf. Mother went into the kitchen before she had finished washing the barley beside the pump. If something had happened to me, Mother would have died too. I returned home late that night. It was a night when a trough of low pressure had settled over all of Ŭngang and it was really hard to breathe. Mother sat completely still. First she asked me about Yŏng-i and then about Yŏng-hŭi. She wanted to talk to Yŏng-i, as she had talked to Yŏng-hŭi, about the traditional duties a woman should perform for her family and home. I didn't know how long Yŏng-i would be in trouble. Yŏng-i's white dress didn't stay clean that day. All Yŏng-hŭi had to do was go on a two-day, one-night fast, chant slogans, and sing the laborers' song. I returned home alone. I thought again that night of the world Father longed for. In the world Father longed for, those who accumulated excessive wealth would be officially recognized as having lost all their love for others, and the homes of those loveless people would be screened off from sunshine, blocked from breezes, cut off from electricity, and disconnected from water lines. The people in that world would work with love and raise their children with love. Love would make the rain fall, love would lead to equilibrium, love would make the wind blow and make it come to rest on the small stems of buttercups. Father believed that laws should be passed in order to punish loveless people. This hadn't sat right with me. But that night I decided to revise my thinking. Father was right.

Everyone was committing sins—without exception. In Ŭngang not even God was an exception.

The Klein Bottle

THERE ARE A LOT of blind people in Ŭngang. This is one of the things that surprised me about living there. Of course I didn't see them in the industrial zone. I learned about them during my walks about the urban district and residential area. One day I saw five blind people in the space of ten minutes. During the next ten minutes I saw three, and in the following ten minutes I saw two more, tapping the ground next to my feet. I found this surprising. There must be cities in the world where you can wander about for more than an hour without seeing a single blind person. I couldn't understand why Ŭngang in particular should have so many blind people. The people of Ŭngang didn't seem to know there were so many blind people all around them. And so there were times when all the people of Ŭngang seemed blind to me.

I thought there was only one way that blind people could see the world. And that was for them to have sight. Mother held to a different idea: It all depended on the eyes through which you saw the world. She knew an old man who saw well with just one eye. Every day Mother went to the lumberyard of a wood products factory that owed its existence to an exclusive license from the Ŭngang Regional Port Authority. Piled there were timber logs from Indonesia. When the tide came up to the lumberyard the logs floated. A log-picker plucked the logs from the water. The people of Liberation Precinct stripped the bark from the Indonesian logs, which had grown tall in the Indonesian sunshine. They stripped the bark and used it at home for fuel. The surplus they sold. Mother and the one-eyed old man stripped the bark together. The old man had worked at the casting plant and lost the sight of an eye. For thirty years he had seen the world through a single eye. He was different from the one-eyed king of the country of the blind. The one-eyed king was convinced that he always saw better than anyone else. But the world he saw was only half the world. He would never know the other half as long as he believed only in that one eye and didn't try to see from a different perspective. Mother stripped the bark from the Indonesian logs and carried it home on her back up the slope of Liberation Precinct. The one-eyed old man followed her. They arrived at his home first. There was bark from the logs throughout the one-eyed old man's small house. That day some students from a church in the residential area paid the old man a visit. One of them asked him, "Grandfather, what do you think your life will be like in the future?" Another read off six answers and asked him to pick one:

- much better
- somewhat better
- neither better nor worse
- a bit worse
- much worse
- no answer

The old man answered simply: "Much better. Mark that one for me."
The students stood at the bark door. Their faces indicated that this reply was unexpected.
"I'll soon be dead," the one-eyed old man said.
That old man, just like Father, would find peace only after he died, said Mother. When the students asked her the same question, she told them: "Our life will be much worse." Mother was anxious on my ac-

count. She believed I had started a losing battle. It didn't sit right with me that Mother was going to the lumberyard.

"Mother, will you please stop?" I said. "Your going to the lumber-yard bothers us. How much is that bark going to help us?"

"All this is because of you." Mother spread out the sea-soaked bark in the sun. "I'm doing this in preparation for when you aren't here any more."

"Am I supposed to be going somewhere?"

"You're always having to leave home."

"But I'm not going anywhere."

"You'll get run out of here."

"By who?"

"Enough, all right?" Mother turned her back to me. "What about the eight days or so you were away from home that last time? Don't tell me you've forgotten?"

"You know—it was because of union business."

"It's all the same. You get beat up and you come home bloody. You'll end up abandoning your mom and your brother and sister and continuing with those crazy activities. And then you'll leave us with a sackful of worries."

"There's nothing to worry about," I said. "Nothing's going to happen."

"There's no need for you to say that." Mother knew. "This is the start," she said as she moved the pieces of bark and spread them out. "This is the start of whatever it is you're up to. I have no idea what it is. What are you going to do? And who for?"

"I don't have the energy to do anything for others."

"Don't think you can deceive me."

"If you know, then why do you say that?"

"All right." Mother stood up. "It was a mistake to come to Ŭngang. Every night I dream about your father."

"So you had a bad dream," Father had said. "You're always having bad dreams, all of you."

"But it's okay!" said Yŏng-ho. "I fly all over the place! I fly across the river!"

"You're growing up," I said. "That's why."

Father rested a hand on my head. "Look at those children."
He pointed outside the gate. The neighborhood children were sitting on the bank of the sewer creek where the lady's-thumb grew; they were eating dirt. As Yǒng-hǔi watched them she ate uncooked rice.

"I used to eat dirt, didn't I?" I asked.

"Not me," said Yǒng-ho.

"Yes, you did," Yǒng-hǔi said as she emptied the rice into her mouth. "Children with worms eat dirt."

"You mean roundworms?"

"Yeah."

"Yǒng-hǔi, please don't eat rice that's not been cooked," Mother said.
"But it's good!"

"When you make some money buy us a big chunk of meat. They're not fed right so they're eating up all our rice before I can cook it."

"All right."

Father stepped outside the gate. He went off into the distance scraping two kitchen knives together as sharpeners do. From that moment on we had waited for Father.

"Father made a mistake, didn't he?" Mother said. "We should have moved to a place in the countryside—anyplace. Then your father wouldn't have passed on."

"What could he do there?"

"Better to work the soil, isn't it?"

"Did we have land to work?"

"Working someone else's land would have been better than being in this place." Tossing aside the remaining bark, Mother turned toward me. "Why can't you just stick to your factory work?" Her voice had risen. "What in God's name do you figure on doing? Why can't you keep to your own job?"

"Mother," I said. "I want to live like a human being."

"Who told you you couldn't?"

"There are bad people stopping us. And the other kids don't know it."

"Let them do their stopping, and let the others keep on not know-ing. Don't listen to me and you'll get yourself hauled off. You commit a crime, you'll go on trial, and then you'll find yourself in jail. Unless you want to see your mom and your brother and sister pounding their heads against the jail door, you had better tone down."

I crawled up into the loft. Mother kept spreading out the bark to dry. The tide cycle in Ŭngang was twelve hours and twenty-five min-utes. Mother probably didn't know that the moon pulled the ocean in and let it out. When a large freighter made its way from the ocean to a dock in the inner harbor Mother would go out to the lumberyard. Along with everything else the logs in the lumberyard only floated at high tide. Mother was obsessed with the thought that she might lose her elder son to Ŭngang. The city of Ŭngang was too large and too complex. As Yŏng-hŭi said, Ŭngang was not only a dangerous city but full of crime. Attached to the bark wall of the one-eyed old man's house were wanted posters. The suspects were charged with murder, attempted murder, aggravated robbery, forcible rape, impersonation of a public official, armed robbery, fraud, bribery, and other crimes. The names of the criminals I knew of did not appear. Some of the photographs of these various criminal suspects were stamped "ar-rested." The big lawbreakers would be found someplace far from us.

The very first thing to startle Mother was the appearance of my name on the blacklist. The employers at the Ŭngang plants had put me on the list of blacklisted workers deeply involved in union activi-ties. In the eyes of the employers I was a little devil. The person they disliked most was the minister at the workers' church. They disliked saintly people, those who epitomized love and sacrifice. The minis-ter seemed a perfect saint to me. Every time I saw the eyes behind the fish-eye lenses I thought of him as a saint. But for me he was al-most impossible to understand. I believed that as long as we made an effort, we could attain salvation for ourselves. When I voiced this thought, all he did was smile. In his presence I was always the young student. Apart from the fact that he had a weakness—the weakness of his body—he was a man of wisdom. There was nothing he didn't know about politics, philosophy, history, science, economics, society, and labor. He likened wealth to water pouring from a spring called Production and said that if it didn't pass from hand to hand it would collect in one place and grow stagnant. When someone who heard these words responded, quite sincerely, "That's how it happens in history," the minister raised his glasses to his forehead and said: "What all of you have to understand is that you yourselves are the producers of wealth. That's the point." This had come up in the Social Studies Group. "I've seen you and your co-workers working hard to produce wealth," the minister said one day. "But I have never seen a single person who received that wealth and then shared it properly." Through a kind of consciousness raising, he installed an engine in my mind.

I learned a lot from a six-month educational program he arranged. I learned about the structure of industrial society, the human social system, the history of the labor movement, current issues in labor/management relations, labor relations law, and more. I learned about politics, economics, history, theology, and technology. There were fourteen of us in all, and every Saturday afternoon we gathered to eat, sleep, and study together until Sunday evening. We students came from the appliances, iron and steel, chemicals, electronics, milling, textile, lumber, railway carriage, aluminum, motor vehicles, glass, shipbuilding, clothing, and other plants. We were all sons or daughters of poor families. We were able to grow close through one thing alone that we had in common: We had all tasted tear-soaked food. We sang a song:

> When I suffered from hunger were you there?
> Were you there when I sought food?
> When I suffered from thirst were you there?
> Were you there when I sought water?
> When I was sick in bed were you there?
> Were you there when I wished to be cared for?

And before we went our separate ways after finishing our course we sang another song:

Together sharing joys and sorrows
Together experiencing hopes and fears

If life was inhuman in those factories equipped with massive production systems, the minister said, we would be remiss if we didn't
single out the problems and restructure them. He emphasized that our
parents never had the experience of working in factories this large. He
categorized us as a generation forced to sacrifice itself in a completely
new environment. Our silence only harms our rights, he said. So fourteen of his students returned to the plants and set themselves difficult
tasks. Six succeeded in organizing a union. Only later did I learn that
in one respect the minister was an utterly conservative moderate. He
was a man who could not live for an instant without his god. As part
of our instruction he called in a man of science. Every Sunday afternoon the man of science would come and talk to us about technology.
As I listened to him, I couldn't help imagining an unskilled laborer
operating one of several coal-black machines. He himself managed a
small workshop. A very small workshop. He called it a tool shop. His
shop's facilities consisted in sum of an automatic lathe, tool lathe,
screw-cutting lathe, screw grinder, drilling machine, milling machine,
and small crucible. At any one time no more than ten workers worked
in his shop operating these tooling machines. The workshop's main
product was a Z-one-and-three-eighths screw. Virtually the entire
output was exported to the United States. His screws were used in the
manufacture of the lunar module and other spacecraft, weather satel-
lites, the Venus probe, remote control rockets, test robots, and com-
puters. All of the small parts he made were used in the manufacture
of intelligent machines. But the man of science was ashamed at the
thought of the work he did. His dream had been to become a scientist.
He hadn't been able to realize that dream. "My circumstances prevented me from becoming a scientist," he said. His feeble voice always
had a metallic ring to it. And he made you feel depressed. His voice
put him at a disadvantage. At first, no one was prepared to accept his
words at face value. According to him, technological developments
caused skilled workers to lose their jobs—and unskilled factory labor

was filled by young laborers working long hours at low pay. And so the population concentrated in the factories and slums appeared in the cities. He spoke, in his usual metallic voice, telling us what we already knew. But the simple suggestion that the workers' loss was the owner's gain struck us forcefully. He showed us that an increase in wealth was always associated with an increase in the number of low-paid workers. Now we believed him.

When at the close of our educational program we went on an outing to the beach we invited him along. We took snacks and things to drink. At the polluted beach we ate, debated, sang. If we jumped in the water we came out smelling of oil. The minister didn't know how to swim. When I broke through the waves and swam out, he waved at me to stop. I swam out a hundred feet or so, then returned. My body was covered with flecks of waste oil. The minister cleaned me off with a towel. The white towel turned black and water drops ran down my oil-smeared skin. I squatted down on the sand and retched. The man of science borrowed a wooden boat and rowed out on the water. He placed a white disk on the surface of the water, which had once been a fishing ground, and used it to measure how far down he could see. At one place in the East Sea that depth was fifty-nine feet, but here the transparency was only nine feet, the man of science said, tsk-tsk-ing in disapproval. We spent the night beside that stagnant sea. I got to thinking about injustice, and I couldn't get to sleep. Yŏng-hŭi and Yŏng-ho were working the night shift that day. Yŏng-hŭi was rushing among the weaving machines and Yŏng-ho was working the polisher—a very unsettled night for Mother. At the time, I was doing almost nothing in my role as elder son. We were living and eating on the money Yŏng-ho and Yŏng-hŭi brought home. Of course I was earning money, but I had to spend it all.

"I'm sorry," I said. "Sorry to Yŏng-ho, sorry to Yŏng-hŭi."

And then my brother and sister spoke up.

"Don't worry, Brother."

"It's all right, Eldest Brother."

Mother was different. "I really wish you would just concentrate on your job at the factory." The same thing she always said. "I don't know how long it will take, but won't the day come when we have peace of mind and body?"

"Haven't you gotten worn down?" I said. "In the long run, we're all getting old and dying."

"No," Mother said in a low voice. "Not you. Your father didn't live out his natural life span."

If I had listened to Mother, I might have moved up from assistant mechanic to mechanic in the Maintenance Department of Ŭngang Textile. My pay would have increased as well. I could not be the son Mother wanted. On my own initiative I chose a difficult path. Right after the educational program at the workers' church I went to the Institute on Labor Issues affiliated with Ŭngang University. To take a three-week course there, an assistant mechanic in Maintenance at Ŭngang Textile had to work three consecutive weeks on the night shift. At a time when people slept, I worked instead. I grew terribly weak. The food was bad enough, but I couldn't eat at regular mealtimes and was always short on sleep. At this time I was told that a man from an industrial complex in the southern part of the country was coming up to see me. The minister had told me about him. And I had heard other accounts of this man. He had experience working at several factories, and his method of labor activism was so unique that labor unions sprang up at the factories where he worked. Not only that, but the workers brought the wheels of the factory owners' wagon to a halt, lessened that wagon's load—profit—and shared it with the employees. I had heard that wounds had been inflicted on various parts of his body. And as was often the case with people who knew a lot, he tended to speak very slowly but was quick to assess. Of course I did not believe everything I heard about him. But I did believe he was someone who had seen a lot of trouble and worked on behalf of others and not in his own interests. When I received word that he had arrived at the workers' church and was waiting for me, I knew I had to rush over there. It was Chi-sŏp. I wasn't surprised. When Mother saw him she could say nothing. A few seconds later she turned away and touched the hem of her sleeve to her eyes. She had thought of our deceased father. Yŏng-ho and Yŏng-hŭi too said they had thought of Father the instant they saw Chi-sŏp. He brought back memories of our last days in Felicity Precinct in Seoul. Through smoky glass we looked back to the past.

"Dying is easier than living," said Mother. "But I've never resented the children's father for that."

"I'm sure you haven't," said Chi-sŏp. There were scars beneath his eyes. His nose looked a bit squashed. With his right hand he covered his left hand, whose ring and little fingers had been severed to stumps. Mother had gone to the market for him. She had bought some beef, used part of it for soup, and grilled the rest. Yŏng-hŭi had lit some bark in the fuel hole. Our home was thick with smoke. Mother had transferred the glowing coals of the bark to the cook-stove and grilled the meat. This was the first time we had sat down to a full table since coming to Ŭngang. And no barley was mixed with our rice. The scene was similar to that of our last day in Felicity Pre-cinct. Chi-sŏp added his rice to the soup and Mother placed chunks of grilled beef in the guest's rice bowl. Mother said she had cooked only a small amount, afraid the aroma would spread. While she was grill-ing the meat the neighborhood urchins smelled it and came to a stop in the midst of their games. Chi-sŏp transferred meat to Yŏng-ho's rice bowl. Yŏng-ho's hand at first blocked it, then dropped. Yŏng-hŭi rose from our cramped veranda, went into the kitchen, and returned with scorched-rice broth. Her face was haggard. Yŏng-hŭi's work and sleep schedule changed from week to week, just like that of all the other young people who worked in factories that operated round the clock. There she stood, the youngest child, whom Father had loved so much, and I saw, spread out behind her face, the gloomy night sky of the fac-tory zone. Father was always offering Yŏng-hŭi a piggyback ride, but she disliked it.

"Not in daytime," little Yŏng-hŭi had said. "The kids make fun of me, and I don't like it."

"Why do they make fun of you?" Mother asked.

"They point at me."

"Look!" the children had said. "The midget's giving a piggyback ride to a kid bigger than he is!"

Yŏng-hŭi would go out riding piggyback on Father only at night. From where we sat we could hear their laughter. For several years our neighbor The Lush would try to get little Yŏng-hŭi to drink, and we could hear him chasing after them. Father with Yŏng-hŭi on his back would return crossing the sewer creek on the plank bridge. Yŏng-hŭi's giggling would precede Father across the creek and home.

"You ought to get married," Mother said. "A man won't settle down otherwise."

"No hope for me," Chi-sŏp laughed. "I'm afraid I'll be wandering about like this for the rest of my days."

"Now don't talk like that—our Yŏng-su is listening."

"Well, what's wrong with that, Mother?"

"I've given up on the boy."

Yŏng-ho and Yŏng-hŭi took Mother's hands.

"What are you doing that for?" Mother said. "Let go."

"Let go," Father had said. "Let go of my hand. You're always using force to stop your dad."

"It's still cold out there, Father—that's why."

"The children don't understand me either," Mother said. "I'm a minority of one."

"Now why should that be?" Again Chi-sŏp laughed.

"Put it in," Father said from where he stood beside the sewer creek. The hard ice of winter had begun to thaw and disappear. I pushed the boat out. Father, who had spent all winter at home, took me aboard the small boat and out we went on the water. Chunks of floating ice hit against the sides of the boat and were pushed aside.

"The children's father doesn't have a burial mound," said Mother. "We had him cremated. Less than a handful of ashes, and we spread it over the water."

"Aren't you cold?"

"I'm fine." Father had drawn in the oars. "You're the eldest son. And so I wanted to have a talk, just the two of us. It wouldn't do for your mother to hear."

"What is it?"

"I'll get to that." Father had glanced back at our house as it receded into the distance. "I've decided I'm not going to live any longer," he said in a voice ever so soft. "Since you're the eldest, you're the only one I'm telling. I've made my decision."

"But why?" I shuddered at the frightening thought of it.

"Why? You ask me why?"

"Yes. Why have you been thinking about dying?"

"Because of you three children and your mom. And because of that house."

"For a while I didn't think I could go on living," said Mother. "But the living just go on living."

"Why us, Father? What have we done wrong?"

"It's not a matter of what you've done wrong."

"Then what?"

"Don't you understand? Do I have to say more?"

"No. I understand," I said. "But is your dying supposed to solve anything?"

"I don't want to be a burden on all of you."

"Who thinks you're a burden? But you'll be a coward if you kill yourself."

"It can't be helped," Father said serenely. "But if you can take my side, I won't think any more about dying."

"All right, then, that's fine." I inched closer to Father.

"I've been thinking about being away from you, but just for a while," Father said. "Remember Humpback, who came to see me once? I'm going to work with him—it's the only way. He has a friend who's crippled. I think you've seen him too—Squatlegs? And there's a medicine peddler who performs feats of strength and acrobat stunts, and he says he'll help the three of us if we join him. He makes big money; he even has a couple of cars to go around in. He goes all over peddling medicine—no place he hasn't been—and he's sent his children to college, has a big house—nothing he doesn't have—and he lives very well. He says he'll treat the three of us as partners, and that's good enough for me. Says he'll split the money equally. It's my last chance. Our house is going to get torn down because it's in a redevelopment zone, and with you three going to work in a factory instead of being in school there's not a day goes by with me having peace of mind. No hopes either. I'm a worm. Got to squirm one last time and get some money together."

"Father, you're not Humpback. And you're not Squatlegs. You know that, don't you?"

"Yes." Father spoke again. "I'm a worm."

"He's probably found peace by now." Mother's voice had grown softer.

"I hope you live a long life, ma'am," said Chi-sŏp. "I'm sure your children will take good care of you in the future."

"Will the day ever come?"

"Surely it will."

"I don't believe it. Somehow I just don't believe it."

Father rowed toward deeper water. The chunks of ice that were pushed aside by the boat sounded like panes of glass being stacked up. I didn't know how deep the water was. The wind still blew cold.

"You should get Mother's opinion," I said. "And please talk with Yŏng-ho and Yŏng-hŭi too."

"Everything will get screwed up then."

"If Mother, Yŏng-ho, and Yŏng-hŭi say fine, then I'll go along with them. And I'll keep quiet. I won't say anything about what you'll wear or what you'll do with Humpback and Squatlegs to draw a crowd. But first ask yourself what the medicine peddler is up to—wanting you in addition to Humpback and Squatlegs. Isn't it obvious he only wants to take advantage of the three of you?"

"That's enough." Father put down the oars. "My heart aches. You have to realize that. It aches."

Father beached the boat on the opposite shore. I remained seated in the boat as Father stepped out onto the dried-up weeds. Several steps away he sat down. I watched as Father lowered his head until it touched his gathered legs. I imagined him stabbed by the blue steel of a knife, his flesh sliced and gouged, the wounds bleeding, and something, its true nature eluding me, sprinkling salt over those wounds. My thoughts about our time in Felicity Precinct were always accompanied by sadness. It was my misfortune, born and raised the elder son of a dwarf, to have never exercised choice in my life. The circumstances of my birth and growing up, though, and my thoughts and experiences along the way, helped me to understand Chi-sŏp. Though Chi-sŏp, after he arrived in Ŭngang, was in many respects similar to the minister and the man of science, in one respect he was completely different. He himself was a worker. To borrow an expression he used, he himself was one martyr among many. We in our family had watched when just after our Felicity Precinct home was torn down he was dragged away bleeding across the empty lot. More or less driven from Seoul, he had bounced from one countryside factory to another working as a temporary laborer. Starting out as a foundry cutter, then a bike shop welder, then an assistant in pouring tempering water in a casting plant, he had been an unskilled laborer doing physical work in the massive factories of new industrial cities. He had picked up at least some experience at a variety of plants—wharf building, shipbuilding, glue, textiles, motor vehicles, appliances, cement, ice making, clothing. My work experience at the Ŭngang factories was only a fraction of his experience at various factories.

That Chi-sŏp, whom Father liked, had become a labor activist during an age that had heaped economic affliction on Father was not entirely coincidental. Who knows? Perhaps the family of a dwarf was for him a subject of observation. The important thing was the warm affection he had extended to Father. At that time, only in his mind did there exist the beautiful, unspoiled world that he called the Land of the Moon. To make that world a reality outside his mind, he came to Ŭngang a brave man of action. He wanted to know what I had done to get my name on the bosses' blacklist. It was a matter of a fifteen percent increase in pay for the work I did at Ŭngang Textile, a hundred percent increase in our bonus, and the rehiring of eighteen workers fired without cause. It was not, of course, a simple matter. While Yŏng-i, the steward of our union local, was taken away for a week to some unknown place for questioning, the union members were holding out by refusing to eat until they collapsed. Yŏng-hǔi was among them, singing, falling silent, shouting slogans, getting dizzy, passing out. Only later did the company people realize that the person who had set fifteen hundred people in motion was an assistant mechanic in the Maintenance Department. I sat in front of the raw cotton store-room listening to the sad song sung by a man with a skein of thread in the Spinning Department. Yŏng-i, whom I hadn't seen in a week, was unrecognizably thin and pale. Yŏng-hŭi brought Yŏng-i home. Yŏng-i burst into tears the moment she saw me. I was lying down, and the tears streaming from her haggard cheeks fell onto my chest. In a dark alley behind Ŭngang Machine Tools I'd been beaten by muscular shadows until I collapsed. Chi-sŏp calculated that I had succeeded in extracting 200 million _wŏn_ from the unfair gains of the industrialists, who had violated their agreement to share. And there was an invisible outcome, too, the awakening of union members. I had revived a dead union, he said. I took his words as praise.

"I didn't do very much," I said.

"I know," he responded.

I didn't know why he had spoken in that way.

"You've only followed in the footsteps of many other people," he said. "And now you had better realize your mistake."

"And what is that?"

"Ignorance is of no help in anything you do," he said in an angry tone.

But I had something to say about that. "As you know, _hyŏng_, I haven't had much opportunity to study. I had to cut short my studies in the high school correspondence course, and college was out of the question. And so I read books that fall into my hands, and whenever I don't know something I find someone and ask. And when we came here, there were many things I didn't know, so I went to the workers' church and studied under two of the grown-ups. And I attended an institute at a college."

"And what did you get out of it?"

"It opened my eyes."

"You talk as if you were born blind!" he said in a loud voice. "If a person like you knows a lot about a situation, what's there to learn by leaving it? Here you've got people whose only knowledge of the situation is what you can tell them, and you're telling me your eyes are opened? You've become completely blind—blind. And so you're all tied up, unable to act on your own. Your ignorance has tied you all up. You've abandoned all the young people who trusted in you."

"That's not true," I said. "I set up fifteen discussion groups. The people on the General Council led them."

"And who led the people on the General Council?"

"The steward did a good job of that."

"And how about you?"

"There were meetings set up by the minister—meetings of labor reps from various industries—and I started leading those meetings some time ago."

"Wouldn't your father be amazed if he were alive now? Yes, indeed, you've got what it takes to be a fine theorist. If you want, you could be a high-level leader of the labor movement."

"I wish I knew why you're speaking that way, *hyŏng*."

"What's your reason for doing something that someone else would do if you didn't?"

"Well, then, what should I be doing?"

"Staying where you are."

"That's the place where I work."

"Then stay there. Don't leave. Think there, act there. Stay at the contact point—the place where workers and bosses meet."

He was a busy man. I had known that from the beginning. He hadn't come up to Ŭngang from the south, changing buses and trains, merely to reminisce about the days in Felicity Precinct. We had a talk as we walked along the shore. "They say that at the ocean the best thing is to walk on the water," he said. "The next best thing is to sail your boat on the water. And next is to look out on the water. Not a thing to worry about. Because we're doing the third best thing now." His voice was very gentle, making me believe he had read poetry. That night, however, he was a completely different person. He gave a one-and-a-half-hour lecture to a gathering of Ŭngang laborers at the workers' church. Everyone was moved. All the time he was speaking, Yŏng-hŭi cried. Yŏng-i, the steward of our local, gave Yŏng-hŭi her handkerchief, but when the tears continued to flow, Yŏng-hŭi covered her eyes with the vice-steward's handkerchief as well. "I thought of God's grace." Yŏng-i relayed these whispered words of Yŏng-hŭi to me. I hoped that Yŏng-hŭi's god was the warmest possible god for her. The greatest gift that Yŏng-hŭi received from her god was that very benevolence. The day Chi-sŏp left, though, Yŏng-hŭi was working her shift and unable to see him off. It was the same with Yŏng-ho and me. Mother had prepared to leave for the lumberyard, and she stood in the dirty alley waving in response to Chi-sŏp's farewell. Yŏng-i and the union's general-affairs director saw him off at the station. The minister, the man of science, and the stewards of several other union locals turned out, Yŏng-i told me. I wondered what influence Chi-sŏp's abrupt visit might have on me in the future. We had wasted too much time trying to figure out what was right, he said.

After Chi-sŏp had come and gone, the first person to read the next change in me was the man of science. "If you think about it, the minister and I are not in line," he said. "I'm not standing at the head of the line, either," I said. "I'm not worthy of it." "But it's your line. How can I stand outside the line and shout for you?" In his room at the workshop he showed me a bottle I could not make sense of at first. I call it a bottle, but it was not the usual type of bottle with an inside and a closed-in space. It was a peculiar bottle formed by making a hole in the wall of a tube and passing one end of the tube through that hole. The man of science called it a Klein bottle. Figure 3 is that very bottle. The man of science had made such a bottle from a glass tube like the one in Figure 1. After flaring one end of the cylinder and tapering the other end, as in Figure 2, he made a hole in the wall and finished up as in Figure 3.

①   ②   ③

Paper has two surfaces, inner and outer, but scholars have done research on "one-surface paper," "closed space," and other things without insides and outsides—queer things that common sense would not lead you to think of. And according to the man of science, this peculiar bottle was described in a research paper by a German mathematician, Felix Klein, that was based on purely abstract theoretical research. The man of science had me wondering. "This is the Klein bottle. No inside or outside, and it has a closed space," he said. I looked intently at the bottle shown in Figure 3. It was simple in appearance and simple to explain, but I had no idea what he was talking about. I believed that since I hadn't received a normal school education, I couldn't understand a problem that was based on the most fundamental ideas. But the man of science said that even someone without educational training could bore his way to the core of a problem through commonsense methods. Sticking to theory makes a problem ever more complicated, he told me, and so I should think in simple terms. I observed that bottle for the longest time. "It really doesn't have an inside," I said. "I can't tell the inside from the outside. And now I understand what they mean by a closed space." The man of science smiled. "We wouldn't have this kind of phenomenon if there was a distinction between the inner and outer parts." That day when I asked why he had shown me the bottle he replied only that I had arrived at the instant he finished making it. It didn't seem coincidental to me, though. What was even less understandable was that the essence of the bottle in Figure 3 was right there before my eyes, but its reality was ignored and it seemed to exist only in the world of imagination. And so I picked up the bottle shown in Figure 3 and asked, "Then what is this?" He merely said, "It doesn't really exist." I said goodbye and left his room.

The machine workers at Ŭngang Heavy Industry had finished their overtime work and emerged from the factory's main entrance and were dispersing into the dark. There was a vacant lot between that factory and the aluminum factory. There dark figures were burning and burying solid industrial waste. I arrived home late to find Mother counting money. It was from the sale of the bark, and she moistened her fingers with saliva to count it. I went up to the loft and lay down. Yŏng-ho returned from the factory and Yŏng-hŭi left for the night shift. From where I lay I could hear the one-eyed old man next door coughing. The working couple who rented a room from him had tipped over their meal tray and were fighting. Their child was wailing. Winter came to Ŭngang. The laborers of Ŭngang hunched up, went to the factories, and worked. It was a terribly cold winter. Everyone grew weaker.

"Yŏng-su," Mother called me one day. "Is something going on at the factory these days? Are you cooking up something again?"

"We'll have elections for our General Council and our steward in the spring. There's some friction with the company people, but nothing's going to happen."

"Then why are you meeting with people from other factories? Any connection with why Chi-sŏp came up?"

"We all work for Ŭngang Group factories. Chi-sŏp too. He works down south, and the Ŭngang Group has a lot of factories there too."

"And so?"

"And so we're trying to do a good job with our union work, discussing what our wage demands should be, and talking about how we should encourage the workers in any factory where friction develops with the company. We have to meet a lot in order to get information. That's all."

"Really?"

"Yes."

"All right, then," Mother said. "I had an awful dream. I dreamed you were arrested. You went to the main office in Seoul and killed one of the higher-ups. It was a terrible dream. Terrible."

"Mother," I said. "Will you _please_ not worry?"

"If something happened to you it would be the end of us."

"I know."

"You've got to listen to me. Just do what you're supposed to do at the factory. You'll be arrested for sure if you don't listen to me. You'll commit a crime, you'll be sentenced, you'll end up in jail."

"I said I know!"

It was too cold and depressing that winter. I suddenly felt as if I had lost everyone. In my sadness I tried to analyze myself. There was nothing to be done about my solitary nature. There wasn't a single person who knew what I was thinking. I went to see the minister wanting to talk about something other than the work we had begun, but returned home without bringing it up. And so it was with the man of science too. When I thought about it, I realized we didn't have time for leisurely talk. The company people had begun to stifle us. I wanted to make the higher-ups in the company realize that we were all in the same boat. But they couldn't see it. They stubbornly insisted that they were in a different boat, and they expressed their own one-sided demands. I couldn't contain my rage toward people who gained such huge profits—not through good work but through opportunism, outside support, ignorance, cruelty, luck, favoritism, and such.

One day when the cold had slowly begun to abate, I sought out the man of science. The Klein bottle was on his windowsill. I considered it.

"Now I understand," I hastened to say. "In this bottle, inside becomes outside and outside becomes inside. Because there's no inside or outside, we can't talk of containing the inside—the notion of closing has no meaning here. If you just follow the wall, you can get out. So in this world the notion of enclosure itself is an illusion."

The man of science looked blankly into my face. "It's just as you say," he said.

He picked up the Klein bottle and turned back toward me, but I had to leave.

The assistant mechanic in the Maintenance Department of Ŭngang Textile walked off quickly toward the factory.

The Spinyfish Entering My Net

FIVE O'CLOCK ALREADY and still it was dark. The first light of day ought to have reached the window by now, where the curtain would absorb it while gloom was driven from my room. I picked up the intercom at the head of my bed and pushed the button that connected me with the kitchen. The speaker diaphragm trembled with the girl's sleepy, tentative voice. I told her I wanted coffee, then rose and drew the curtain. Fog draped the window; it crept toward the ground. I watched the old dog moving in the fog. Still it lived, scattering and dispersing the fog, this dog that had belonged to my departed grandfather. The dog had been a gift to my uncle from a German businessman. Uncle in turn had presented this gift to Grandfather, letting it be known that the dog's pedigree made reference to none other than the royal house of Hohenzollern. The old dog's more recent ancestors had taken part in the Second World War, patrolling the Normandy coast and crossing the deserts of Africa. This story excited me. It was good to obey a leader's orders unconditionally. The old dog's ancestors had accompanied their masters to war, keeping watch over their trenches and standing guard. The leader had given the order to charge. "I am always right—trust in me, obey me, fight!" he had said. Typical of Europeans, who received a sound education, those people had fought with all their might. I admired their history. Sitting beside the pond, Grandfather's dog struck out with its forefeet and killed a sparrow that had lit in search of food. Father said he had never seen such an alert, intelligent hunting dog. Whenever he went hunting, the car returned full of bloody animals. Grandfather had the animals dragged into the living room, staining the carpet, and he would roar with laughter. And then the dog, whom you could count on to be out in front of Grandfather, cornering the animals he shot, went out to the doghouse and chewed on an ample portion of ribs. That was when it was young. The old dog moved slowly. I picked out a thick book and threw it at the dog. It fell wide of the mark on the tile deck of the swimming pool, and the old dog disappeared into the fog.

The dog wouldn't eat after Grandfather died. Uncle was going to take the dog. Father told him no. The dog was past its prime, it was an old dog, but Father wanted Uncle to know that he had assumed all of Grandfather's prerogatives. At the time of Uncle's death from the knife of a worker at the Ŭngang plant, Father, standing next to my aunt and cousins, had dabbed at the tears poised at his eyelids. I had to force myself not to laugh. From my seat in the visitors' gallery at the courthouse I had watched the worker who killed Uncle. The old dog was out of sight. I heard a voice, and Father's security guard broke through the fog and retrieved the thick book I had thrown hoping to kill the old dog.

The girl appeared with the book and coffee. "Your aunt is here with the young master." Her voice was still sleepy. She wore a white apron over a dress the faint color of sky. "Anyone else?" I asked. "They brought the lawyer." I slept naked from the waist up. And so the girl couldn't look directly at me. She'd arrived at the age of fifteen the year I'd entered college, and I hadn't realized how she'd grown in the two years since. Extraordinary how she bulged out at the chest. I took her by the hand as she was about to leave. "Bet you don't have this on the television in your room." I selected a video cassette and pressed the start button on my VCR. The previous night's sleep seemed stuck to her. I brought my cup of coffee to her lips. "I'll be sent home," she said as the music of Berlioz scattered the hair of the girl on the screen.

What is it with these Europeans nowadays? No matter what your country, you don't use Berlioz with this sort of tape. The title was *Sixteen*. A sixteen-year-old girl in a red sweater was waving goodbye to her friends. I fast-forwarded to the end. Something startling was playing out on the screen. "What's wrong? I didn't do anything to you." The girl wouldn't answer. I sensed that her body had awakened from its sleep. Her gaze moved from the screen to regard me with cold reproach, and she freed her hand from mine.

The three people who had arrived at dawn to see Father sat like a portrait in the second-floor living room. Father and Mother were still asleep. The lawyer brought by my aunt had closed his eyes. I felt like retching the moment I saw those two. My cousin sat across from them leafing through a newspaper.

"*Hyŏng*," I called out to him. "Come here."

"You're up early," said my aunt. I ignored her.

The lawyer, eyes open now, adjusted his glasses and stared at me. He had been Aunt's lawyer from the day Uncle died. My cousin walked up the spiral staircase to where I was standing. "You're early," I said. We walked down to the end of the hall and stepped down to the fire escape. The fog had lifted. The first of the sun's rays fell across the corner of the landing where we'd arrived, and then the white wall of the house, and then the leaves of the tall trees. My cousin wore a black suit and tie.

"What are you doing here?"

My cousin made a sad face.

"They should have stayed in bed. How come she brought the lawyer?"

"Let's not talk about that."

My cousin had been in America when Uncle died. My two older brothers were also studying there, but they weren't the sort to return for their uncle's funeral. If it had been Father, they would have been frantic to get home. But they wouldn't have shed a tear on the plane. No, their main worry would be to make sure of their share of Father's estate as soon as possible. Thinking about them kept me awake at night. It was clear in my mind that they would go to absurd lengths to minimize my share. We passed the rose garden. The security guard was patting the old dog. Apparently my aim hadn't been so bad after all. Tending to the wound in its head, he led the old dog away.

"Go on back to the States."

At the side of the pool I kicked off my shoes. My cousin sat down on the bench in the wisteria arbor and lit a cigarette.

"You must think I'm a bother too," he said in a sad voice.

"No," I said. "There's no one who thinks you're a bother. I merely had your interests in mind when I said that."

"Thanks."

I didn't hear what he said next. I bounced several times on the diving board and plunged into the water. The bottom of the pool was still murky and the water felt ice-cold. I stayed under for a minute or so. That minute—or so it felt—of holding my breath crouched in the corner of the pool, that minute of make-believe despair, made me tense, changing into a feeling of distress that my world would eventually be lost, was even now growing distant. I kicked and floated to the surface, and there sat my cousin at the far end of a procession of ripples that were lit up by the sun's rays. I stretched out, kicking and stroking, one arm and then the other, clawing at the water. I relaxed my ankles, knees, hips as I kicked. I rotated my head, breathing in when my mouth broke the surface, then breathing out into the water. I climbed out and my cousin threw me a towel. The sun felt warm this early in the morning. Beads of sweat had formed on the forehead of my dressed-up cousin. Through the spindle trees I saw Father's chauffeur pull up in his car and get out.

"Aunt seems to have misunderstood something," I said. "I guess you know how stupidly she's been behaving."

"I don't know what to make of it. Like you said, I'd better go back to America and get on with my studies."

"That's the first thing you should tell Father when you see him. There's nothing to be gained by doing things Aunt's way."

"All right. That way, Uncle ought to be satisfied," he said.

"He'll emphasize that you're a member of the Ŭngang Group. Remember, *hyŏng,* our companies pay four percent of all the tax in this country, they account for four point two percent of everything sold on the domestic market, and they produce five point three percent of our exports."

"Amazing."

"You better believe it's amazing!" I said. "Father doesn't believe in running a dumb business. Do you think her request for Uncle's share of the business will register with him? The most logical thing is for you to finish your studies, come back, get used to the work, and take part in running the business. You're the only one Father's acknowledged. You're not going to like this, but Aunt is no longer part of our family."

"How's that?" My cousin looked completely out of sorts.

"I believe that's what Father said."

My cousin looked at me as if he didn't understand. Compared with my two brothers, he was a paragon of virtue. "Why did that young man from Ŭngang have to kill with a sharp knife?" he had asked others. He was inherently good. He had wanted to know if Uncle had been in pain from the knifing when he breathed his last. When he learned it was actually Father that the murderer had targeted, he had fallen silent. My cousin saw the criminal as a schizophrenic whose powers of reasoning and emotion were out of balance with his will. He shouldn't have stood trial, my cousin had said. Not until he went to the courthouse and saw for himself did he admit that the defendant was a normal person. He tried the patience of those around him by insisting that the premeditated murder committed by this person who had killed his father was a case of justifiable self-defense. The visitors' gallery was crammed with factory workers.

Through the very same spindle trees Father's young secretary could be seen going inside with his briefcase. Father's car gleamed in the sun. It was a luxury car manufactured by the Germans. My car, also made in Germany, was smaller and made for the masses, a cute white car. My cousin lit another cigarette. One day American workers began chanting something, he had said. "How much do Korean textile workers make?" With a union rep leading the chorus, the workers had shouted: "Nineteen cents an hour!" As the workers, more than ten thousand of them, marched about the square, their voices ringing, my cousin had decided they were lying because they wanted to restore the balance of trade with our country. He didn't believe there was a managerial group that would force the workers to work for the equivalent of $45.60 a month. And so from my cousin's standpoint it was only natural that the young man from Ŭngang Textile had drawn a knife. Our system was about to be destroyed from the inside, he said. He went so far as to say that we lived in a three-dimensional world, while the person with the knife, his co-workers, and their families lived in a two-dimensional world. Reality had stripped itself of one dimension. In the two-dimensional world there were fixed boundaries and limits. My cousin had a way of overanalyzing and inhibiting himself. He was a tiresome person of whom one couldn't expect improvement.

"The lawyer's leaving, isn't he?" he asked.

"Father's secretary is getting rid of him," I said. "He should have gone to see Father's lawyer. He's wasting his time with Aunt."

"A lawyer sees a situation for what it is. He locks onto the core of a problem much faster than the average person. I trusted him. Mother telephoned him at daybreak to come out here. She didn't sleep at all. Without him there's nothing she can say. He's good at presenting the facts in a systematic way, and now that he's gone there's no use in Mother seeing Uncle."

"Wait a few years and you'll automatically be on the board of directors," I said with a smile. "Go on in—Father's up now."

"I wish we didn't have so much money," my cousin said in a tired voice.

It was a trying day for him. My aunt sat alone in the living room. I went upstairs to my room, changed, and came back down, and still she was sitting there. On the north wall, behind her back, there hung a large painting of Grandfather looking out at Ŭngang Shipbuilding. He didn't appear to be in a good mood. Grandfather feared change. Long before, he had made great profits selling various products he had manufactured utilizing technology and machinery. Detailed management of a few import-export firms and companies that made consumer products had enabled him to safeguard shareholder investments, stabilize the financial affairs of those businesses, and succeed in making his fortune. To Grandfather there was no special reason to be in the very forefront of the changes demanded by society. As long as you continued to make money, there was no need to bother your mind with untried methods and new technology. Together Father and Uncle broke Grandfather's resistance to change. We were wrong, Father said. If we limited ourselves to the management methods we'd used so far, he said, then one year from now profits would decline, in two years it would become difficult to maintain the status quo, and in three years we would lose our position as the leading group. I was young then, but I knew Father was right. When I grew old and had my own grandchildren, they would hear stories about the absurd times in which their great-grandfather and great-great-grandfather had lived and would grow shame-faced. They would be told that ethics, morals, order, and responsibility were considered counterproductive in that economically convulsive age, and our noteworthy legacy would be dismissed. Father used his head. The scale of the economy had grown, its structure had become more sophisticated, and so the patterns of business activity had to change, he thought. Grandfather's group of enterprises, centered in light industry, were going nowhere. Using only his mind and some subventions, Father had turned it into a comprehensive organization of heavy chemical industries, including machinery, iron and steel, electronics, shipbuilding, construction, automobiles, and petrochemicals. In his last years Grandfather professed to get dizzy at the frightening pace of Ŭngang's growth. To Grandfather the golden era of the 1960s was just child's play in comparison with the years of upheaval into which Father and Uncle had dived. Father now met with my aunt and cousin in his reception room.

"Are you back here for good?" Father asked my cousin.

"No," he said. "I'm thinking of going back and resuming my studies."

"It's fine that you've seen your father buried, but you could have gone back right away. Instead you're wasting all these months here— why? Do you think I ought to siphon off one of our companies and place it in your mother's hands?"

"I really don't know."

My aunt's face blanched.

"Well, you ought to know," said Father. "Your father would consider this unforgivable. And I'm the same as your father."

"But Brother-in-Law," my aunt finally managed to say.

Father ignored this and continued with his nephew: "You're the very person to succeed to your father's position. You must finish your studies, return, and take up your father's work. You'll find out what it's like to have no time to rest. We have a lot of interests we've got to protect. At the same time, we're always trying to think of a revolution that we can achieve through action. There are quite a few people who don't think we earned our success, and given the opportunity they'd try to hammer us down. If we can't persuade them, then we need the strength to drive them off. There are too many people who don't realize how thankful they should be for what we do for them. Until my eyes close for the last time I'll remember what happened to your father. We have never made such a great sacrifice. If this had happened between nations, we would have an all-out war. It's sufficient reason for a holy war."

"I see your point, Uncle," said my cousin. "And in that respect the factory workers would say the same thing. They'd present the issue in terms of a holy cause, too, saying they've got to take action to protect themselves."

"Let's talk about that later. Get the money you'll need in the States from our branch office there."

Father then turned to regard my aunt. As my cousin had indicated, she couldn't speak a single word properly. Father wanted to bring an end to this business once and for all. And so he proferred her an envelope containing several photographs, asking what she thought she was doing when the grass on his younger brother's grave wasn't even dry. The instant she felt my cousin's gaze she turned away. To Aunt this was unbearable. With utter ease Father had driven a wedge between my aunt and my cousin. She had taken Uncle's death as a liberation. If not for that, she wouldn't be committing such an outlandish act with a younger man who was just starting up a company. I couldn't see these photos of Aunt sleeping with the man. The instant she peered at the photos, eyebrows drooping, a brief gasp escaped from her parched lips. There was nothing more to the interview. My aunt left by herself.

My cousin and I had breakfast in the dining room. He asked if I swam early in the morning every day. I told him I'd been after Father to have a yacht built, and if it ever became a reality, I wanted to set out on an adventure and so I was doing some endurance training in preparation for a solo voyage across the wide ocean. A look of surprise came over my cousin. He wanted to know if we in our country, with our technology, could build the kind of boat that Chichester had sailed. And was I really at the stage where I could talk openly of an adventure? Of course, I answered. I presumed he knew, I said, that the United States, with less than eight percent of the world's population, consumed half the world's resources, and that the daily caloric intake of one affluent American was no less than the weekly amount of calories derived by the poor of Africa and Asia from their meager meals. As long as it's acknowledged that the strong have such an impact on the weak, it was only fair, I argued, that the position of our country be acknowledged as well. I gave an impassioned explanation of the technology we had imported. But my cousin said he couldn't understand what I was saying. And the way he talked, it really did seem that way. And so I told him that no one else would think of launching such an adventure when there was a family matter to be resolved. And I mentioned the natural differences in sexual development.

"I feel a sexual urge more often than other boys my age. And I've probably had a lot more opportunities to satisfy that urge with girls."

My cousin looked at me. "You're a strange one. You keep jumping from one thing to another."

"You're the one who's strange, *hyŏng,* feeling like that."

"I know, I haven't been my normal self. I have a headache. Was there something Mother was unhappy with? I suppose a lot of people have seen those photos?"

"Got me," I told my cousin. "If I were you, I'd go back to the States after the guy who stabbed Uncle is sentenced. I'd forget everything, get my fill of life over there. Just relax, *hyŏng*—your share of the profits will pile up."

"I guess that makes sense," my cousin said as he rose. "You know all the angles, don't you?"

I decided not to worry about him anymore. Refusing my offer of a ride, he walked out the door. It was very hot outside. The midsummer sun fell on my cousin's suffering body. He once said that on the basis of my mindset, constitution, and habits, my nationality was becoming less and less clear. Here his observations were correct. He was as much as admitting that nothing was wrong with me.

Now and then I thought about what I would do in the future. It was clear I would end up working with my brothers before too long. Before Father passed on, my cousin would end up working with us too. I had never considered my cousin to be a problem. Ever since I was small it was my two brothers I had feared. They were both smart and they were both strong. We weighed my small desires for certain toys against one another, but I always lost out to them. I had my steam locomotive taken away—and my tank, armored car, airplane, artillery pieces, machine gun, pistol, even my toy soldiers—and I played with my sister putting dolls to bed in dollhouses. "Daddy, turn off the light, our baby's asleep," my sister would whisper, and as I carefully turned the bean-sized light switch and the lights went off my heart would flutter as I wondered if my brothers would fire their artillery, bring in their forces, and shatter the peaceful world of the dolls. And then my brothers would tell me to pee sitting down, and if Mother's friends happened by they would take me in their arms and kiss me countless times, saying, "Look how pretty Kyŏng-hun is, prettier than a girl, he's so pretty!" It was at my studies that I wanted to show them up, but my two brothers, who thought only of cheating on their teachers, took the wind out of my sails by getting good grades without ever really cracking a book. My very first tearful prayer in this world was for those two devils to be dead and gone from my side—they could even go to heaven, for all I cared. The second time I offered up a prayer was when my oldest brother had an accident. He was grown up by then and tool-ing around in a car with some girl. His car hit a tree and the girl who tagged along with him, naked and sucking his filthy semen, died at the scene. My brother was taken to the hospital and attended to while he lay on a bed bandaged like a mummy. That prayer didn't come true either. Less than two weeks later my brother was out of the hospital. Instead of my brother it was Mother's chauffeur who went to the po-lice station, though at the time of the accident he'd been asleep in the room where the boiler man and the chauffeurs slept. Grandfather then summoned Father and told him to pay the dead girl's parents a siz-able sum. When Grandfather passed on, I shed not a tear. During his lifetime the word Grandfather always harped on was *sacrifice,* but that word bore no relation to his own life. After my brothers left home I convinced myself that Father would have to acknowledge me. Father was beside himself with delight when he learned I was very interested in his work and wanted to grow up soon and follow in his footsteps. What Father feared most was war. It was strange, but various social changes held the same significance as war for him. In an instant such changes could strip Father of everything. It didn't take a lengthy ex-planation to make me aware of this. For I thought the same way. I was most scared of my two brothers. There was nothing frightening about my cousin. He was weak. I sat with him in the visitors gallery in the courtroom listening to a man named Han Chi-sŏp from our factory in the south say that the murderer who stabbed Uncle had committed no crime.

"Bastard!" He was no different from a rebel inciting a revolt.

"Who?" asked my cousin.

"That bastard defense witness."

"Don't be narrow-minded."

"Are you out of your mind, *hyŏng*? There's a guy on trial for doing something to somebody—remember?"

"He's only saying what he's thinking. All these workers crammed into the gallery think he's right. Why do you suppose that is?"

It was just as well not to talk with him. I couldn't forgive Chi-sŏp.

He'd appeared in shabby clothes on purpose. He was extremely preju-
diced, arrogant, evil-minded even. The truth was covered up while he
lumped us together as criminals.

At midday the midsummer sun poured heat over the buildings, the
roadside trees, the crawl of cars. People dragged their squat one-thirty
shadows along the street, hastening toward any shade that presented
itself and mopping faces and throats with handkerchiefs already satu-
rated with perspiration. Many had abandoned Seoul. Considerably
fewer vehicles as well. I pulled up across from the holding room for
those appearing in court, and as soon as I opened the car door I was
hit by a suffocating blast of steamy air. People from our company's
secretariat emerged from the holding room and proceeded toward the
courthouse. To their left, in the shade of a tree, stood some workers.
My aunt and cousin weren't to be seen. I hadn't seen them for the last
three days, ever since they had arrived at our house together at dawn
and left separately. As I passed by, the workers in the shade stood motionless watching me. At the crest of the gentle slope to the courthouse
was a long line exposed to the sun. Half of those people would fill the
courtroom to overflowing, but as I continued on, the line kept growing. The majority of them were workers no older than twenty who had
come up from the Ŭngang mill. There were also many factory kids
who had given up hope of gaining admittance and instead had found
shade at the concession or sat with their backs to the courthouse,
waiting for court to commence. As I approached two girl workers
standing near the concession stand's pay phone I asked if it was true
that the defendant's father was a dwarf. They studied me with blood-
shot eyes—our plant operated round the clock and they probably
worked the night shift and hadn't slept. One of the girls hesitated, then
said she didn't know. The girl next to her was different. All in a breath
she said she didn't want to tell me since she didn't know who I was
and didn't know why I wanted to know, but she would anyway, since
it seemed I really did want to know: The father of the defendant, who
would shortly hear the verdict, was actually a huge giant of a man.
As I listened to this, several factory boys left the line and approached

me. As did some of the kids in the shade. One of the boys said, "Look here, mister." I asked what he wanted. "They say you're the son of our chairman—is it true?" he asked in an uppity tone. Something flared inside me, but I had to keep it there. Nothing to say, really. These kids surrounded me, only the eyes in their sallow, pointy faces seeming distinctly alive and moving. And then I heard a short song, the kind that expresses hostility, that's meant to provoke:

> Our chairman's
> a good-hearted man.
> He rakes in his change
> to pay us.

A short song, yes, but unthinkable. I found it impossible to look at the worker singing this song. He would never grow up properly, I told myself, because of the rage and confusion crammed in a body too small for his age. Now the kids in front of me were peering at my expression and mouthing the words in all seriousness, softer than the chirping of the cicadas in the trees: *Our-chair-man's-a-good-heart-ed-man. He-rakes-in-his-change-to-pay-us.* And so I was in a state of great fear. Those lined up before the courtroom notice board didn't know what was happening behind them; but weren't the people from our secretariat watching, wherever they were? This was a matter that involved our prestige. I couldn't defend my prestige, not to mention Father. If it were my brothers, it would have been different. That thought put me in a wretched state of mind. My thoughts sped homeward. I imagined myself slipping Father's twenty-two-caliber revolver into my pocket, loading his automatic rifle with exploding bullets, and running back. I took aim at them.

But it wasn't necessary to shoot. The workers surrounding me had flocked to the side of a woman who had just arrived—a woman who had come to hear her son's verdict. The murderer who had killed Uncle was her oldest son. Her second son and her daughter stood beside her. The woman wasn't small, and I tried to imagine the kind of sex life she had had with the dwarf. The workers escorted her to the courthouse door. My aunt and cousin were yet to be seen. There are differences from one case to the next, but an authoritarian father always makes his family suffer—and the more incapable of family responsibilities he becomes, the more he enjoys giving orders and demanding obedience. I thought about this dwarf I hadn't known. He would never forgive his children for the slightest mistake. He would beat them frequently, would mete out harsh punishment. To his children he would be an autocrat who never slept. His power was not merited, though, because his constitutional shortcomings—his ignorance of love, respect, and trust—made him resort to terrible beatings and punishments. Because he was dead, his older son had lost the object of his aggression. But the uncertain aggressiveness of this son, who had grown accustomed to doing poorly in society at large, had remained within him, and ultimately he had killed Uncle. Just then my cousin arrived and walked up the slope to the courthouse. I drew him near and told him my thoughts, but he merely waved me off without listening.

"No," he simply said. "You're wrong. You ought to believe what he said in court. I know what kind of work Father was helping Uncle with."

I made up my mind that if my brothers were to cook up a plot to disown my cousin even before Father died, then I'd be more than happy to take their side. Cousin mopped his perspiring face in the fiery sunshine. The courthouse door opened and the workers milled inside. We went in through another door. It was refreshingly cool inside.

"What did he say your father and mine did?"

"Made life miserable for them," my cousin whispered as he turned to look at the workers in the gallery. "Said they claimed to work on behalf of human beings when actually they despised human beings."

"Wonderful words, coming from you," I said. "The fact is, they built a plant, gave them work, paid them money. Those people right there are the ones who benefited the most."

My cousin smiled. At that moment, in that courthouse, there was no one else smiling. For the son of the murder victim to smile while awaiting the verdict, whatever the reason, was not a good thing. I saw a girl who seemed to be one of the union leaders at the Ŭngang mill. She was with the wife and children of the dwarf I hadn't known, and she ushered them to a bench behind the defendant. Already the visitors gallery was filled to capacity and confusion reigned at the entrance, where others were still trying to enter. The court clerk waded through the crowd and closed the door to the gallery. My aunt hadn't arrived. My cousin, who lived in the same house she did, said he hadn't seen her face for three days. We sat among a group that included the directors from our group's headquarters and people from the secretariat, who were present so they could report the results of the trial to Father. The air conditioner at the base of the back wall spewed cold air. The court clerk, irritated at having to admit spectators, asked the workers to straighten their clothing and be quiet.

"You there in back, please button your shirt," the court clerk said. "And the last time, several people were crying—for heaven's sake don't do that today."

"We can't even cry?" asked a woman worker in a husky voice.

"I don't care if you cry. Just don't do it out loud. This isn't a movie theater, and if you start blubbering it doesn't help anybody."

"You think we can afford to go to movies and such?"

"So, you always cry like you did last time?"

"Yes. Every day. Because we just can't stand it."

With a puzzled expression the court clerk walked away. I looked for the factory woman with the husky voice. A very ugly girl was standing there. Like most factory operatives, this girl was characterized by a flat face, a squat nose, jutting cheekbones, broad shoulders, thick arms, big hands; she was short from the waist down and had abnormally sallow skin. She could have been nineteen or maybe twenty, but she didn't look like a woman. You could be sent with her to a desert island for a thousand days and still wouldn't think of sleeping with her. Factory labor was this girl's destiny, something she did for subsistence. All we needed from her was her muscle. If factory labor ever became enjoyable for these workers crammed into the visitors gallery, rather than miserable, then even Father would lose all his control over them.

I was bored. Everything was ready in the courtroom, the time had arrived, but nothing was happening. There was no reason for me to fret, however. The first person to enter was the defense lawyer with his envelope of documents. He approached the wife of the dwarf I had never seen, said a few words, and squeezed her hand reassuringly. She rose and bowed to him. He surveyed the visitors gallery, then sat down at his place below and to the right of the bar. He was a young man who wore glasses. He seemed to believe he enjoyed the favor and respect of the spectators. Resentment seethed up from the pit of my stomach the instant I noticed him. I couldn't understand how a legal system like this, where counsel insinuated themselves into a felony trial to protect criminals, could be left in place. From the beginning he had treated Uncle's murder as if no crime were involved and had tried to misrepresent the nature of the incident completely. A different prosecutor might have been dragged into this scheme if he had misunderstood the chain of events. But this was an excellent prosecutor. As one who was absolutely qualified to represent the public interest, he gave the impression of spotlessness, even in his attire. After the judge had verified the identity of the dwarf's elder son, Uncle's murderer—his name, age, birthplace, address, occupation—the prosecutor presented a summary of the indictment. He listed the charges—murder, sedition, aggravated extortion, aggravated destruction of property, preparation of explosives, conspiracy, and so on—and outlined in detail the date, location, and method of the crimes. Before proceeding with the direct examination the judge advised the defendant of his rights, saying he could refuse to testify in response to any part of the examination. And yet the dwarf's older son readily answered all the prosecutor's questions.

"Is it true that while working as an assistant mechanic in the Maintenance Department at Ŭngang Textile you organized fifteen discussion groups?"

"Yes, it is."

"And the members of these groups numbered approximately one hundred fifty? And they all worked at the same mill?"

"That's correct."

"Those one hundred fifty could each try to recruit ten co-workers. And if you gave each group leader something to announce, then fifteen hundred plant employees would know of it within a short time. Correct?"

"I'm not sure what you mean."

"All right. On the X day of the month of X, 197X, didn't you issue instructions for all the employees to stop work and gather outside?"

"I did."

"And all of them did so, did they not?"

"Yes."

"You advised all the employees to go on a fast. And later you and some radical workers entered your workplace and destroyed machinery—is that true?"

"No, it is not. When the president of our local told me some people had gotten worked up and gone to the Weaving Section intending to damage the machines, I ran there and stopped them. One of them had damaged a loom slightly, but it's my understanding it was easily repaired and is back in operation."

"Sodium nitrate, sulfur, and charcoal were found in your room. Who obtained these?"

"I did."

"Why did you need them?"

"I was going to make explosives."

"And did you?"

"I started to, but I gave up."

"And so you were aware, were you not, that a combination of sodium nitrate, sulfur, and charcoal is powerful, that it has absorptive properties, that you can make an explosive device with it and use it immediately?"

"Yes, I was. But I didn't have a suitable testing spot, and I was afraid that even if I did succeed in manufacturing it, innocent people would be injured. So I gave it up."

"So you gave up the idea of manufacturing an explosive device and purchased a knife?"

"Yes."

"Is this the knife?"

"That's it."

"Now, could you tell us what you did at six-thirteen p.m. on the X day of X, 197X, at the Ŭngang Group headquarters."

"I killed a man."

"With this knife?"

"Yes."

The trial needn't have continued. The dwarf's elder son, this terrible criminal, had told all with no sign of remorse. He had come here with the intention of killing Father, he testified, but had mistaken Uncle for him—Uncle who so resembled Father. At that hour Father had been in his office going over sales figures for each of the companies and Uncle had taken the elevator downstairs for a meeting with some business people. The criminal, taking advantage of a moment of negligence on the part of the security people, sprang out from behind a marble pillar where he'd hidden himself, and Uncle had taken the knife in his heart and collapsed. My cousin wanted to know if Uncle had felt pain, but there hadn't been time—because of the location, the stab was quite lethal. Here, however, was the point of departure for the trial. We had liberal laws even for the most vicious felons. If I had my way, the instant the confession was found to be consistent with the evidence, I would have hung the murderer before a large crowd. If we didn't render such treatment to one who had broken another's bones, then everyone in the world would end up with broken bones and carry their deformities to the grave. Uncle was already buried. And yet the dwarf's older son, who should have been hung at the site of the Ŭngang plant for all the workers to see on their way to work, continued to appear in court, protected by the prison guards. To judge from the defendant's testimony during the defense lawyer's cross-examination, the people who wrung sweat from the Ŭngang workers' brows, who exhausted them body and soul, who ultimately saddled them with tribulation, were none other than us. It sounded to me as if each of the defense lawyer's questions was posed in order to justify the defendant's actions. The way the two of them harped on details that had no direct bearing on the criminal action at hand, the one with his cross-examination and the other with his testimony, in spite of the prosecutor's objections and the judge's rulings, you might have thought they had uncovered a corrupt society and dissected it to shreds. As far as he could tell, the lawyer said, at home the defendant was an elder son who led the family, a good brother to his younger siblings. And at the plant he was an industrial warrior with a strong sense of responsibility, a considerate co-worker, a loyal comrade who shared the suffering of those in difficulty and was the first to help them, a student and leader who at meetings to thrash out labor issues always advocated mutual understanding, reconciliation, and love. And yet he saw that there was a reason, for better or worse, why such a person had come to the point of thinking one day of committing that terrible murder. And so he had raised the questions of pay, vacation, and reinstatement of workers dismissed without just cause. And although he had tried to find areas on which he could work with the company for improvements, he was unable to obtain its agreement—apart from which the employers' unilateral breach of worker/management harmony by trampling on the efforts of trade union members to hold peaceful elections of union representatives and officials had, not surprisingly, shattered industrial harmony to the detriment of both labor and management. And the instant the defendant witnessed this, was it not the case, the lawyer asked, that he had resolved upon a misguided mission to kill the person with primary responsibility for leading the Ŭngang Group—namely, its chairman? The dwarf's older son was bent over coughing. This was the first time I had seen his head bowed. His sister had pressed a handkerchief over her mouth to stifle her weeping. She was successful but several people weeping behind her couldn't silence themselves. The court clerk told the women workers to stop.

The dwarf's older son lifted his head. "It wasn't misguided," he said.

"I beg your pardon," said the defense lawyer. "Would you please repeat what you just said?"

"I said it wasn't a misguided mission to kill."

An awkward expression crossed the lawyer's face. "In that case, could you briefly describe for us your state of mind at that time?"

"I was standing right there when the mill workers, who ought to know better, who have gone through hardship after hardship, all at once burst into tears and started sobbing. Those fifteen hundred people, who should have been immune by then to a full dose of hardship, did that, all of them, together. I've had occasion to tell this story to people outside the mill, people with a good education and deep understanding of matters, but they have trouble believing such a thing is possible. People just don't believe me."

"No, I believe you."

"That gentleman did not think about human beings."

"This was the motive behind the homicide?"

"Son of a bitch!" I shouted. But no one paid attention, not even my cousin sitting beside me. Why would Father have had to think about such stuff? This vicious little creature didn't know that Father was a busy man with countless better things to do—planning, making decisions, giving instructions, following up. I was well aware that there lived this ilk—retarded development, smaller and weaker than us, but a small body stuffed with cruel thoughts. They denounced the life we enjoyed as a result of our distinctive efforts—our capital, entrepreneurship, competitiveness, and monopolies—and concluded that they were slowly being poisoned by lethal toxicants. Suppose they were to say that this poisonous substance was poverty and it was Father's plant where they all worked; even so, they shouldn't hold Father responsible. Just as they had chosen to go to work at the Ŭngang plant out of their own free will, so they could quit and leave anytime they wanted. In fact their livelihood actually improved while they worked at the plant. But never had they tried to remove the scowls from their faces. In their minds they inhabited a "meaningful" world, a society where everyone laughed together—a society that could never exist. And so they always suppressed their desires, were always criticizing, always held fast to their denial of pleasure and happiness.

I was fed up just thinking about this brand of stoic who was always comparing the ideal with the real. And now one of them had gone so far as to kill. And his defense lawyer, in order to save him, was calling as a witness the same brand of human being. This was Han Chi-sŏp.

He went up to the witness stand, and when he swore to tell nothing but the truth, straightforwardly and without exaggeration, as dictated by his conscience, and to accept punishment for perjury if he should lie, I began to suspect that he was a master criminal. Supposedly he had come up from a southern plant, and he had only eight fingers. He must have lost the other two at Father's plant. His nose was squashed down and disfigured and below his eyes there were scars. I decided from the beginning not to listen to him. A person with only eight fingers appearing as a witness—that didn't sit right with me. Those two fingers, I thought, had warped his understanding of things. But he had lost something more—his objectivity. I closed my eyes. The color of a lake, hot sun, trees and grass, a breeze blowing through them, a motorboat cleaving the lake, skiing on a lawn, a girl with strange proclivities, a delicious nap—these were the things I called to mind in order to block out what those two were saying. Beehives and deer farms. And after the nap a meal waiting for me. I decided to read. The books I should read were about engineering the future and about economic history. Father liked his sons to read such books. Already I had read considerable portions of the latter. I had to laugh at the places where Walter Scott was quoted. After looking around a mill district where poor laborers were exploited, he worried that this was a country chock full of explosives and might some day blow up. It appeared that blowhard moralists were alive and well during that period too. Imagine the mill owners' expressions after they heard his words. In the eyes of this moralist, this first stage of development at Manchester and Bradford could only be seen as some insane thing careering toward a nationwide explosion. In the end, though, I lost out to my curiosity. I couldn't help but listen to that pair sitting in the courtroom. As far as he could see, Chi-sŏp was saying, the defendant had been forced into the act. The defense lawyer jumped on those words and asked who had forced him—would the witness be more specific? As proof that he had been forced into the act by violence and by threats to his life and person and those of his loved ones, Chi-sŏp cited the worn-out budget book filled out by the dwarf's wife and the primitive life his family led on the earnings from their three children's employment at the Ŭngang mill. I got so angry I could hardly listen. He read off the price of everything from bean sprouts, salt, and shrimp relish to pain relievers for headaches and toothaches, then rambled on incoherently about the minimum cost of living for urban laborers, about their pay that didn't reflect the contribution they made to production, about living conditions that made it hard for the labor force to regenerate its productive energy. Of course, I had to hear about the enormous financial power of the Ŭngang Group with Father at its head, about the continuous support and protection it received as a conglomerate, about the highly educated management team formed of outstanding minds, about the policy of low wages and high profits they pursued. By this point, anyone could see that this was a clear case of human degradation, environmental damage—and even an insult to God, Chi-sŏp went so far as to say. Therefore, what the dwarf's older son had said about Father was sad but indeed true. And what he had borne in mind for Father was something unavoidable, because Father was at the very heart of the repression. The defense lawyer asked Chi-sŏp to explain what he meant by repression. To this Chi-sŏp replied that the repression Father wielded against the employees of subsidiary companies was always connected with subsistence expenses—that is, living expenses—and accordingly, it meant the thing that everyone was inevitably most afraid of: financial straits. There could be no one, he said, who was not continually frightened by such repression. If anyone was directly vulnerable to such repression but had never thought of acting on his right to resist, then that person was either an idiot or had given up on his life. The more I heard, the angrier I grew. To listen to him, you'd think that the most evil people in this world were not them but us. Not only had we destroyed human dignity and worth, but we recognized a special class that on the basis of social position discriminated among people who were equal before the law—and, moreover, had stripped many people of their right to live as human beings. I sat there suppressing my anger. The defense lawyer asked Chi-sŏp if he knew that a wage increase and the firing of people without just cause were the initial problems between labor and management. Of course, he replied. If you considered the wage increase in terms of the company's increased profits, the rise in the price of goods, and the laborers' cost of living, then it was entirely justified. And the demand to reinstate workers fired without just cause on trumped-up charges—alleging that these union members took classes offered by the union and they prayed and sang in a church other than the company church—was also completely justified. Because in terms of paid work, they had learned only one sort of work during their time in the factory. And because firing without just cause was a violation of article 1, section 27, of the Labor Standards Act, which was meant to ensure balance in the nation's economic development.

"And I understand there was concern about the upcoming election of the General Council and union staff, since there was no dialogue with management," said Chi-sŏp. "So I advised the union members to postpone it. But apparently that was impossible."

"And why was that?" the defense lawyer asked.

"Supposedly the company was thinking about getting it over with quickly. They even formed their own election committee."

"And where is this supposed to take place?"

"The election committee is supposed to be elected at a meeting of the General Council."

"And the company committee was therefore illegal?"

"Yes."

"And what happened next?"

"The company people put forth their own candidates, then shortened the deadline for people to declare their candidacy. And so the steward of the local called a general meeting, but the company wouldn't permit it. I went to Ŭngang just after the defendant here, Kim Yŏng-su, and some union staffers were beaten by a band of unidentified thugs."

"While being treated they left intending to go to Seoul—were you aware of that?"

"I was."

"Why do you suppose they wanted to go to Seoul?"

"My understanding is that they intended to meet with the top people at headquarters. Yŏng-su had come to the conclusion that the management people being sent down to the mill were no longer acting rationally. But they were spotted at the bus terminal by that same band of thugs and couldn't carry out their plan. I learned from Yŏng-su that all of them were taken to the building where raw cotton is stored, and attacked once again."

"And it was the following day that all the employees stopped work and gathered outside on the mill grounds?"

"Yes."

"Could you briefly describe to us what you witnessed at that time?"

"The steward of the local chose to report to the union members what had happened to that point. When the report was finished, many of the members embraced the union staffers in tears. Those who had become upset shouted and started running outside the mill, and off to one side they began singing the union anthem. Yŏng-su calmed them down, then told them they had to protect their union from those who wanted to take it away—because it was the workers' one and only organization; it was their life. He suggested that to show their determination they should stop seeing, listening, speaking, or eating for a certain period. And that's what they did."

"Did Kim Yŏng-su destroy machinery along with agitated workers?"

"Destruction of anything is bad. And to destroy expensive machinery would be out of the question. I have never heard Yŏng-su talk about destroying anything in this world."

"If you'll forgive me for moving quickly to the end of the story, what became of the union after that?"

On and on it went, this ridiculous behavior that showed their true colors. The union was of course broken up, Chi-sŏp replied. This was incorrect. At his monthly meeting with the company presidents Father had said that obviously a trade union, even if led by people who cooperated with us, no matter how restricted its activities, would be of no benefit to our enterprise. One day, he warned, the people who discovered embers in the ashes of a charcoal brazier would ignite those embers, rise up, and harm the enterprise and all of us. And so any manager with wisdom would resolve the matter now, at the cost of a bit of noisy resistance, and not entrust the workers with the company. I saw this in a memo in Father's office. That was all he had said—not one word more. Father must have had his own position in mind. He had always said that the labor union was a devil's cauldron that weakened our entire structure, but he hadn't put that down in the memo. Let's suppose Father had to reprimand the executives at one of our affiliates for allowing a trade union to be established at a company plant. Or let's say that during a period of worker unrest in one of our companies a union was formed and Father had to be the one to dismantle it. You can imagine the damage this would do to his position. Then the defense lawyer asked if there was anything Chi-sŏp wished to add in conclusion. Anything indeed! He knew the dwarf's older son well, Chi-sŏp said. They enjoyed a close relationship and had continued to exchange thoughts while working in the labor movement. Ultimately the dwarf's son had suffered hardship on account of his ideals, and the reason he now stood in the defendant's box was that he had reacted to the shattering of those ideals. At this point I was confirmed in my beliefs. Chi-sŏp continued. What the dwarf's son dealt with was not a certain class, he said, but humanity itself. From the beginning, he explained, he and the dwarf's son had understood clearly that the worker and the employer were both producers, not two classes with different interests, and that this was common knowledge. He tried to speak in measured tones with precise pronunciation. By then the two hands resting on the witness stand were trembling. All together the fingers on those two hands were no more than eight. The dwarf's son kept his head up. Directly behind him in the gallery his mother was managing to stifle the weeping that had risen to her throat. I had no doubt about my suspicions. The person who had awakened the dwarf's eldest son like a ray of light was Chi-sŏp. They held the same ideal—one based on love. *They* did not cause human beings to suffer. *We* did. They were the victims. He curled up his eight fingers and withdrew them from sight, then produced a dirty handkerchief from the pocket of his dirty pants. With that dirty handkerchief he dabbed at the sweat around his eyes.

We waited some more.

"I've decided to leave the day after tomorrow," my cousin said.
"Good idea," I said. "And I think I'll go to Germany pretty soon."
"What for?"

"That's where Krupp and Thyssen are located. I need to see how they do things. Father's dream now is to have an ironworks. When my brothers return, I'll have to go to Germany to study."

We sat waiting with the secretariat people and the executive directors from group headquarters. The court clerk entered, went to his place in the center of the area below the bar, and sat. At every session of this trial, I saw him sitting there in the center below the bar. The courtroom grew hotter. Because all the windows were closed, the air was stale. From the bodies of the dense throng of workers issued a nearly unbearable odor. The cold air spewing from the air conditioner could not subdue their body heat. If only they could have kept their body odor to themselves, I could easily have endured being there. My cousin turned toward the gallery, as if something had occurred to him. Chi-sŏp couldn't be seen, he said. I looked back as well. It was true. I had no idea why he hadn't presented himself here at court for the actual verdict. Like us, the dwarf's younger son looked back. The dwarf's wife pulled him down. So he'd gotten scared, had he? Han Chi-sŏp was a coward!

People were dragging their lengthening shadows along the street as I returned home from the trial. Though the shadows were lengthening, the fiery heat remained. The fresh young women didn't mind the heat. There remained, guardians of frantic, desperate Seoul, only the languid bodies of the girls who hadn't left yet. When those girls were ready to leave, I told myself, the girls before them who had let themselves turn copper would return and guard Seoul. The girls wore thin clothing. What we thought about in summer was the pleasure hidden beneath those thin clothes. The summer pleasures I had tried to recall the previous winter—hot sun, salt water, a kiss that held the salt taste of seawater—were unchanging abstractions. As I entered our neighborhood I lowered the window of my small car and let in some air. The smell of flowers and grass rode the breeze in. That smell was something utterly different from the body odor of the workers packed into the courtroom gallery. They gave off a smell that was simply filthy. I got home and the first thing I did was shower. Mother said they gave off a sweaty smell because they didn't wash thoroughly after their sweaty work. And if we were to provide all the factories with sufficient shower facilities, we would have to make a breakthrough in cutting production expenses or else slow down the rate of pay increases. I laughed. If there really was such a thing as an eternal soul that left the flesh, I said, then I wondered how Uncle's soul felt today.

"Yes. And so what happened to that man?" Mother asked.

"I didn't tell you?"

"No."

"He was sentenced to death."

Well, well, oh God—Mother mouthed the words. The dwarf's older son had entered, escorted by prison guards, the prosecutor had entered, then the judge had entered, and the last stage of the trial proceeded very quickly. And when the judge found the defendant guilty of all charges and sentenced him to death, as sought by the prosecution, the workers waiting in the gallery, who earlier had reacted in disbelief to the prosecutor's request for the death sentence—"no, no, it can't be"—gave themselves up to a short gasp of surprise. Their tongues, once so supple, became stiff and hard. For once they had regained their senses, they finally realized the enormity of the crime and the enormity of the punishment. The head of the dwarf's older son, once held high, dropped, and his brother and sister embraced their mother, who had sprung to her feet then collapsed with a visceral shriek. The defense lawyer, who had painted us all with the same brush intending to save the dwarf's elder son, merely looked up at the ceiling. During the course of the trial he had provided the workers, whose powers of judgment were never very strong, with much confusion and misunderstanding. The prosecutor, who appeared to be a good-hearted man, sat with a benign expression. I had learned something very important from these events, I told Mother. At that, she looked at my face and said it was because they were related to people's lives and their suffering.

"Of course," I said. "But that's not what I want to tell you now. I've discovered a way for the workers at our plants to be happy while they do their work."

"Oh, Kyŏng-hun." Mother smiled. "You don't have to think about such things. No matter how good a factory is, how can so many people all be happy together?"

"Just use drugs."

"Drugs?"

"We make a drug that makes them happy just to work. We'd have to put it in what they eat and drink at the factory. We'd have to form a first-rate research team and have them develop it. It would take a lot of money to begin with, but in the long run there's no better way."

"That's enough," Mother said. "You think about such awful things."

"It's not me who's awful," I said. "The thing that's really awful is this world. Some countries already inject people who want to break away from their social system."

"Those people must be sick."

"Disease has nothing to do with it."

"At any rate, don't be telling your father notions like that. He judges all of you on every little thing. I want to see that you get the same opportunities as your older brothers. You understand, don't you?"

Not once had I doubted Mother's love. The measure of her love for each of her children was always equal. Father was different. He liked to tell us that the most essential ability for a manager was a talent for taking several heterogeneous elements and synthesizing them into a whole. In doing so he was giving us notice that he could never hand over power to somebody lacking this talent. Talk about what went on at the factories had never made its way inside the household before Uncle's passing. But that wasn't the case these days, Mother said. And this time, she added, there seemed to be something serious going on at the machine shops. So that's it, I thought to myself. The machine shop was in the south. A man with eight fingers used to come up from down there. He wore dirtier clothes than the workers, used a dirtier handkerchief. If my thick-headed cousin had heard this news, he would have said, "I'm not surprised—he's different." It seemed Chi-sŏp was giving me a wake-up call from a distance. But he hadn't been able to come up to comfort the dwarf's family. Here was a man who stood opposed to us. Here was a person who had grown unhappy analyzing himself, analyzing his co-workers, analyzing us, the people who suppressed them with our economic power. Mother prepared to leave for a Patriotic Women's Volunteer Corps fundraising meeting for needy neighbors. Her young secretary helped her. I went right up to this woman and told her we didn't owe a speck of debt to this society. Smiling awkwardly, the young woman stepped back. She wore thin clothes. I imagined the little instruments of delight hidden beneath those clothes. My lust threw my mind into disorder. I went up to my room and watched the young woman depart with my mother. The watchman pushed open the iron gate. Mother's car disappeared in the grove of broadleaf trees. A short time later our steward came to ask me something. The water in the pool needed changing, and he wanted to know if it was all right for the girls to go in and splash around for a bit before it was drained and cleaned. Before answering I asked him to get in touch with our island house, where I was thinking of taking some friends a few days later. And then I told him of course it was fine with me as long as it helped them do a good job of cleaning the pool. But one of the girls would have to come up and help me put away my books. For the first time I heard him say thank you. I put the tape with the Berlioz music into my VCR. The sixteen-year-old girl with the blond hair wrapped her arms around a man. The girl from three mornings earlier came up without a sound. One by one she picked up the books that lay scattered all over and cradled them in her arm. A book titled _Human Engineering_ pressed against her swelling chest. I couldn't remember when I had first heard Berlioz. My sister immediately below me liked me because I liked Hindemith. I took hold of the girl's arm and the books dropped. The blond girl's clothes loosened and fell from her shoulder line. "Look!" I said. "Different from your television." The girl did as I said. Something astounding was happening on the screen. The girl stood stock still. She breathed with her chest and shoulders. My hand went to her, touched her, and she trembled. It never ceased to amaze me that girls harbored the river of life in their little bodies. The man on the screen had violated the blond girl's body. *You're a woman now,* he said. "All right, go on down," I said to the girl, whose body was hot by now. "Take a dip before the water's drained." The girl looked up at me with a face grown pale. A tear welled up, she turned and went downstairs, and I lay down on my bed. I read a book. I thought I would read some economic history before Father returned home. The author quoted another economist as saying that economists would have broader responsibilities in the future. I read awhile, then fell asleep, and just before I woke up I had a dream. In the dream I was casting a fishnet. I went into the water wearing goggles intending to watch the fat fish that came into my net get caught in the mesh. A school of fish came toward my net. But they weren't fat fish. They were only some big-spine fish—a collection of bones and spines with two eyes and a pectoral fin. Hundreds, thousands, of these big-spine fish making bony, spiny sounds were caught in my net. I grew scared. I got out of the water and pulled out the net. Countless big-spine fish came up, caught. They freed themselves from the mesh and came up at me spitting thousands, tens of thousands, of phosphorescent rays. Every time the spines touched me my skin was torn open. I woke up screaming for help, in pain from being torn to shreds. Poppy red twilight touched the west-facing window. Beautiful, I felt; I went to the window and looked down. I could see the tiniest particles in the atmosphere carrying the light. The white wall reflected the twilight toward the woods. Deceased Grandfather's old dog crept out from those woods. The girl who had been ready to accept me with her heated body called the dog. After setting the dog's bowl in front of her she clasped the dog's neck tightly in her arms. As the dwarf's older son was being led out, the dwarf's wife had done the same to him. The workers had gone outside and wept. Chi-sŏp hadn't been able to come up. People's love saddened me. At that moment I saw the watchman push the iron gate shut. Father's car emerged from the grove of broad-leaf trees and slid to a stop. I thought I would visit a psychiatrist the following day, without anyone knowing. If Father learned of my weakness, I'd be the first person he would skip over. Love would gain me nothing. Rehearsing the brave words I would speak in a hearty voice, I opened my door and went out.

Epilogue

THE MATHEMATICS TEACHER entered the classroom. The students saw he didn't have the textbook. The majority of the students trusted this teacher. As many as one-fifth doubted him. They were the ones who hadn't scored well in mathematics on the college preparatory exam.

"Gentlemen," he began. "This has been a challenging time for you. You've really put your heart into your studies, all of you. But the math scores, which are my responsibility, are lower than ever before. I can't tell you how sorry I am. This may sound like an excuse, but the responsibility for these lower math scores on the preparatory exam does not lie with the math teacher alone. To discover precisely who or what is responsible we would have to list numerous things: the authorities who devised this system, the educators and parents who accepted it, the designers of the multiple-choice questions where you select one of four answers, the people who print the exam questions, the manufacturer of poor-quality pens, the exam inspectors, the key-punchers, the supervisors, the programmers, those responsible for the level of humidity in the computer room, the computer that assumed the role of judge—and of course you gentlemen yourselves who took my class, the guidance counselor, who always makes irrelevant requests of me, your teacher, who must stand before you gentlemen and teach, and above him the vice-principal and principal, and finally the plans and their implementation, the schemes, the failures, and whatnot, of those elements outside the school that influence the state of mind of you gentlemen and myself, the teacher and the taught. In spite of all this, I can't help taking upon myself the full responsibility."

"Who did it?" a student asked. "Who placed that responsibility on you, sir?"

"They did," the teacher said.

Another student rose. "Could you please be more specific?"

"They did. Who can be more specific than that? One of their characteristics is that until the day they die they won't assume responsibility for a single thing. They all have plausible alibis. Until now you gentlemen have put your heart into your studies, and since this is the last class hour you will have in high school, I hope you'll understand if I talk about something unrelated to the entrance exam. Through no choice of my own, I've given up the subject of mathematics. I've received notice that starting next semester I'll be teaching ethics. As you gentlemen are well aware, ethics are principles realized in practice as moral standards. If you gentlemen were the decision makers, would you take a person who had been stigmatized as a failure in the teaching of mathematics and saddle him with the teaching of ethics? No one knows this, but there is some terrible scheming going on. What it comes down to is removing ethics from the curriculum. It's also a scheme to develop you gentlemen and your successors as human capital. Gentlemen, we are not the ends, you and I. Rather, we've become the means without realizing it. I should have sensed their intent, but you gentlemen and I have been in a rush—you in order to go to college, I in order to see that you pass the examination—and we haven't been able to read their true intention. We've been too busy. But was this busyness something we did for our own self-esteem, as one might expect? It's a short hour, but please give this some thought. I'm going to make myself comfortable now—please forgive me."

Hunger awakened Humpback. It was black inside the tent. The darkness was total and nothing was visible. Whether he opened or closed his eyes, there was only darkness. He realized he had made a mistake not eating those instant noodles. Instant noodles for breakfast, instant noodles for lunch, and when again at dinnertime he had heard "instant noodles," he had gone for a walk instead of eating. After the girl had been put in the hospital he'd eaten nothing but rice gruel and instant noodles. He couldn't stand it—he wasn't some laboratory mouse. The tonic peddler they called The Boss had said the girl would rejoin them, but they'd gone through three towns and eleven villages and she still hadn't shown up. She was a dirty, homely girl but she made good rice and good soup. She had grown up in an orphanage. Suddenly she had developed a high fever, and The Boss had taken her to the hospital. It seemed to Humpback he would continue to eat instant noodles until she hooked up with them again.

Humpback rose carefully so as not to disturb the strong man they called The Master, sleeping beside him. His shoulders touched the side of the tent. He would certainly be beaten up in the darkness just for disturbing and waking the strong man. The strong man wasn't eating well these days, either, and appeared to be losing strength. When he broke rocks he avoided the hard ones, and he could pull a car with his teeth only half the usual ten yards. And he was reluctant to perform the knife trick—the one where he strapped the long sharp blade of a knife to his palm with nylon cord, pressed the tip to his stomach, and then released it. It was a frightful stunt whenever he saw it. Watching it gave him the sensation that his body tissues, skin and all, were being shredded by the blade. If a lot of tonic was to be sold, then this trick was essential.

Although the strong man was losing strength, he was still a mighty man. Humpback had no intention of suffering a useless beating by disturbing him in the dark. He placed his feet carefully, stopped, listened. Only the sound of Squatlegs breathing. He groped with his hand. The strong man wasn't there. Humpback struck a match and lit the lantern. No one but Squatlegs. Squatlegs was asleep on his back with his legs, which were perpetually flexed at the knees, drawn up.

Humpback went outside. The call of some small creature came to him from a dense grove off at a distance. Humpback didn't know the name of this small creature producing the faint cry. He didn't know it was suffering from water it had drunk from a branch of the river tainted by wastewater from a factory upstream. Humpback felt utterly dispirited as he looked about. He went back in the tent and shook Squatlegs awake.

"Get up!"

"What's the matter?" Squatlegs pawed at the air and Humpback helped him sit up.

"Nobody's around," Humpback said.

"What?" Squatlegs slowly asked. "You mean they left us behind?"

Humpback raised the tent flap. Squatlegs quickly scooted outside. His small body was enveloped in darkness.

"Don't see The Boss's tent, do you?" Squatlegs asked. "Or his car, either."

"Like I said, they're gone."

"Leaving us by ourselves?"

"I'll bet The Boss did the same thing with that girl who cooked for us."

"She's in the hospital."

"How do you know?" Humpback asked. "Did you see her there?"

"I saw him take her to the hospital."

"So did I. I'll bet he took that sick girl any old place, then drove back."

Squatlegs bit his lip. Then he held his breath and listened.

"What's that?" Humpback asked.

"Hmm?"

"I thought I heard something."

"Birds flying around," Squatlegs said. "Looking for food."

"In the middle of the night?"

"Shit." Squatlegs grew angry. "How many times have I told you? It's a goatsucker. It sleeps during the day. Keeps to the trees and sleeps."

The two friends held their breath and listened to the fluttering wings of the goatsucker as it flew low overhead. The sound disappeared into the mass of darkness held in the dense grove's embrace. Almost simultaneously the two friends thought of their wives and children, who had come to this dismal place outside Seoul.

"How much have we been sending them a month?" asked Humpback.

Squatlegs answered. "Three thousand _wŏn_ for the first six months and two thousand for the last seven months."

"Think they're managing on that?"

"My kids are tough."

"Let's get out of here!"

"Where are we going to go?"

"We've got to catch them," Humpback said. "Every day is a living hell for us—what's the use of thinking about the future?"

"I needed that lump sum. Needed a hutch for the baby rabbits."

"Put on your gloves."

Squatlegs fished out his leather gloves and put them on. Balling up his fists and pushing against the ground, he lifted himself and moved out ahead. Humpback went into the tent and emerged with the lantern. He made up the few paces between himself and Squatlegs, who was scooting ahead. Insect calls came from the woods. The small creature whose name Humpback didn't know was silent. The children would be sleeping now in the rented room outside Seoul. Perhaps one of them had awakened and was crying? And wouldn't one of them be sick and crying? Humpback turned onto a narrow road. Squatlegs rolled himself sideways down a small hill, coming to rest in front of Humpback. Humpback bent over and Squatlegs grinned, his teeth white in the darkness.

They left the narrow road and came upon the branch of the river. The rocks in that river were extraordinarily hard. For the strong man Humpback only gathered rocks he expected would break easily, but when the strong man practiced with them he got bloody. He slapped Humpback with his bloody hands. Humpback's nose bled. The Boss pretended not to see. He sat in his car counting money and the items in the medicine chest. Squatlegs, dangling from the rope, plopped down, scooted over, produced some cotton balls from his pocket, and plugged Humpback's nose. The water in the river was absolutely filthy. Fish floating belly up were caught among the weeds. Humpback picked out several whose spines were bent and buried them in the sand. The sand had turned reddish brown.

They passed the unlit amusement park and Humpback came to a stop. Squatlegs couldn't be seen; there was only the sound of him scooting along. Humpback found the well and lowered the little bucket. He drank until his face was raised toward the night sky, drank to fill his empty stomach. He pulled up a second bucketful and waited for Squatlegs. Squatlegs scooted up, breathing hard. He looked up, his face a mixture of sweat and dirt, and removed his leather gloves. He drank from the bucket Humpback passed to him. Drank a little and poured the rest over his head.

They left the amusement park and turned up a steep, narrow path toward the expressway. Where the slope was severe, Squatlegs climbed sideways. Ahead, Humpback set down the lantern and descended. He lifted Squatlegs, carried him in his arms to the lantern, set him down, and plumped himself down. Squatlegs saw Humpback's breathing and the large movements it created along his bent spine. And then while Humpback rested, Squatlegs continued on, scooting up sideways. Catching his breath, Humpback again climbed ahead, descended, and picked up Squatlegs in his arms. Repeating this process until they reached the expressway, the two friends lay down and rested on the asphalt. Humpback lay on his side and Squatlegs lay with his flexed legs upraised, as when he slept. In that position Squatlegs laughed. His laughter became intermittent, then ceased. A huge freight truck roared up on the opposite side of the center strip and sped past. This monster with lights for eyes shredded the night air with its frightening speed.

"No curfew once you're on the expressway," Humpback said.

"So that's where we catch a ride to Seoul. The Boss is probably parked in front of a toll booth, waiting for it to open. If he gets onto the expressway, we'll never catch him."

"And what do we do when we catch him?"

"We'll get rid of him," Squatlegs said.

"Let's just get the money. Together we can get what's left."

"I'm going to cut open his stomach."

"Put away that knife."

"Never you mind. I'll do it myself—cut that son of a bitch's stomach right open," Squatlegs said again.

"All right," Humpback said. "If that makes you feel better. But like I said, that's not the answer."

"You're going to tell me again you don't like me anymore?"

"No, it's just that you scare me. And the thing that scares me is your state of mind."

And when he looked at Squatlegs, Squatlegs was shivering all over. The water he'd poured over himself at the amusement park had left his clothes wet. There was also the dampness from his perspiration, and the night air lacked warmth. Insects sang in a weed patch to their right. Except for the insects that lived in the weeds, nothing was safe.

Humpback jumped over the drainage ditch beside the highway and the cries of insects abruptly stopped. He pulled out two signposts standing among some little pine trees. He set down the posts and plank signs in the ditch and broke them with rocks. He gathered the pieces, poured kerosene from the lantern onto them, then put a match to them. Squatlegs scooted to the fire. They heard a lone car. The car sped toward their fire. Humpback ran out onto the asphalt and hailed it. The small car swept by.

Squatlegs retreated from the fire and sat back. Steam rose from his body. The pocket on the right side sagged limply. In it were wire and the sharpened blue steel of his knife. Together with these were the three thousand _wŏn_ in emergency money that he carried with him. He had added a zipper to the pocket. "No matter what happens," he would say, "I have to head for the little ones and their mom."

"Sure," Humpback would say.

Next to speed up was a bulky refrigerator truck. Humpback removed his shirt and waved it. The truck had just passed Humpback when it changed lanes and came to a stop. Humpback ran to the truck and knocked on the driver's door, hopping up and down in agitation. Squatlegs clenched his teeth ferociously.

The driver, exhausted from driving at night, stuck his head out the window. He saw a hunchback with a horribly bent spine waving toward a small creature scooting over the asphalt. The driver was spooked. He barely heard the knocking on his door as he drove off.

"Son of a bitch!" Squatlegs shook his fist at the bulky truck.

Again they could hear insects.

"Look at that!" Humpback suddenly shouted.

"Look at what?" said Squatlegs. "What do you see?"

"It flew into the woods."

"How do you know? Your night vision's no good."

"I saw the light!"

"You mean a firefly?"

"Yeah, a firefly."

"Your eyes are playing tricks on you," said Squatlegs. "Fireflies are extinct."

"How come?"

"The people in this world have ganged up and killed them off."

"They must have missed one."

"I said your eyes are playing tricks on you."

"And I'm telling you I saw it."

"Shit," grumbled Squatlegs. "No cars coming. And now fireflies— what the hell. We can't let The Boss get away. I've got to cut that son of a bitch's stomach open, then get back to the baby rabbits. Got to buy a rabbit hutch."

"Come here."

"Cut it out."

"Maybe my night vision's no good, but I can see *that*."

As Humpback had said, it was quite visible. There below them, alongside the river's outline revealed in the starlight, stood a large building. It was at a distance, but its numerous lights made it seem as if the building had bored a hole in the darkness.

"A factory, isn't it?" said Squatlegs.

"That's what it looks like."

"You mean it's not?"

"It's a penitentiary."

"You mean a jail?"

There were still no vehicles on the expressway.

Now it was Humpback who asked. "You know who was in there?"

"Huh?" Squatlegs didn't catch his friend's meaning. And so he sat back. All he could think of was the knife in his pocket.

"Remember that midget in Felicity Precinct?" Humpback asked.

Squatlegs nodded. "The one who died in the brick factory smokestack?"

"That's right. Well, the midget's elder son used to be in there."

"How come?"

"He killed a man."

Squatlegs said nothing.

"The midget was always bragging about that son of his."

"Yeah, he bragged quite a lot." Then Squatlegs hesitantly asked, "You said he _used to be_ in there?"

"He's out."

"How can he be out if he killed somebody?"

"He came out dead."

"He did?"

"He was different from his father."

"Completely different death."

"The midget's wife came here with her boy and girl and claimed the body. They were beyond tears. They sat for a while beside the water, then left."

"It shouldn't have happened."

"So you ought to get rid of that knife in your pocket right now."

Quite a long time passed, and still no vehicles appeared. The expressway was still concealed in darkness. There was no way to tell the time. The two friends were sad. Just then Humpback discovered a small living thing that was sending out light in the darkness. It flew low over the asphalt. "Look!" he shouted. And then, by the sheerest coincidence, Squatlegs heard a vehicle. He saw Humpback run onto the asphalt. He braced his hands and pushed against the ground. "Look! A firefly!" came his friend's voice. "How did it survive?" But Squatlegs couldn't be seen. Humpback was running toward the center strip. The approaching vehicle was a tanker truck. To make it stop, Squatlegs rolled himself into its lights and stuck up his hand. The truck driver momentarily closed his eyes, stepped on the emergency brake, then released it. He couldn't stop the truck all at once or pull it to the side. He was impartial. The tanker regained speed and drove on. The two friends were motionless. Nor did the insects sing. When they started singing again, Squatlegs lifted himself up. With one hand he scooted toward his friend, whom he had seen in the truck's headlights. "Look!" Humpback was sprawled on his side next to the center strip. Squatlegs pointed. Tail glittering, a lone firefly flew toward the woods on their right.

The teacher rested his hands on the podium. He spoke to his charges.

"I wanted to write something I could share with all of you. But I couldn't write a single line. Obviously I'm disappointed. I'm very sad at having to give up mathematics, and I wasn't able to finish a single line. I wanted to write about the very first humans, who came down from the trees, and about animals, which get their nutrients from eating plants and other animals because they don't have the ability to manufacture organic substances from inorganic substances the way plants do. And if I still had some time left, I was going to write about the people who are trying to smother the creativity of you gentlemen. They don't want the slightest detail of our present circumstances to be revealed for what they really are, and they don't want reform. A pot of coffee, a barrel of liquor, and I couldn't write a decent word; all I could do was cry—understand me. But you shouldn't feel sorry for me. I've decided to leave on a space voyage for a small planet you gentlemen haven't heard of."

This set the students buzzing. "Have you ever met an alien?" a student asked.

"Yes," said the teacher. "I've met them on a mountaintop I often visit. This small map I've just taken from my pocket, which I got from them, is an HR map. The planet I'm going to is located midway along a diagonal line from the upper left corner to the lower right corner. The beings who live there have the ability to manufacture organic substances out of inorganic substances the way plants do. Have you gentlemen ever heard of anything better than this?"

"I have a question," said a student in the very last row.

"What is it?"

"I once heard that sightings of aliens or flying saucers are a defense mechanism appearing at a moment of societal stress. How are we to understand your case, sir?"

"Believe me when I say I will leave with the aliens for that planet, and that when I do, sparks will soar up and brighten the western sky. A long explanation is out of the question. The only thing I don't know yet is what I'll encounter the moment I leave. What will it be? The silence of a public cemetery? Maybe not. Do outcries come only from the dead? Time is up. Whether we live on Earth or another planet, our spirit is always free. I pray that all of you get good grades and succeed at the college of your choice. Why don't we just leave it at that and skip the thank-yous and goodbyes."

"Attention!" shouted the class monitor as he sprang to his feet. "Salute!"

The teacher returned the students' bow and stepped down from his platform. Then he left the classroom. The way he walked was peculiar. Maybe that's how aliens walk, thought the students.

The winter sun was already slanting downward and the classroom grew dark.

Afterword

Cho Se-hŭi and The Dwarf

When the Republic of Korea (South Korea)'s first five-year economic development plan was launched in 1962, the nation's economy was one of subsistence agriculture. Within four decades, South Korea had become one of the most high-tech countries in the world. This rapid transformation was made possible in part by President Park Chung Hee's long-range economic program of export-led development, which in turn was predicated on the transformation of South Korea from an agrarian to an industrialized nation. Park, a former military man, was able to expedite this transformation after assuming dictatorial powers in the early 1970s. Industrialization during the Park regime (1961–1979) was gained at the cost of civil, labor, and environmental abuses of the sort that attracted the attention of muckraking journalists in the United States in the early 1900s. The cast of characters in this national drama included a huge number of laborers, many of them recent immigrants to Seoul from the countryside; an incipient urban middle class suddenly faced with civil and social issues larger than those encountered in the hometown village; and the crony capitalists who headed a few powerful conglomerates.

Cho Se-hŭi's purpose in *The Dwarf (Nanjangi ka ssoaollin chagŭn kong)* was to describe, without running afoul of Park's strict national security laws, the societal ills caused by industrialization. His solution to this daunting challenge was to inject a subtle irony in his narratives and at the same time, in order to reach the widest possible audience, to write in syntax simple enough to be understood by any Korean with a rudimentary education. The result is a book whose basic message—the human costs of reckless industrialization—is evident but whose deeper meanings—the spiritual malaise of the newly rich and powerful and the confusion of a working class subject to forces beyond its control—await discovery by the careful and deliberate reader. Cho succeeded admirably in his undertaking: In his native Korea the book is approaching its two hundredth printing and has sold almost a million copies since its publication in 1978. Ch'oe Yun, who cotranslated the novel into French and who was a graduate student when the novel was first published in book form in Korea, notes that South Koreans in the 1970s tended to view the world in terms of white and black. Readers of *The Dwarf* were thus already receptive to the notion of a contest being played out between powerless laborers and the corrupt families who led the conglomerates, and it is likely that the book was read by the great majority of college students in South Korea in the 1980s. Outside of Korea Cho's works have been translated into English, French, German, Bulgarian, and Japanese.

The Dwarf is a linked-story novel—a collection of stories that can be read independently but are all linked by character, theme, and setting. The characters are in turn a laboring family, a family of the newly emerging middle class, and a wealthy industrialist's family that looks for inspiration to German big business. The twelve stories are written in a lean, clipped style that features abrupt shifts of scene, time, and viewpoint. Long paragraphs of narrative alternate with stretches of terse dialogue. Reproductions of bureaucratic forms and an extract from a working family's budget book give us a taste of a dwarf's life—the dwarf epitomizing the "little people" on whose backs the South Korean economic miracle took place. These details of life in South Korea in the 1970s are juxtaposed with snippets of information on science past and present and allusions to the workings of the universe. Two stories, "The Möbius Strip" (Moebiusŭ ŭi tti; 1976) and "The Klein

Bottle" (K'ŭllain sshi ŭi pyŏng; 1978), are built on the concept of spatial form, their titles referring to objects whose inner and outer surfaces are interchangeable. This notion of interchangeability and the references to the history of science and space exploration suggest to us that the dualities, contradictions, and anomalies of industrialization described in *The Dwarf* are not unique to Korea but result in large part from global economic forces that have accumulated over the centuries.

Ch'oe Yun has also observed that although writing by and about the working class predated *The Dwarf*, it tended to be political and ideological. In comparison, *The Dwarf* focuses on the concrete detail of the lives of three major groups of people. The minutiae of workplace conditions are particularly vivid, giving us an almost tactile sense of factory life: In "The Cost of Living for a Family of Ŭngang Laborers" (Ŭngang nodong kajok ŭi saenggyebi; 1977) we learn that Yŏng-hŭi's job requires her to walk seventy-two hundred steps in an hour; that the decibel level in her workplace is deafening; and that the *nighttime* temperature inside the factory is a hundred and two degrees. Environmental degradation is especially vivid in "City of Machines" (Kigye toshi; 1978), and indeed *The Dwarf* is one of the first contemporary Korean novels in which concern for human and natural ecology is evident throughout.

Abuse of power is a vivid presence in *The Dwarf*. Typically power is exercised through intimidation and violence, as in "Knifeblade" (K'allal; 1975) and "A Little Ball Launched by a Dwarf" (Nanjangi ka ssoaollin chagŭn kong; 1976), and through sexual domination, evident also in the latter story. Violence begets violence—as when in the penultimate story a captain of industry is assassinated. Here the author is obliquely critiquing the authoritarian leadership that has plagued much of modern Korean history, as well as questioning Korea's traditionally patriarchal social structure.

South Korea's spate of industrial accidents and economic troubles in the 1990s—as well as the more desperate environmental degradation and food shortages in the Democratic People's Republic of Korea (North Korea)—have reinforced the contemporaneity of *The Dwarf* and confirmed its status as the most important postwar Korean novel.

If Cho Se-hŭi had written nothing else, he would remain one of modern Korea's most important writers on the basis of this work alone. In the new millennium, as South Korea continues to develop into one of the most technologically advanced nations in the world, *The Dwarf* stands as a constant reminder of the millions of nameless people who made possible the industrialization of their society.

Cho Se-hŭi *was born in 1942 in Kap'yŏng, Kyŏnggi Province, and graduated from Kyunghee University with a degree in Korean literature. If he had written nothing else besides his linked-story novel* The Dwarf, *he would remain one of modern Korea's most important writers. Such is the significance of that work in the history of modern Korean letters. After making his literary debut in the* Kyŏnghyang shinmun, *a Seoul daily, in 1965, Cho published but a single story during the next ten years. But then in short order, from 1975 to 1978, he published the twelve stories that would form* The Dwarf. *Two books have appeared since:* Time Travel *(1983) and* The Roots of Silence *(1985).*

Bruce and Ju-Chan Fulton *are the translators of several volumes of modern Korean fiction, most recently Hwang Sun-wŏn's novel* Trees on a Slope *(2005). They are the recipients of several translation awards and grants, including the first U.S. National Endowment for the Arts Translation Fellowship given for a translation from Korean literature. Bruce Fulton is the inaugural holder of the Young-Bin Min Chair in Korean literature and literary translation at the University of British Columbia. He is the co-translator, with the late Kim Chong-un, of the award-winning* A Ready-Made Life: Early Masters of Modern Korean Fiction *(1998) and is co-editor with Youngmin Kwon of* Modern Korean Fiction: An Anthology *(2005).*

Production Notes for Cho / THE DWARF
Cover and interior designed by University of Hawai'i Press production
    staff in Minion Condensed, with display type in Gill Sans
Composition by BW&A Books, Inc.
Printing and binding by The Maple-Vail Book Manufacturing Group
Printed on 55 # Sebago Antique, 360 ppi